P9-BBN-483

"If I could transform myself into a man this instant, I would do so,"

she snapped. "All my life I have been made to feel I had no value because I was a female. But worthless as I am, Brys, I care about you...." Her voice trailed off. Then Gisele almost jumped when she felt his hand touching her shoulder.

"And I for you, though I know you will not believe it, Gisele," he said, his voice husky. "I have been fighting my desire for you ever since I found you in the Weald. But you didn't want to become a wife, and I thought you deserved better than me." He looked away, adding, "Yet I could not resist trying to seduce you in the garden. Damn me for a double-minded rogue."

"Deserved better than you, my lord?" she asked, honestly puzzled. "Why on earth would you say that...?"

Dear Reader,

Welcome to Harlequin Historicals, Harlequin/Silhouette's *only* historical romance line! We offer four unforgettable love stories each month, in a range of time periods, settings and sensuality. And they're written by some of the best writers in the field!

We're very excited to bring you *My Lady Reluctant,* a terrific new medieval novel by Laurie Grant. This book has something for everyone—intrigue, emotion, adventure and plenty of passion! Spurned by her betrothed and forced to find another husband, the heroine travels from Normandy to England to attend court. En route, she is attacked by outlaws but is rescued by a mysterious knight…who protects her by day and invades her dreams by night!

The Outlaw's Bride by Liz Ireland is a fresh, charming Western about a reputed Texas outlaw and a headstrong "nurse" who fall in love—despite the odds against them. Deborah Simmons returns with a frothy new Regency romance, *The Gentleman Thief,* about a beautiful bluestocking who stirs up trouble when she investigates a jewel theft and finds herself scrutinizing—and falling for—an irresistible marquis.

And don't miss Carolyn Davidson's new Western, *The Bachelor Tax.* In this darling tale, a least-likely-to-marry "bad boy" rancher tries to avoid a local bachelor tax by proposing to the one woman he's *sure* will turn him down—the prim preacher's daughter....

Enjoy! And come back again next month for four more choices of the best in historical romance.

Sincerely,

Tracy Farrell
Senior Editor

MY LADY RELUCTANT

LAURIE GRANT

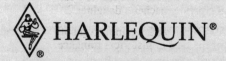

HARLEQUIN®

TORONTO • NEW YORK • LONDON
AMSTERDAM • PARIS • SYDNEY • HAMBURG
STOCKHOLM • ATHENS • TOKYO • MILAN • MADRID
PRAGUE • WARSAW • BUDAPEST • AUCKLAND

If you purchased this book without a cover you should be aware that this book is stolen property. It was reported as "unsold and destroyed" to the publisher, and neither the author nor the publisher has received any payment for this "stripped book."

ISBN 0-373-29097-7

MY LADY RELUCTANT

Copyright © 2000 by Laurie A. Miller

All rights reserved. Except for use in any review, the reproduction or utilization of this work in whole or in part in any form by any electronic, mechanical or other means, now known or hereafter invented, including xerography, photocopying and recording, or in any information storage or retrieval system, is forbidden without the written permission of the publisher, Harlequin Enterprises Limited, 225 Duncan Mill Road, Don Mills, Ontario, Canada M3B 3K9.

All characters in this book have no existence outside the imagination of the author and have no relation whatsoever to anyone bearing the same name or names. They are not even distantly inspired by any individual known or unknown to the author, and all incidents are pure invention.

This edition published by arrangement with Harlequin Books S.A.

® and TM are trademarks of the publisher. Trademarks indicated with ® are registered in the United States Patent and Trademark Office, the Canadian Trade Marks Office and in other countries.

Visit us at www.romance.net

Printed in U.S.A.

Please address questions and book requests to:
Harlequin Reader Service
U.S.: 3010 Walden Ave., P.O. Box 1325, Buffalo, NY 14269
Canadian: P.O. Box 609, Fort Erie, Ont. L2A 5X3

To my wonderful agent, Maryanne Colas, for her
guidance (and help with my French!) and friendship,
and always, to Michael, my very own hero

Prologue

Normandy, 1141

"He rejected me? The Baron of Hawkswell rejected *me*, Sidonie Gisele de l'Aigle? Is he so rich that he has no interest in wedding an heiress?" Indignation laced Gisele's voice and sent a rush of heat up her neck to flush her cheeks. By the Virgin, she would never survive the humiliation, the shame!

Her father, Charles, Count de l'Aigle, smirked. "Nay, he's but a fool. Not only is Alain of Hawkswell not overwealthy, but he's spurned you for a lady whose family are adherents of Stephen's!"

Gisele felt her jaw drop with shock, and for a moment she forgot the affront to her own pride. For one of the Empress Matilda's lords to refuse her choice of a bride for him, the heiress of a Norman family whose alliance with the empress was bedrock-solid, was beyond foolish, unless...

"Is he changing sides, then? Does he now side with King Stephen?" she mused.

Her father's brow furrowed, and he rubbed his chin.

"Nay, that's the mysterious part. The word is he's as much Matilda's man as before, yet he's apparently married the woman with Matilda's blessing."

Gisele sighed as the pain of rejection mingled with envy in her soul. It wasn't so mysterious, not to her. Lord Alain had married for love. He had loved this woman enough to risk the empress's displeasure and had been rewarded by not losing her favor. Ah, to have a man love *her*, Gisele de l'Aigle, like that! And the name *Alain* had had such a *kind* sound to it. Gisele had thought that here was a man who might understand her, who might value *her* for what she was, and not merely what she could bring him by marriage. Her heart mourned the passing of that dream.

"There must be more going on there than meets the eye," her father continued, oblivious of her grief, "but in any case *my* problem is not solved. Here I am, an old man with no heir for my lands but a mere girl, a girl who's of marriageable age, and not a husband in sight."

Being seen as of no value by her father, at least, was an old and familiar hurt. He had always treated her as if being born female were somehow a fault she could have remedied in the womb if she'd only been industrious enough. *I may be but a girl, but I'm worth your love,* she wanted to cry, but knew it was no use. He could not love her, would never love her as he would have if she'd been the son he'd hoped for. Now she only represented a pawn he could use to obtain a son, at least one by marriage. Well, she'd have no more of it!

"Don't think you can palm me off on some sprig of nobility on this side of the Channel, then, my lord father! I'll just stay here at l'Aigle and be your chatelaine," she announced, stalking over to the open window to look down on the swirling currents of the Risle that flowed just beyond the curtain wall.

"And when I die?" her father interrupted, his face darkening.

"I'll be the Lady of l'Aigle in my own right."

"Foolish wench!" Her father's voice was a lash that cut her heart. "Did you just crawl out from underneath a cabbage leaf? No mere *female* can hold a castle, l'Aigle or any other!"

"But the empress is her father's heir to the throne in her own right."

"Yes, and you have heard what a merry time she's having trying to hold on to that throne, have you not?" the count retorted. "England is torn apart while she wrangles with her cousin, Stephen of Blois! And you'd be overrun by our nearest neighbor in a se'enight. Nay, Sidonie Gisele—" he always used both her names, both the one she went by, Gisele, as well as her first name, which had been the name of his despised dead wife, when he meant to make an unpleasant point "—a noble female has two choices in this world—the marriage bed or the convent. I cannot even allow you to chose the latter, for I have no heir and *I will not give l'Aigle back to the duchy of Normandy when I die!*"

His last words, shouted so loudly that they echoed off the stone walls, merely strengthened her resolve to be owned by no man. But before she could voice her resistance, her father spoke again.

"I haven't given up my dream of having a holding in England, even if only through my daughter," the count replied in his condescending way, "and actually, the empress has not left me without remedy," the old man said, joining her at the window. "She bids me send you to wait upon her. As a lady-in-waiting to the empress, you are bound to catch the eye of some powerful and marriageable vassal of hers.''

"I? Go to England alone?" How could he send her to a country he had just described as torn apart by civil war? Yet, there were advantages to the idea, not the least of which was the pleasure of leaving behind a father who could not love her or even respect her. The empress was a powerful woman, even though she was having to fight to keep the crown her father, Henry, had bequeathed her. Matilda, a woman unhappy in her own marriage, would surely understand Gisele's wish to control her own fate, and allow her to remain unwed.

Mayhap, once she was in England, she'd see this Alain, Baron of Hawkswell, and the lady he'd chosen over her.

"Nay, of course you would not be alone," the old man snapped. "I believe I know what's due to the heiress of l'Aigle. I would have to send a suitable escort of my knights along—a half dozen should be an impressive enough number, though I can ill spare them, you know—and old Fleurette to attend you. The knights will return as soon as they've delivered you to the empress, while Fleurette can remain with you.''

Thus ridding you permanently of two mouths to feed rather than one, eh, Father? The idea of her old nurse, now more of a beloved companion than a servant, coming with her was comforting enough to prevent Gisele from commenting on her father's begrudging her even the temporary use of six of his knights.

Once she was in England, all would be different.

Chapter One

"I vow, there is nothing more to bring up but my toenails," moaned Gisele in the sheltered aftcastle of the cog *Saint Valery*.

"Yes, you're no sailor, that's sure," Fleurette murmured soothingly as she smoothed the damp brown locks away from Gisele's forehead as her lady lay with her head pillowed in her old nurse's lap. "The Channel's been smooth as glass from the moment we left Normandy. I'd hate to see how you'd fare in rough seas."

"Well, you never shall, for I'm never setting foot on a ship again my entire life," muttered Gisele, then grabbed the basin at her nurse's feet as a new round of spasms cramped her belly.

"What, never returning home?" asked the old woman in shocked tones. "Of course you shall return to Normandy, if only to allow your father to meet the fine lord you will marry, and to show him his grandchildren."

Gisele had yet to confide in her former nurse that her plans were different from those her father had made for her, and she didn't have the energy to do it now, so she merely played along.

"Of course I shall go to Normandy to show off my husband and the babes he shall give me," she told Fleurette with a wan attempt at a smile. "I'm sure we shall be so blissful that it will be no effort at all to just *float* across the waves...."

"Ah, go on with you, then!" Fleurette said, giving her an affectionate pat. "You always did have a ripe imagination!"

"*I* have an imagination? 'Tis *you* imagining me with a husband and babe in a triumphal return to l'Aigle, long before we have so much as landed in England, let alone met any of Matilda's marriageable lords."

"Eh, well, I don't know what your lord father can be thinking of, sending you off to a country in the grip of civil war—"

"*England lies ahead!*" called the lookout in the crow's nest.

Within an hour of landing, they were on their way to London. Gisele, exhausted from the hours of retching aboard the tossing cog, would have liked to lie overnight in Hastings, and she knew the elderly Fleurette would have been better off with a night of rest. But Sir Hubert LeBec, the senior of the knights, was a hard-bitten old Crusader who clearly saw escorting his lord's daughter as an onerous chore, to be accomplished as swiftly as possible. He allowed Lady Gisele and her companion just time enough to take some refreshment at an inn, but no more.

Gisele had thought just an hour ago she'd never be able to eat again, but now, revitalized by a full stomach and delighted to be back on firm ground again, did not begrudge her father's captain his hurry. She was eager to get on with her new life, the life that would begin once she reached London, which was now held by the empress.

Lark, the chestnut palfrey she had brought from l'Aigle, had smooth paces and gentle manners, allowing Gisele to savor the beauty of the coastal area as they left the town behind. The countryside was decorated in the best June could offer. Blue squill garnished grasslands nearest the sea, giving way to white cow parsley banking the roadsides, mixed with reddish-purple foxglove. Some fields were dotted with grazing sheep; others looked like they were carpeted in gold, for the rape grown to feed pigs and sheep was now in flower. In the sky, skylarks and kestrels replaced the gulls that had ruled the air over the harbor.

So this is England, she thought with pleasure. Her father had called it a foggy, wet island, but today at least, she saw no evidence of such unpleasant weather. *This is my new home. Here I will build a new life for myself, a life where I am my own mistress, at no man's beck and call.*

After she had been a-horse for some three hours, Gisele urged her palfrey up to the front of the procession, where the captain was riding with another of the men. "How far is it to London? Will we reach it tonight, Sir Hubert?" Gisele asked LeBec.

He wiped his fingers across his mouth as if to rub out his smirking grin. "Even if we had wings to fly, my lady, 'twould be too long a flight. Nay, we'll lie at an abbey tonight—"

"An abbey? Is there not some castle where we might seek hospitality? Monastic guest houses have lumpy beds, and poor fare, and the brothers who serve the

ladies look down their pious Benedictine noses at us,''
Gisele protested, remembering her few journeys in Normandy.

"We'll stay at an abbey," Sir Hubert said firmly.
"'Twas your father's command, my lady. Much of
southern England is sympathetic to Stephen, and the
even those who were known to support the empress may
have turned their coats since we last had word on the
other side of the Channel. You'd be a great prize for
them, my lady—to be held for ransom, or forcibly married to compel your father to support Stephen's cause."

His words were sobering. "Very well, Sir Hubert. It
shall be as my lord father orders."

He said nothing more. Soon they left the low-lying
coastal area behind and entered a densely forested area.

"What is this place?" Gisele asked him, watching as
the green fastness of the place enshrouded the mounted
party and seemed to swallow up the sun, except for
occasional dappled patches on the forest floor.

"'Tis called the Weald, and I like it not. The Saxons
fleeing the Conqueror at Senlac once took refuge here,
and the very air seems thick with their ghosts."

His words formed a vivid image in her mind, and as
Gisele peered about her, trying to pierce the gloom with
her eyes, it seemed as if she could see the shades of the
long-dead Saxons behind every tree.

"Then why not go around the Weald, instead of
through it?" she inquired, trying not to sound as nervous as he had made her feel.

"'Tis too wide, my lady. We'd add a full day or more
onto our journey, and would more likely encounter Stephen's men." Evidently deciding he'd wasted enough
time in speech with a slip of a girl, he looked over his

shoulder and said, "Stay alert, men. An entire garrison could hide behind these oaks."

Gisele, following his gaze, looked back, but was made more uneasy by the faces of the other five knights of the escort. Faces that had looked bluff and harmless in the unthreatening sunlight took on a secretive, vaguely menacing, gray-green cast in the shadows of the wood. Eyes that had been respectfully downcast during the Channel crossing now stared at her, but their intent was unreadable.

For the first time Gisele realized how vulnerable she was, a woman alone with these six men but for the presence of Fleurette, and what good could that dear woman do if they decided to turn rogue? What was to stop them from uniting to seize her and hold her for ransom, figuring they could earn more from her ransom than a lifetime of loyal service to the Count de l'Aigle? Inwardly she said a prayer for protection as she dropped back to the middle of the procession to rejoin Fleurette.

Fleurette had been able to hear the conversation Gisele had had with LeBec, and it seemed she could guess what her mistress had been thinking. But she had apprehensions of her own. "'Tis not your father's knights we have to worry about in here," she said in low tones. "'Tis outlaws—they do say outlaws have thriven amid the unrest created by the empress and the king both striving for the same throne. 'Tis said it's as if our Lord and His saints sleep."

Gisele shivered, looking about her in the murky gloom. The decaying leaves from endless autumns muffled the horses' plodding and seemed to swallow up the jingle of the horses' harnesses, the creak of leather and the occasional remark passed between the men. Not even a birdcall marred the preternatural quiet.

Gisele could swear she felt eyes upon her—eyes other than those of the men who rode behind her—but when she stared into the undergrowth on both sides of the narrow path and beyond her as far as she could see, she saw nothing but greenery and bark. A pestilence on LeBec for mentioning ghosts!

Somewhere in the undergrowth a twig snapped, and Gisele jerked in her saddle, startling the gentle palfrey and causing her to sidle uneasily for a few paces.

Gisele's heart seemed to be ready to jump right out of her chest.

She was not the only one alarmed. LeBec cursed and growled, "What was that?"

Suddenly a crashing sounded in the undergrowth and a roe deer burst across the path ahead of them, leaping gracefully into a thicket on their left.

"*There's* what frightened ye, Captain," one of the men called out, chuckling, and the rest joined in. "Too bad no one had a bow and arrow handy. I'd fancy roast venison for supper more than what the monks'll likely serve."

"Those deer are not for the likes of you or me," countered LeBec in an irritated voice. Gisele guessed he was embarrassed at having been so skittish. "I'd wager the king lays claim to them."

"What care have we for what Stephen lays claim to?" argued the other. "Is my lord de l'Aigle not the empress's man?"

"You may say that right up until the moment Stephen has your neck stretched," the captain snapped back.

For a minute or two they could hear the sounds of the buck's progress through the distant wood, then all was quiet once more. The knights clucked to their mounts to resume their plodding.

In the next heartbeat, chaos descended from above.
Shapes that Gisele only vaguely recognized as men
landed on LeBec and two of the other men, bearing
them to the ground as their startled horses reared and
whinnied. Arrows whirred through the air. One caught
the other man ahead of Gisele in the throat, ending his
life in a strangling gurgle of blood as he collapsed on
his horse's withers.

"Christ preserve us!" screamed Fleurette, even as an
arrow caught her full in the chest. She sagged bone-
lessly in the saddle and fell off to the left like a limp
rag doll.

"Fleurette!" Gisele screamed frantically, then whirled
in her saddle in time to see the rear pair of knights
snatched off their horses by brigands who had been
merely shapeless mounds amidst the fallen leaves seconds ago. Then Lark, stung by a feathered barb that had
pierced her flank, forgot her mannerly ways and began
to buck and plunge. Gisele struggled desperately to keep
her seat while the shouts and screams of the men behind
her and ahead of her testified to the fact that they were
being slaughtered by the forest outlaws. The coppery
smell of blood filled the air.

With no one left to protect Gisele, the outlaws were
advancing on her now, their dirty, bearded, sweat-
drenched faces alive with anticipation, holding crude
knives at the ready, some with blades still crimson with
the blood of the Norman knights dead and dying around
them. She was about to be taken, Gisele realized with
terror, and what these brigands would do to her would
make LeBec's mention of being held for ransom or
forcibly wed sound like heaven in comparison. They'd
rape her, like as not, then slit her throat and sell her
clothes, leaving her body to be torn by wild animals

and her bones to be buried eventually by the falling leaves.

But her palfrey was unwittingly her ally now. As Gisele clung to Lark's neck, her mount plunged and kicked so wildly that none of the brigands could get near her. One of them picked up his bow and nocked an arrow in the bowstring, leveling it at the crazed beast's chest.

Then another—perhaps he was the leader—called out something in a guttural English dialect unknown to Gisele. The gesture seemed to indicate that they were not to harm the palfrey—no doubt that man, at least, realized the mare was also a valuable prize. The brigands fell back, but their eyes gleamed like those of wolves as they circled around Gisele and her mare, looking for the opportunity to snatch the wild-eyed horse's bridle.

In a moment they would succeed, Gisele thought, still striving to keep her seat, and then they would rend her like the two-legged wolves they were. *Our Lady help me!* Then, on an impulse, she shrieked as if all the demons in hell had just erupted from her slender throat.

It was enough. Terrified anew, the mare sprang sideways, knocking a nearby outlaw over onto his back, then bolted between two other outlaws and headed off the path into the depths of the wood at a crazed gallop. Gisele bent as low as she could over the mare's straining neck as branches whipped by her face, tearing at her clothes, snatching off her veil and scratching her cheeks.

The sounds of the brigands' foot pursuit grew more and more distant behind her. If she could just circle her way back out of this wood, Gisele thought, she would ride back to the nearest village. She'd find someone in authority to help her go back and find the rest of her party, though she was fairly certain none were alive. Fleurette had probably died instantly, Gisele thought with a pang of grief, but there was no time to mourn now. A parish priest would surely help her find assistance to get to London and the empress—and she'd send the sheriff back to clean out this nest of robbers!

But Gisele had no idea which way the mare was headed. She had lost her reins as well as her sense of direction in the attack. For all she knew, the terrified beast was going in a circle that would lead her right back into the brutal arms of the outlaws!

She ducked just in time to avoid a painful collision with a stout oak branch, and after that she did not dare to raise her head again. The ground blurred by beneath her. Saints, if she had only been riding astride, it would be easier to hug the horse's neck, but ladies did not ride astride.

Ladies did not usually have to flee for their lives, either, Gisele reminded herself. When a quick glance revealed no low-lying branches immediately ahead, she renewed her clutching hold on the beast's streaming mane and threw her right leg over the mare's bunching withers. There was no stirrup to balance her on that side, of course, but she gripped with her knees as if her salvation depended upon it. Without reins, she would just have to wait until the palfrey wore itself out, and hope that the Weald was not as deep as it was wide. Surely she'd come out before she was benighted here, and find some sort of settlement on the other side.

A log loomed ahead of them, and Gisele tried in vain to persuade the mare away from it by pressure from her knees and tugging on her mane, but having come so far on her own impulses, the palfrey was seemingly loath to start taking direction now. The horse gathered herself and leaped the log, with Gisele clinging like a burr atop her, but then caught her hoof in a half-buried root at her landing point on the other side.

Whinnying in fear, the mare cartwheeled, her long legs flailing. Gisele had no chance to do more than scream as she went flying through the air, striking the bole of a beech with the side of her head. There was a flash of light, and then—nothing.

Chapter Two

Gisele awoke to a gentle nudge against her shoulder.
Lark? But no, she thought, keeping her eyes closed,
whatever pushed against her shoulder was harder than
the soft velvety nose of her palfrey. More like a booted
foot…

*The outlaws had found her, and were poking her to
see if she lived.* She froze, holding her breath. In a moment they would try some more noxious means of eliciting a response, and she would not be able to hold back
her scream. Doubtless that would delight them.

She waited until her lungs burned for lack of air, then
took a breath, eyes still closed.

"The lady lives, my lord."

"So 'twould seem."

They spoke good Norman French, not the gutteral
Saxon tongue of the outlaws. Gisele's eyes flew open.

And looked directly up into eyes so dark and deep
that they appeared to be black, bottomless pools. The
man who owned such eyes stood over her, gazing down
at her with open curiosity. He had a warrior's powerful
shoulders and broad chest, and from Gisele's recumbent
position he seemed tall as a tree. He wore a hauberk,

and the mail coif framed a face that was all angular planes. The lean, chiseled face, firm mouth, and deep-set eyes shouldn't have been a pleasing combination, but despite the lack of a smile, it was.

Next to him, the other man who had spoken leaned over to stare at her, too. Even taller than the man he had addressed as my lord, he was massively built, and wore a leather byrnie sewn with metal links rather than a hauberk. Possibly a half-dozen years younger than his master, he was not handsome, but his face bore a stamp of permanent amiability.

"Who—who are you?" Gisele asked at last, when it seemed their duel of gazes might go on until the end of the world.

"I might ask the same of you," the mail-clad man pointed out.

Gisele wondered if she should tell him the truth. By his speech, the quality of his armor, and the presence of the gold spurs, she could tell he was noble, but whose vassal was he? If he was Stephen's and found out she was the daughter of a vassal of Matilda's, would he still behave chivalrously toward her, or treat her with dishonor? She dared not tell him a lie, for in the leather pouch that swung from her girdle, she bore a letter her father had written to introduce her to the empress. If the man standing over her was the dishonorable sort, he might have already have searched that pouch for valuables, and discovered her identity and her allegiance. But he did not *look* unscrupulous, despite the slight impatience that thinned his lips now.

"I am Lady Sidonie Gisele de l'Aigle. And you?"

He went on studying her silently, until the other man finally said, "He's the Baron de Balleroy, my lady. What are you doing in the woods all alone?"

"Hush, Maislin. Forgive my squire his impertinence, Lady Gisele. My Christian name is Brys, since you have given me yours. Might I help you to your feet?" he asked, extending a mail-gauntleted hand.

Up to this point Gisele hadn't moved from her supine position, but as she pushed up on her elbows preparatory to taking his hand, it suddenly seemed as if the devil had made a Saracen drum out of her head and was pounding it with fiendish glee. With a moan she sank back, feeling sick with the intensity of the pain.

"She's ill, my lord!" the squire announced anxiously.

"I can see that," she heard de Balleroy snap. "Go catch her palfrey grazing over there, Maislin, while I see what's to be done. I can see that your face is scraped, my lady, but where else are you hurt? Is aught broken?"

She opened her eyes again to find de Balleroy crouching beside her, his face creased with concern. He was reaching a hand out as if to explore her limbs for a fracture.

"Nay, 'tis my head," she told him quickly, before he could touch her. "It feels as if it may split open. I...my palfrey fell, and I with her. I...guess the fall knocked me insensible. How long have I lain—" she began, as she struggled to sit up again.

"Just rest there a moment, Lady Sidonie," he began.

"Gisele," she corrected him.

He looked blank for a moment, until she explained, "I go by my middle name, Gisele. I was named Sidonie for my mother, but to avoid confusion, I am called Gisele." There hadn't been, of course, any confusion in the ten years that her mother had been dead, but de Balleroy needn't know that.

She started to lever herself into a sitting position, but he put a hand on her shoulder to forestall her. "As to how long you lay there, I know not—but 'tis late afternoon now. And as my squire asked, what were you doing in the Weald alone?" There was an edge to his voice, as if he already suspected her answer.

And then she remembered. "Fleurette! I must go to her! And the men! Maybe I was wrong—even now, one or two may still live!" She thrashed now beneath his hand, struggling to get up, her teeth gritted against the pain her movement elicited.

"Lie *still,* my lady! You gain nothing if the pain makes you pass out again! You traveled with that party of men-at-arms, and the old woman? My squire and I...well, we came upon them farther back, Lady Gisele. There is nothing you can do for them. They are all dead."

He could have added, *And stripped naked as the day they were born, their throats cut,* but he did not. Lady Sidonie Gisele de l'Aigle's creamy ivory skin had a decidedly green cast to it already. If he described the scene of carnage he and his squire had found, she just might perish from the shock.

She ceased trying to rise. Her eyelids squeezed shut, forcing a tear down her cheek, then another. "We were set upon by brigands, my lord," she said, obviously struggling not to give way to full-blown sobbing. "They jumped out of the trees without warning. I saw the arrow pierce my old nurse's breast...but I hoped..."

"Like as not she was dead before she hit the ground, my lady." Brys de Balleroy said, keeping his voice deep and soothing. "I'll come back and see them buried, I promise you. But now we must get you to safety—'twill be dusk soon, and we must not remain in the woods any longer. Do you think you can stand?''

She nodded.

"Let me help you," he told her, placing both of his hands under her arms to help her up. Over his shoulder, Brys saw that his squire had caught the chestnut mare and stood holding the reins nearby, his face anxious.

Lady Gisele gave a gallant effort, but as she first put her weight on her left foot, she gasped and swayed against him. "My ankle—I cannot stand on it!" Pearls of sweat popped out on her forehead as he eased her to the ground. Her face went shroud-white, her pupils dilated.

Leaving her in a sitting position, he went to her foot and began to pull the kidskin boot off.

She moaned and grabbed for his hand. "Nay, it hurts too much...."

He took the dagger from his belt and slit the kidskin boot open from top to toe, peeling the ruined boot from around her swollen ankle before probing the bone with experienced fingers.

He looked up to see her gritting her teeth and staring at him with pain-widened eyes. "'Tis but sprained, I think, my lady, though I doubt not it pains you, for 'tis very swollen. You cannot ride your mare, that's clear, so you will have to ride with me."

"But surely if you'll just help me to mount, I can manage," she insisted, trying once again to rise.

"You'll ride with me," he said, his face set. "You still look as if you could swoon any moment now, and I have no desire to be benighted in this forest with no one but me and my squire to fend off those miscreants. They may come looking for you, you know, so I'll hear no more argument. Maislin, tie her palfrey to a tree and bring Jerusalem over. I'll mount and you can lift her up behind me, then lead her mare. You can manage to ride pillion, can't you, Lady Gisele? I'd hold you in front of me, but I'd rather have my arms free in case your attackers try again before we get out of the wood.''

She nodded, her eyes enormous in her pale oval face. Brys could not tell what hue they were, not in this murky gloom, but he could see she was beautiful, despite the rent and muddied clothes she wore. She had a pert nose, high cheekbones and lips that looked made for a man's kiss. Beneath the gold fillet and the stained veil which was slightly askew, a wealth of rich brown hair cascaded down her back, much of it loose from the thick plait which extended nearly to her waist.

Once. Brys was mounted on his tall black destrier, Maislin lifted Lady Gisele up to him from the stallion's near side, his powerfully muscled arms making the task look effortless.

''Put your arms about my waist, my lady,'' Brys instructed her. ''Jerusalem's gait is smooth, but 'twill steady you as we ride.''

A faint essence wafted to his nostrils, making him smile in wonder. After all she had been through, Lady Gisele de l'Aigle still smelled of lilies. He felt her arms go around him and saw her hands link just above his waist; then felt the slight pressure of her head, and farther down, the softness of her breast against his back. God's blood, what a delicious torment of a ride this would be!

''You have not said how you came to be here, Lady Gisele,'' he said, once they had found the path that led out of the Weald.

He felt her tense, then sigh against his back. He could

swear the warmth of her breath penetrated his mail, the quilted *aketon* beneath, and all the way to his backbone.

"I suppose I owe you that much," she said at last. "But I must confess myself afraid to be candid, my lord. These are dangerous times...."

Stung by her remark, he said, "Lady, I do not hold my chivalry so cheaply that I would abandon you if I liked not your reason for being in this wood with such a paltry escort. And even if I wanted to, Maislin wouldn't allow it. He aspires to knighthood and his chivalry, at least, is unsullied."

He heard her swift intake of breath. "I'm sorry," she said at last. "I have offended you, and 'twas not my intent, when you have offered me only kindness. But even in Normandy we are aware of the trouble in England, as one noble fights for Stephen, the other for the empress. I know not which side you cleave to, my lord, though I know I am at your mercy whichever it is."

The idea of this demoiselle being at his mercy appealed to him more than he cared to admit. Aloud, he said, "Then I will tell you I am a vassal of the empress. Does that aid you to trust me? I swear upon the True Cross you have naught to fear of me, even if you are one of Stephen's mistresses."

He felt her relax against him like a full grain sack that suddenly is opened at the bottom. "No, I am assuredly not one of those. The de l'Aigles owe their loyalty to Matilda as well, Lord Brys. In fact, I am sent to join her as a lady-in-waiting."

"Then we are on the same side. 'Tis well, is it not? And better yet, I am bound for London with a message for the empress, so I will consider it my honor to escort you to her court."

"Our Lord and all His saints bless you, Lord Brys,"

she murmured. "I will write to my father, and ask him to reward your kindness."

"'Tis not necessary, lady. Any Christian ought to do the same," he said. He felt himself begin to smile. "I am often with her grace, so we shall see each other on occasion. If I can but claim a smile from you each time I come, I shall ask no other recompense." He could tell, from the shy way she had looked at him earlier, that she was a virgin. Alas. *Lady Gisele, if only you were a noble widow instead of an innocent maiden, I'd ask an altogether different reward when I came to court.* Brys felt his loins stir at the thought.

Behind him, he heard Maislin give a barely smothered snort, and knew his squire was struggling to contain his amusement at the fulsome remark. He would chasten him about it later, Brys was sure.

"And when did you come to England, Lady Gisele?" he asked, thankful she was riding behind him and could not see the effect his thoughts had on his body.

"We landed at Hastings but this morning, my lord."

Brys considered that. "Lady Gisele, forgive me for asking, but if your father is as aware of the conditions here as you say, why would he send you with but half a dozen men and an old woman?"

She was silent, and Brys knew his words had been rude. What daughter could allow a parent to be criticized? "I'm sorry if I sounded harsh—"

"Nay, do not apologize, for you are right. There should have been a larger escort. I know that had my horse not bolted, I would have been lucky to escape those brigands with my life, let alone my honor." Her voice was muffled, as if she fought tears. "Poor Fleurette—to have died because of my father's...misalculation. And those six men, too. They did not deserve to perish like that, all unshriven.''

He was ready to swear she'd meant some other word when she'd said *miscalculation,* and he wondered what it was—and what was wrong with the Count de l'Aigle that he valued his daughter so cheaply.

"You have a tender heart, lady.'' He only hoped it would not lead her astray at Matilda's court.

"Fleurette had been my nurse from my earliest childhood, so 'tis natural I would grieve at her death,'' she said, sounding a trifle defensive. "The men...well, I have difficulty accepting that because my lord father ordered them to escort me to London, they lie dead now.''

This was an uncommon noblewoman, to spare a thought for common soldiers. "Dying violently is the risk any man-at-arms runs, but doubtless their loyalty will outweigh their sins, Lady Gisele.''

"God send you are right.''

Perhaps it was best not to allow her to dwell on such things right now. After a moment he said, "You go to court to wed, my lady?''

He felt her stiffen against his back. He glanced back over his shoulder and saw that her eyes had the light of defiance dancing in them.

"'Twas my father's wish, my lord.''

He was quick to catch the implication. "But not yours?'' he asked, glancing over his shoulder again.

He saw her shrug. "I shall have a place at the empress's court,'' she said. "That will be enough for me. What need have I for some lord to carry me off to his castle to bear a child every year till I am no longer able?''

An image flashed before his mind's eye of this

woman nursing a babe—*his* babe. Sternly he banished the picture before he grew too fond of it. There was no place in his life for such feelings, and the lady had just indicated there was none in the life she wanted, either. But he could not stop himself from probing further, though in a carefully neutral tone of voice, ''You do not wish to fulfill the role that nature and the church has deemed fit for a woman?''

''There must be more for a woman than the marriage bed or the convent, no matter what the church tells us,'' she said with a passionate insistence. ''There *must* be.''

''Lady, has a man hurt you in some manner?'' he asked in a low tone that would not carry to Maislin's ears. Had he been wrong about her? Had some man robbed her of her innocence?

Her answer came a little too quickly. ''Hurt me? Nay, my lord! Just because the lord the empress selected for me chose to marry some other lady, you should not think that I am not heart-whole.''

She was lying, he'd wager his salvation on that. There was a wealth of wounded pride in her voice. But something about her last few words sounded familiar....

''Nay, my lord,'' she went on in a breezy voice, '''Tis merely that I see no need to w—''

Suddenly he realized who she was. ''Ah, you're the one Matilda offered to Baron Alain of Hawkswell, aren't you?''

''And how did you know such a thing?'' she asked, her voice chilly.

He felt her remove her arms from about his waist and draw a little away from him. Instantly his body felt deprived. He wanted to demand that she put her arms back around him—he didn't want her to fall, of course!

''Fear not, proud lady—'tis not a thing bandied about

court—the only reason I know is that Alain is a good friend.''

"How nice for you to have such a friend," she said, as if every courteous word cut her like a dagger.

"Nay, do not bristle at me," he said, patting her hands that were still clasped around his abdomen with his free one. "Alain would not have suited you at all— a widower with two children? Claire is much more his sort, for all that her family are adherents of Stephen's. You'll see what I mean if you ever meet them."

"Mayhap," she said noncommittally, but he could tell she was lying again. She'd move heaven and earth to avoid encountering the man who had rejected her, sight unseen. What a proud, fierce maid she was!

"I think you have the right idea, Lady Gisele—enjoy your life at court just as any bachelor knight enjoys his freedom," he told her. "You'll enjoy the empress's favor and all her lords will covet you."

"I told you," she began, impatience tingeing her voice, "I care not about the opinion of men—"

"Of course, of course," he said. "Hold to that course, my lady, for we are knaves one and all." But Brys could guess how Lady Gisele's coolness would affect the men in the empress's orbit—they'd be panting all the more after Gisele de l'Aigle, like brachets after a swift doe. He felt acid burn in his stomach at the thought. And Brys could only wonder how long Matilda would allow such a beauty to indulge her whims before she used her as a pawn in making an alliance.

Chapter Three

At last they came to a Benedictine priory just beyond the edge of the Weald. Gisele, exhausted by the day's events and longing to have some time to grieve in private, told Brys before he even assisted her to dismount that she was too tired to dine in the guest house and would seek her bed early instead.

"Very well, then, my lady," he said. "Doubtless you'll feel better on the morrow. I will send the infirmarer to you with a salve for your cuts and a draft to help you sleep. Your ankle will have swollen since this afternoon, and the pain is apt to keep you wakeful."

"You seem very familiar with what this house has to offer, my lord," she said. Now that they were beyond the forest gloom, she saw that his eyes were not black, but a deep, rich brown, like the color of her palfrey's coat.

"I have sought remedy for injury here before," he said, without elaborating.

She could tell that Brother Porter was scandalized by the way de Balleroy handed her down to his squire, then took Gisele back into his arms and bid the monk to lead the way to the ladies' guest quarters. But the disapproving Benedictine did not remonstrate with him, just directed another pair of monks to stable the horses, before gesturing for de Balleroy to follow him.

Gisele awoke and hobbled her way to the shuttered window, throwing it open to see if it was yet light. She was alarmed to see that the sun was already high in the sky. The infirmarian's potion had been powerful indeed! She hadn't even heard the chapel bells call the brothers to prayer during the night. Her ankle still throbbed, though less than it had last even.

Then a sudden thought struck her. *Dear God, what if Brys de Balleroy had grown tired of waiting and had ridden on to London without her? What of his promise to have Fleurette and the men-at-arms buried?*

Hopping awkwardly over to the row of hooks by the door where she had left her muddied, torn gown hanging, she found the garment miraculously clean and dry again. Propped up against the wall beneath the gown was a crutch with a cloth-padded armrest. She silently blessed whichever Benedictines had done her these kindnesses, and with the crutch to help her, ventured out into the cloister and across the garth until she came to the gate.

"Where is my lord de Balleroy? Has he left?" she asked Brother Porter.

"Aye," replied the monk. "He and the big fellow, his squire, left at Prime—along with a wagon and a pair of our brothers. He said he promised you he would bury your dead. Some other brothers are already digging the graves in our cemetery."

"Oh." So de Balleroy was as good as his word, Gisele thought, warmed by the idea that he had been up and about and fulfilling his promise while she had still been deep in slumber.

The party returned at midday. Gisele, waiting just inside the gate, saw a grim-faced de Balleroy riding behind the mule-drawn cart with its ghastly load.

"Make ready to leave, Lady Gisele," he said as he dismounted.

"But may we not remain until they are buried? Fleurette—" she began, her voice breaking as she saw the monks begin to unload the sheet-wrapped, stiffened forms. She could not even tell which one was her beloved nurse.

"Is at peace already, my lady, and if we stay for the burial we will have to spend another night here. We will have to pass one more night on the road as 'tis, and I think it best to get you to the empress as soon as I can. Do not fear, the Benedictines will see all done properly."

She could see the prudence of that, of course, but nevertheless, her heart ached as she rode away from the priory within the hour, once more riding pillion behind de Balleroy.

The next day, as the distant spires of London came into view ahead of them, de Balleroy turned west.

"We do not go directly to London?" Gisele questioned.

"Nay. The empress resides at Westminster, a few miles up the Thames, my lady," de Balleroy told her. "But you'll see the city soon and often enough. Now that Matilda has finally been admitted to London, and will soon be crowned, she likes to remind the citizens of her presence."

Gisele nodded her understanding and reined her palfrey to the left, where the road led over marshy, sparsely settled ground. Though her ankle was still slightly swollen and painful, she had insisted she would sit her own horse this morning, not wanting to arrive at the empress's residence riding pillion behind the baron as if she had no more dignity than a dairymaid. It was bad enough that outlaws possessed every stitch of clothing she owned, except for what she had on her back. Seeing her in the enforced intimacy of this position, however, someone might take them for lovers. Having her good name ruined would *not* be a good way for Gisele to begin her new life!

Perhaps de Balleroy had guessed her thoughts this morning. Instead of arguing about her ankle's fitness, he had lifted her up into her saddle as if she weighed no more than an acorn, sparing her the necessity of putting her weight on the still-tender ankle to mount.

Gisele took the opportunity to study de Balleroy covertly, an easier task now that she was no longer sitting behind him. The sun gleamed on his chin-length, auburn hair. Somehow she had not expected it to be such a hue; his dark eyes and eyelashes had given no hint of it, and she had never previously seen him without his head being covered. This morning, however, he had evidently felt close enough to civilization to leave the metal coif draped around his neck and shoulders.

"Faith, but 'tis hot this morn," he murmured, raking a hand through his hair, an action which caused the sun to gild it with golden highlights that belied the dangerous look of his lean, beard-shadowed cheeks. "I believe the sun is shining just to welcome you to court, Lady Gisele." He flashed a grin at her, making her heart to do a strange little dance within her breast.

Firmly she quashed the flirtatious reply that had

sprung ready-born to her lips. She owed this man much for her safety, but it would not do to let him think his flattery delighted her, after telling him before that such things were unimportant to her. From the ease at which such smooth words flowed from his lips, she supposed he had pleased many women with his cajolery—but she was not going to join their number!

"*I* believe too much sun has addled your brain, my lord," she said tartly.

"Just so, Lady Gisele," Maislin agreed from behind them. "From the color of his hair, 'tis obvious his skull must have been singed at one time or another, and his brain beneath it, too!"

Apparently, however, de Balleroy took her retort for bantering. "Ah, Lady Gisele, you wound me to the heart with your dagger-sharp tongue. I'll be but a shadow of my former robust self by the time I bid you farewell at Westminster." His merry smile didn't look the least bit discomfitted, however.

"Oh? You're not remaining?" she said, then wished she could kick herself, for his smile had broadened into a grin. But she was dismayed at the thought she would have to navigate the strange new world of Matilda's palace without the presence of even one familiar face.

"Ah, so you *will* miss me," he teased. "I'll be back at court from time to time, never fear."

"Oh, it's naught to *me*, my lord," she assured him with what she hoped sounded like conviction. She made her voice casual, even a trifle bored. "No doubt the empress will keep me so busy I should scarce know whether you are there or not. Do you return to a fief in England? Or mayhap you have a demesne and wife in Normandy?"

"Mayhap," he said, shrugging his shoulders.

His evasiveness, coupled with her nervousness about the new life she was about to take up, sparked her temper.

"You're very secretive, my lord. I was merely making conversation."

"If you wanted to know if I was married, Lady Gisele, you should have asked me," he said with maddening sangfroid.

Devil take the man! "As I said, 'tis naught to me," she replied through clenched teeth. "I was just trying to pass the time. And after all, you know much about me and I know virtually nothing about you."

She could read nothing in those honey-brown eyes, neither anger at her sharp tone nor amusement at her expense.

Finally he said, "I'm sorry, Lady Gisele. The responsibilities I bear for the empress have required that I keep my own counsel, and 'tis a habit hard to break."

She averted her face from him. "Well, do not feel you must change your habit for me."

"I am not wed," he continued, as if she had not spoken. "I am the lord of Balleroy in Normandy, and in addition, hold Tichenden Castle here in England. I have a sister two years my junior, who acts as my chatelaine at Tichenden, two younger sisters being educated in a Norman convent—perhaps one of them will take the veil—and the youngest is a brother still at home. Our parents are dead. Is there aught else you would know?"

She refused to express surprise at the sudden flood of information. "Where is Tichenden? In the west, I assume, where the empress's forces are strong?"

"Nay, 'tis on the North Downs."

"But I thought Stephen's adherents held that part of England?"

"And so they do, for the most part." She saw that shuttered look come over his eyes again, and knew she must not delve further in this particular subject.

After ferrying themselves and their mounts across the Thames, they arrived at Westminster just at the hour of Sext. De Balleroy had just assisted Gisele to dismount and their horses were being led away by a servitor when Gisele's stomach growled so loudly that even the baron heard it.

"Ah, too bad," he mocked, "for I fear we've missed the midday meal, and 'twill be long till supper. Shall I take you first to the kitchens for something to fill your empty stomach?"

"That won't be necessary," she told him, wishing he'd allow her to keep her dignity, at least until she'd been presented to Matilda! "If you would direct me in finding the empress, or someone who knows where she may be found—"

Visibly making an effort to smoothe the teasing grin from his face, he murmured, "Very well, follow me, my lady. Maislin," he called over his shoulder as he led her across the courtyard, "see that Lady Gisele's palfrey is given a good stall, and all our mounts grained and watered, but tell the stable boy yours and mine are to be kept in readiness. We'll likely depart by midafternoon. Oh, and don't force me have to come and find you off in some shadowy corner with a scullery wench, Maislin."

"Yes, my lord!" the squire called back, but his voice sounded undismayed by these strictures.

I wonder if you practice what you preach, my lord,

Gisele wanted to say, but she was too intent on keeping up with him despite her painful limp.

At last he seemed to realize how far behind she was falling, and turned around. "Your dignity will have to wait until your foot is better, Lady Gisele," he said, picking her up.

She only hoped no one important would see them.

He carried her into the palace, and through a maze of corridors, doors and antechambers. He strode along as surely as if he carried nothing, and this mysterious warren was his own castle. At last they came to a door guarded by two hefty men-at-arms, who crossed their spears to bar their way.

"Who would enter the empress's presence?" one growled.

"Tell her chamberlain 'tis de Balleroy," the baron responded easily, a slight smile playing over his lips as he set Gisele down.

One of the guards disappeared within, and a moment later, the door was opened, and a harried-looking man in a robe trimmed with squirrel stuck his head out and gestured that they were to enter.

Before the two could do so, however, a throaty female voice called, "Brys, is that you? Come in, you rascally knave!"

De Balleroy grinned at her as if to say, *See, I told you we were knaves all!*

They entered a spacious chamber into which the noonday sun streamed through several wide, arched windows, illuminating a feminine figure who glided toward them. As Matilda drew closer, Gisele saw that she was still strikingly attractive, with a slender waist that belied the fact that she had given her husband three sons. Worry had etched a sharpness to her features, though, and her gray eyes had a shrewd, penetrating quality to them. She wore a veil and wimple over her hair, with an ornate circlet of gold keeping the veil in place.

De Balleroy went down on one knee before the empress, bowing his head, while behind him Gisele awkwardly knelt also, uncertain what was proper for her to do.

"Brys," Matilda purred in that caressing, faintly German-accented voice as she held out an ivory-white hand and extended it to de Balleroy to kiss, "Isn't it wonderful that I am finally in Westminster Palace where I belong? I tell you, Geoffrey de Mandeville is a miracle worker, persuading those stiff-necked Londoners to let me in! Did you have a good journey? And who is this lovely maid behind you?"

Seemingly used to the empress's flood of words, de Balleroy rose and said, "You glow like a jewel in its proper setting at last, Domina. My journey was uneventful until I traveled through the Weald, and found this lady lying unconscious, the only survivor of a massacre. May I present Lady Sidonie Gisele de l'Aigle? She goes by her middle name, Gisele."

The empress's eyes widened, and she glided past de Balleroy and placed her hands on Gisele's blushing cheeks. Her hands were cool and smooth. "God in Heaven! A massacre? I have been expecting you, child—but what on earth happened? Your face—it is all scratched!" she said, tracing the scrapes on Gisele's face, left by the tree branches during her wild ride.

"Outlaws, your…highness," Gisele said hesitatingly. "My escort was attacked in the Weald—" She felt emotion tighten her throat.

"They were slaughtered to a man," de Balleroy finished for her. "The miscreants even killed an old woman with them, the lady's servant. If Lady Gisele's horse hadn't bolted, doubtless she would not be standing before you now, Domina. As it is, the robbers got everything she brought with her but the clothes she wears."

"God be thanked you were preserved, child," Matilda said, extending a hand to Gisele to assist her to her feet. Gisele arose, awkwardly because of the still-painful ankle, and she could feel Matilda assessing her, judging her appearance and her worth. If only she had had something more to wear than the travel-stained *bliaut*.

"I went back and buried the bodies, Empress," de Balleroy said. "Would that I could return with a force of knights and clear out the rats' nest of outlaws in the Weald as well."

"Always, he is the soul of chivalry," she said to Gisele. "Ah, Brys, if only I was already crowned, and Stephen of Blois banished across the Channel where he belongs! Then I would grant you that force! Since my cousin has been on the throne, felons and thieves have multiplied, and honest folk are murdered. It was not so in my father's day, and will not be so in this land as soon as I have won—but who knows how long that may be?" She sighed heavily. "A deputation of the wealthiest merchants of London just left before you came, Brys, and they did not like it when I told them Stephen had left the treasury bare as a well-gnawed bone. And they took it very ill that I told them they would have to supply the funds for my crowning! Can you imagine it? They thought I should be crowned in the same threadbare garments that I brought from Anjou."

Gisele did not think the purple velvet overgown,

banded at the neck and sleeves with golden-threaded embroidery, looked at all threadbare, but possibly it was not ornate enough for the widow of the Holy Roman Emperor to wear to her crowning.

Gisele wondered, though, if it was wise for Matilda, who had been refused entrance into London for so long, to have immediately demanded money of the independent-minded Londoners. Even in Normandy it was known that the Londoners had long favored Stephen, Matilda's rival. Surely it would have been prudent to wait a while before making financial demands?

Fortunately the empress did not seem to be expecting an answer to her question from de Balleroy, for she immediately turned back to Gisele.

"Ah, but you must be too fatigued to listen to such things, my dear, after what you have been through!" exclaimed the empress, putting her arm around Gisele's shoulders. "I must immediately write a letter to your lord father, telling him what has befallen you and assuring him that you, at least, are unharmed!"

He won't care, Gisele wanted to blurt out. *He will begrudge me the loss of his six knights much more than he values my safety, at least until I make an advantageous marriage and provide him with a male heir.* But she did not say what she was thinking; she could not bear for this worldly, sophisticated woman who had been through so much herself to pity her.

"Thank you, Domina," Gisele managed to say, calling the empress by the title she had heard Brys use.

"Things will appear better to you after you have rested and refreshed yourself, Gisele, my dear," Matilda said. Her husky, accented voice had a very soothing quality, and all at once Gisele could see why so many men had been willing to follow and fight for this woman, even though her fortunes had often been precarious.

"Talford!" Matilda called to the chamberlain who had been hovering in the background. "Find Lady Gisele a suitable chamber in the palace! See that she has everything she needs between now and the supper hour, and that someone comes to show her the way to the hall. Lady Gisele, I will see you again at supper, where you will meet my other ladies and members of my court."

It was a dismissal; Matilda was already drawing de Balleroy over to two carved, high-backed chairs over by one of the windows, and the harried-looking chamberlain was gesturing for her to follow him out the door. But Gisele had wanted to bid farewell to Brys de Balleroy and thank him for his and his squire's kindness to her. She hesitated, willing de Balleroy to turn around. "I would thank my lord de Balleroy...." she said at last, when it seemed she would be ushered away with no chance to say anything further to him.

Brys de Balleroy turned, a curious light dancing in those honey-brown eyes, and smiled encouragingly at her.

"'Twas my honor to render you such a paltry service, my lady. No doubt when I next see you, you will have blossomed like a rose, a rose every man will want for his garden."

Easy words, glibly spoken while Matilda smiled tolerantly, then pulled Brys toward the chairs.

She wanted to ask when that would be—when would he be returning to Westminster? But she felt he had already forgotten her, and so there was nothing to do but limp after the chamberlain as he led her from the room.

Chapter Four

"I do believe the Norman damsel has stolen your heart, my lord," Maislin commented as they rode away from Westminster, following the river back toward London. White-headed daisies and purple loosestrife waved on the riverbanks; overhead, gulls flew eastward back toward the mouth of the Thames, following a barge.

"Oh? And how many buckets of ale did you manage to swill in the short time I was gone from you?"

Maislin blinked. "I? I'm sober as a monk at the end of Lent, my lord! In fact, I was just about to ask that we stop and wet our throats at that little alehouse in Southwark. Why would you ask such a thing?"

"Why? Because I've rarely known you to say such a foolish thing, Maislin."

To give him credit, the shaggy giant didn't try to pretend he didn't know what Brys meant. "My lord Brys," he retorted, "you looked back at the palace walls thrice since we left. Will you try to tell me it's the empress you're longing for, so soon after departing her presence?"

Brys chuckled. "Nay, I'm not so foolish as to get involved in Matilda's coils."

His squire nodded sagely. "Aye, then 'tis the Norman maiden you're already missing. She's stolen your heart," he insisted.

"I have no heart to steal, don't you remember?" Brys reminded Maislin, with a wry twist of his mouth. "At least, that's what you always say when I won't stop at every alestake between here and Scotland. Nay, I'm just pitying poor Lady Gisele. I feel like an untrustworthy shepherd who has just tossed a prize lamb in among a pack of wolves."

Maislin grinned. "Could a man who never had a heart speak so, Lord Brys? Aye, you've got feelings for the Norman lass, I'll be bound! And why not? She *is* a toothsome damsel, with those great round eyes and soft rosebud lips and that thick chestnut hair. Tell me your loins never burned while you were carrying her into the priory, or while she was ridin' behind you with her softness rub—"

Brys put up a gauntleted hand to forestall his squire's frankness. "Careful…" Damn Maislin, he could feel his aforementioned loins tingling as Maislin reminded him of the exquisite torment he'd experienced the past two days due to his enforced contact with the Norman maiden. "You're confusing a heart with a *conscience,* Maislin," he said. "I merely don't like to think of an innocent such as Lady Gisele at the mercy of every lecherous knight at Matilda's court."

"Innocent?" Maislin mused consideringly. "Aye, I think you've the right of it there, my lord. The wench is innocent as a newborn kitten."

"She can spit like a kitten, too," Brys murmured, recalling the indignant way she had spoken of her rejection by his friend Alain of Hawkswell. "I merely fear she has not claws enough for the savage dogs that lurk about the empress,'' he added, as some of the faces of Matilda's supporters came to mind.

"There is a remedy, if you are truly worried, my lord," Maislin said, mischief lurking in his blue eyes.

"Oh? And what would that be, pray?" Brys asked, suspicious.

"'Tis obvious! Take her to wife yourself, my lord! I'd vow you could have that kitten purring in your arms well before dawn!"

Suddenly the conversation had gone on too long. "Cease your silly japing, Maislin," Brys commanded, turning his face from his squire. "You're making my brains ache."

"But 'tis no jape, my lord Brys," Maislin protested. "Why not wed Lady Gisele? She's comely enough for a *prince,* and is an heiress in the bargain! Why not make Hawkswell's loss your gain? You must marry *some* lady and give a son to Balleroy!"

"Maislin, you forget yourself," Brys snapped. "I'll brook no more talk like this! You would do well to remember that we have been entrusted with a mission, and keep your mind upon it. Not upon your lord's private business."

"Yes, my lord," his squire said, his usually merry face instantly crestfallen, his cheeks a dull brick red.

They rode in silence for the next few minutes. His squire's words echoed back to him—*You must marry some lady and give a son to Balleroy*—as if Balleroy were not his castle in Normandy, but a greedy pagan god to be appeased by the offering of a male infant. He had sisters, and no inclination to tie himself down to a wife just now. If he was caught while he played his dangerous game, and paid with his life, one of his sisters could marry and provide Balleroy with its heir.

Then why could he not banish Gisele de l'Aigle's face from his mind? Her creamy oval face, framed by glossy chestnut hair. Her eyes. Once they had left the forest gloom behind, he had discovered her eyes were a changeable hazel—now amber, now jade green shot with gold, depending upon her surroundings. And yes, that pair of soft lips his squire had compared to rosebuds, curse him. His loins ached as he thought of kissing those lips.

Well, he never would. He had no time for marriage, and hadn't Gisele herself indicated she wanted no part of the wedded state? She wanted to be free and independent of either a husband's control or that of the Church. Good luck, my lady, for I doubt you will find such a state anywhere in Christendom!

"I can see the alestake from here, Maislin," he said, when they were halfway across the bridge to Southwark. He was determined to eject Gisele from his mind.

"Aye, my lord."

Glancing over at the young giant, he saw that his squire's eyes were fixed firmly between his mount's ears. He had looked neither to the right nor the left, even when Brys had spoken. Brys felt shame stab at him. His squire was as strong as a young ox, and excelled at swordsmanship, yet his feelings were as easy to hurt as a puppy's.

"Isn't that the alehouse with the buxom serving wench you had your eye on last time we passed this way, Maislin? Here, tuck this into her bodice—" he held out a silver penny "—and I'll wager she'll invite you to the back chamber where she can serve you more privately."

Maislin brightened immediately. "Thank you, my lord! I have no doubt she will! But...what of you, Lord

Brys? She had a cousin working there too, as I recall…a cuddlesome thing nearly as pretty as she, if you don't mind the pox scar on her cheek—I'm sure she'd do the same for you, my lord.…''

Brys smiled. ''No doubt, but I'll just drink my ale while you…ah…sate another appetite.''

''Why do they call the empress 'Domina?''' she asked, not only because she wondered, but because she wanted to slow the chamberlain down. He set a quick pace in spite of his short legs.

''Because 'tis the proper title for a queen before she has been crowned,'' Talford said, as if Gisele should have known it. ''Until her coronation, she is 'Domina' or 'the Lady of England'—or one uses her former title of Empress.''

''I see,'' Gisele said, trying not to pant.

''It is to be hoped one of the other ladies can furnish you with a suitable gown, until you can obtain some of your own,'' Talford sniffed, eyeing her brown *bliaut* with distaste.

Gisele said nothing. She guessed the supercilious chamberlain had been listening when the empress was told about the attack in the Weald.

He sniffed again as they stopped in front of a door. ''Here is your chamber. You will share it with Lady Manette de Mandeville.''

De Mandeville—the empress had mentioned that name. Ah yes, Geoffrey de Mandeville, the man whom Matilda had claimed worked a miracle by getting the Londoners to let her in.

''She is the daughter of Lord Geoffrey de Mandeville?''

''Lady Manette is the niece of the Earl of Essex—or

at least 'tis what I've been *told*," the chamberlain said, lifting a brow as if he doubted the relationship—making Gisele wonder why.

He knocked at the door, but no one answered within. He knocked again, harder this time, and from inside the chamber came a breathless, muffled shout: "Go away!"

Talford's face hardened and he rolled his eyes heavenward. "It is I, Talford! Lady Manette, you must open this door!" He added softly, as if to himself, "And there had better not be anyone in there with you."

Gisele heard a scuffling within, and a muttered curse in a voice which sounded too deep to be a woman's, then a rustling as though someone walked across rushes toward the door. A moment later it creaked open, revealing a heavy-lidded flush-faced blond girl whose hair had mostly escaped the plait that hung to her slender waist. A heavily embroidered girdle was only half-tied at her hips.

"Yes?" she said, her gaze flicking from Talford to Gisele and back again.

"I did not truly did not think to find you here at this hour, my lady."

Manette de Mandeville raised a supercilious pale brow.

"You knocked on the door and called my name, but you did not think to find me here?"

"It is past midday, my lady. I did not think to find you abed," he said in his sententious way, nodding toward the interior, where bed with rumpled linens was clearly visible from the corridor. "I knocked only as a courtesy. I thought you would be about your duties with the rest of the empress's ladies."

"I was ill," Lady Manette said, a trifle defensively. "My belly was cramping—my monthly flux, you know.

And now," she said, glancing meaningfully over her shoulder at the bed, "if you will excuse me…"

Gisele watched, fascinated, as the chamberlain's face turned livid, then crimson.

"Such plain speaking is neither necessary nor becoming of one of the empress's ladies," Talford reprimanded her. "And I regret that you will have to rise to the occasion despite your um…*ill health.* The empress's new lady has arrived, and she is to share your chamber. Not only that, but you will need to find her something suitable to wear—immediately," he added, as Manette opened her mouth and looked as if she were about to protest. "Lady Gisele de l'Aigle has fallen upon misfortune and has naught but what she is wearing, and that will never do in the hall at supper, as I'm sure you can see."

Manette's eyes, which had only briefly rested upon Gisele, now darted back to her and assessed her frankly. "Ah, so you're the heiress from Normandy," she murmured in her sleepy, sultry voice. She looked at least mildly interested. "Well, in that case, *you* may come in," she said to Gisele. "She'll be fine, my lord," she added, waving a hand dismissively at the chamberlain, who once again sniffed and stared as Manette took hold of Gisele's hand and pulled her none too gently inside, then shut the door firmly in Talford's face.

"The pompous old fool," she said, jerking her head back toward the door to indicate the chamberlain.

Gisele was not sure how she should reply to that, although she'd found the chamberlain's manner annoying, too. "I regret to disturb you while you are ill, Lady Manette," she began diffidently. "If you will but indicate where the rest of the empress's ladies are working, I will join them and you can go back to bed—"

A trill of laughter burst from Manette. "Oh, I'm not *truly* ill, silly, unless you count lovesickness! That was but a ruse to get Talford to leave the quicker! I thought if I embarrassed him enough—but never mind." She went to the bed, and bent over by it, raising the blanket that dangled from the bed to the rushes. She said something in the gutteral tongue Gisele knew was English, though she didn't understand it.

A moment later, a lanky, flaxen-haired youth crawled out from under the bed, and blinking at Gisele, bowed, then straightened to his full height, looking at Manette as if for direction.

"This is Wulfram. A gorgeous Saxon, isn't he?" drawled Manette in Norman French, running a hand over the well-developed youth's muscular shoulder. "And speaks not a word of French, so we may discuss his attributes right in front of him and he'll never know. Nay, I wasn't ill—Wulfram and I were just indulging in a little midday bed sport. Wulfram is um...very talented at that. Is he not handsome? A veritable pagan Adonis, if one may call a Saxon by a Greek name?"

The lanky Saxon looked distinctly uncomfortable, and Gisele was sure he had a very good idea that he was being discussed, even if he did not speak French.

Gisele, feeling the flush creeping up her cheeks, cleared her throat. "Yes...very handsome."

She was startled when the Saxon extended his hand, touching her scraped cheek with unexpected gentleness. He asked Manette something.

"Wulfram wants to know what happened to you. He asks if 'twas over-rough lovemaking?" She giggled.

Gisele found herself flushing at the Saxon's supposition. "Nay!" she said, then quickly told the other girl about the attack.

"Oh." Manette seemed disappointed as she translated for Wulfram.

"I am intruding upon your…time together," Gisele said. "Perhaps I might share another lady's chamber, so you are not forced to…interrupt your trysts with Wulfram?" She started for the door, determined to escape this embarrassing situation.

Manette laid a detaining hand upon her wrist. "Nay, stay," she said, laughing as if Gisele had said something hilarious. "It was inevitable I should be made to share with some lady sooner or later, as some of the other ladies are three to a bed! Besides, Wulfram and I can resume our play another time. We can work out an arrangement, you and I, so that neither of us interrupts the other in this chamber when we have male…company."

Gisele felt her jaw drop open. "But I shall not be doing any such…" She couldn't find a polite word for what she meant. Manette's behavior was beyond her experience.

Manette's eyes narrowed, and she studied Gisele again. "A virtuous demoiselle, are you? Never mind, you may begin to see things differently here, as you meet the courtiers about the empress. Or not," she added with a shrug, as Gisele opened her mouth to deny it. "In any case, we shall get along very well, you and I. And you must not join the other ladies—they'd devour you, in your present state, dear Gisele," she said, indicating the travel-stained gown. "It will take us the rest of the afternoon, but that will be sufficient, since Wulfram is here to fetch the seamstress to alter one of my gowns to fit you. I am bigger here than you," she said, indicating Gisele's bust, so that Gisele, aware that Wulfram was watching, blushed all over again. "But you have a lissome figure nonetheless. You will have knights and lordlings agog to meet you.'' She rattled off something in English to the flaxen-haired lackey, then turned back to Gisele. ''I told him to fetch Edgyth the seamstress, and have a wooden tub and hot water brought for a bath.''

Chapter Five

Two hours later, Gisele had bathed, submitted to Manette's washing her hair, and donned the gown of mulberry-dyed wool the other girl had given her from her own wardrobe.

"Turn around and let me see," Manette commanded.

Obediently, Gisele twirled around, feeling the pleated wool skirt bell around her, then settle against her legs. The gown had smooth, close-fitting sleeves with inset bands of embroidery just above the elbow; below the elbow the wool fell into flared pleats that came to midforearm in the front, and fingertip length in the back, revealing the tight sleeves of her undergown. Bands of embroidery that matched those on her upper arms circled her bodice just below her breast and made up the woven girdle that hung low on her hips. Her hair had been parted in the middle and encased in mulberry-colored bindings. Manette had even furnished her with a spare pair of shoes to replace her other pair, of which the left one had been clumsily repaired by the monks.

"Your hair is so thick and long, it doesn't even need false hair added to lengthen it to your waist, as most of the ladies at court must do," Manette approved, reaching out a hand to bring one of the plaits which had remained over Gisele's shoulder when she had whirled around, back over her breast.

"Thank you—for everything," Gisele said, a bit overwhelmed by the girl's generosity. "I will return the gown to you as soon as I am able to purchase cloth and sew my own...."

"Pah, never mind that," Manette said with an airy wave of a beringed hand. "'Twas one I was tired of, for the color looks not well with my fairness." She patted her own tresses, in which the gold was supplemented, Gisele guessed, with saffron dye.

"And now for the finishing touch." Reaching into a chest at her feet, Manette brought out a sheer short veil, which she placed atop Gisele's hair, then added a flared and garnet-studded headband that sat on Gisele's head like a crown.

"Ah, no, Manette, 'tis too much," Gisele protested, reaching up to remove it. "I could never accept such a costly—"

"Don't worry, silly, the headdress is but on loan," Manette said, laughing at her as she reached out a hand to forestall Gisele from removing it. "Uncle Geoffrey is sure to find you *very* attractive, and that is all to the good," she added in a low murmur, as if to herself. Her green eyes gleamed.

For reasons that Gisele could not understand, the strange remark, coupled with the avid glint in Manette's eyes, made her uncomfortable.

"Come, they will be gathering in the hall for supper now," Manette said, taking her by the elbow and steering her toward the door.

"I understand Lord Geoffrey de Mandeville is your

uncle,'' Gisele said, more to fill the sudden silence than because she had any desire to learn more of the man.

"Yes, and dear Uncle Geoffrey is the Earl of Essex and Constable of the Tower," Manette boasted as they walked down the long drafty corridor, "So 'tis Matilda's good fortune that he decided to favor her, for 'twas he who persuaded the Londoners to grant her imperial haughtiness entrance to the city."

Gisele looked uneasily about her, for while Manette had been speaking so plainly, they had drawn near to others, lords, ladies and servitors, all thronging in the direction of the hall. "You...you do not like the empress?" she whispered. "But...you are her attendant."

Manette gave her a sidelong glance. "For now. While the winds of fortune favor the empress, yes."

"But what of your parents? Where are they? Surely you are here because they owe allegiance to the empress?"

Manette gave a casual shrug as they began to descend, single file, the winding staircase that led from the residence floors to the hall below. "They are dead. I am my uncle's ward."

"'Twas good of him to bring you to court, then, rather than shut you away in a convent as some guardians would do until they arranged an advantageous marriage for you," Gisele said.

Again, that casual lift of one slender shoulder. "Mayhap I shall not marry," Manette said. "I enjoy myself here at court. I like the freedom to do as I please, to take a lover if I want. Why should one surrender all one's control to a man? Gisele, do you not agree?"

Hadn't Gisele been longing for this same sort of freedom Manette spoke of? The freedom to control her own destiny, rather than be like a puppet whose strings were controlled by a man? She had been profoundly shocked earlier, though, when she saw how Manette used that freedom—how she had casually revealed the presence of her lowborn English lover in the bedchamber, and the manner in which she had spoken of their "bed sport"—as if what they did together were no more important than any other game!

"But never mind. Here we are. Follow me to where the empress's ladies sit," Manette said as they entered the high-ceilinged great hall with its several rows of trestle tables that were set at right angles to the high table. Expertly threading her way among the throng of scurrying servitors and chattering noblemen and women, she led Gisele to a place at a table very near the center. Half a dozen other ladies had already positioned themselves there.

"Manette, I trust you are recovered?" one said in a voice oozing with skepticism.

"But of course," Manette purred. "I sent for Wulfram to massage my...brow. It works every time, like a charm. You should try it, Aubine."

While Aubine was still exchanging looks with her fellow attendants, Manette continued: "But I have not introduced our newcomer. Ladies, this is Lady Gisele de l'Aigle, newly arrived from Normandy. Gisele, that is Aubine on your left, and Cosette across from you, and beyond them, Halette, Emmeline, and from Germany, where Her Highness was empress, Winifride and Rilla."

All of them eyed her assessingly, their welcoming remarks blending into a meaningless blur. Gisele was very sure she would never remember which of them was which, for though each was dressed differently from her neighbor, and they all had differing heights and figures, they seemed alike in the suspicious manner in which they stared at her.

Then a horn was blown, and everyone who had not found their places hastened to do so. The procession to the high table began.

"Here comes Brien fitzCount, Matilda's faithful knight," Manette explained as a sturdy-looking man with graying hair strode by, his head held proudly. "Some say he is *more* than just her faithful knight," she added in a silky, insinuating purr.

"Manette, hold your tongue," the lady named Wilfride commanded in her thickly accented French.

But Manette was irrepressible. "Pooh, Wilfride. I say nothing that all the realm is not *thinking*." Her eyes went back to the procession. "And that is Robert, Earl of Gloucester, the empress's half brother—born on the wrong side of the blanket, of course. The late King Henry was a lusty man."

"Manette, be *silent!*" snapped the tallest of the ladies—Cosette? "Someone will hear you!"

A churchman, dressed in rich purple robes straining at the seams to cover his bulk, his cloak trimmed with ermine, entered next.

"That is Henry, Stephen's brother, Bishop of Winchester and the papal legate."

Gisele stared at the corpulent churchman in his rich, ermine-trimmed robe. She had heard of this brother of Stephen, who had lately allied himself with Matilda, his brother's rival. He did not look as if his choice sat easily upon his conscience.

Just then the steward, standing in front of the dais, announced, "Her highness the Holy Roman Empress, Lady of the English, Matilda, daughter and heir of King Henry!"

"She can't wait to be called *queen* instead of just *Domina*," Manette whispered as both watched the empress make a regal entrance. "She's already signing charters as queen!"

"*Hush*, Manette. Her majesty's coronation will be soon enough," reproved one of the other ladies, who was as angular as Manette was voluptuous—the one called Emmeline, Gisele thought.

To get to her place on the dais, Matilda had to pass right by her ladies-in-waiting, and as she did so, she paused, studying Gisele until Gisele began to fear she had a hole in her borrowed gown, or that some smudge of dirt remained on her face.

At last, the corners of her lips lifted in a half smile. "Ah, Lady Manette, you have done well with our new lady. Very well indeed. Welcome to our court, Lady Gisele."

Both Manette and Gisele inclined their heads respectfully and in unison, murmured, "Thank you, Domina," as the empress swept on, past the men standing in front of their places at the high table, waiting for her. One place, at the empress's left, remained empty.

Manette looked triumphant at Matilda's compliment, but then, as they were about to sit, both spotted a man who had just entered the hall. Manette's smile broadened.

"Ah, there is my uncle at last, late as usual. Is he not the most handsome of men?"

Gisele stared at the wiry, whip-thin man striding hurriedly into the hall. "I thought you believed Wulfram was the embodiment of masculine beauty?"

"Wulfram's all very well for an Englishman—all flaxen hair and brawn. My uncle, on the other hand, has a *mind* to match his attractive form,'' Manette countered.

Gisele darted a glance at Manette, once more experiencing a frisson of unease. Manette's tone was so... *fervent.*

Yes, Geoffrey de Mandeville was beautiful, in the same way a sinuous adder possessed beauty. Perhaps Lucifer had been beautiful in that same way, just before being cast out of Heaven. She expected that when de Mandeville opened his mouth, a thin, forked tongue would emerge and his voice would possess a hissing quality.

De Mandeville did not pass in front of them, but stepped onto the dais from the far side. Gisele saw the sitting empress look up as the Earl of Essex seated himself at her left. Matilda's lips thinned. Clearly she did not like anyone to arrive after she had made her entrance, but de Mandeville seemed oblivious to her annoyance.

Gisele looked back to her side and saw Manette's eyes meet those of her uncle. Geoffrey de Mandeville smiled.

Then Gisele saw her nod, ever so imperceptibly, in *her* direction.

Puzzling over her new acquaintance's action, she felt rather than saw Geoffrey de Mandeville's gaze fix upon her. She looked up to see his eyes, black and unblinking as a serpent's, devouring her.

''Ah, I can tell he thinks you're very attractive,'' Manette confided softly, her tone jubilant.

''I'm sure that is the veriest nonsense, Manette,'' Gisele said, chilled by the girl's odd words. ''Why should a powerful nobleman such as your uncle pay *any* attention to a maiden such as me?''

Just then, however, Bishop Henry rose and began a sonorous, lengthy grace, so Manette never answered. Following that, the lackeys began to offer trays with sliced meats, venison and capon and pork, bowls of fruit and loaves of freshly baked manchet bread. Gisele, re-minded by her stomach that it had been long since she had broken her fast, decided to postpone asking why Manette had made such a curious remark.

"I thought I was going to have to go upstairs, sword drawn, and set you free," Brys growled when his squire at last clumped down the ladder that led to the rooms where the serving wenches entertained their customers in a more personal manner.

"Pardon, my lord, but the woman was insatiable." Maislin's grin was unrepentant. "She said it been too long since she had had a man as well-equipped as I."

Brys nearly choked on his ale.

"'Tis the truth, my lord, I swear she said it!" he protested in an aggrieved tone. "I have the scratches on my back from that she-cat to prove it! And the tricks she knows..." Maislin sighed, still grinning. "If I died tonight, I should die happy. She'll do until the right lady comes along, at least."

"The right lady won't be happy if this wench's given you the pox," Brys retorted, then realized he sounded like a sour old man. Was he envying his squire's care-free hedonism, after encouraging him to indulge this once in it? It wasn't as if Maislin ever shirked his duties. "But we've dallied long enough. 'Tis getting late—I'd thought to press on toward Kent, but now I think we'll stay the night at my London house, and depart in the morning."

"Yes, my lord. We're going to visit Stephen's queen?"

Brys nodded. "I think it's time I checked to see what Matilda of Boulogne is up to while her lord husband is imprisoned. She isn't one to take this enforced separation lightly. Perhaps she'll have a letter she wants delivered to Stephen at his Bristol gaol—" He stopped speaking as a pair of men-at-arms in waist-length shirts of boiled leather strode into the tavern, ruthlessly shouldering aside an old man who was just leaving.

"Ho, tavern master! Ale, qvick!" one of them said, his accent thickly foreign.

"Flemings," Brys breathed.

"I wonder what they're doing here?" Maislin muttered, eyeing the two who had their backs to them. "I heard Queen Matilda had sent for Flemish mercenaries, but I thought she kept them with her at her stronghold in Kent?"

"So I thought, too. Let's just keep our mouths shut, and see what we may learn from these blustering blowhards."

"Here you are, my good sirs," the tavern master said, handing the Flemings their mugs with anxious alacrity. "A farthing apiece will call it even."

"Ve pay ven ve leave," growled one of the foreigners, whose greasy, tow-colored locks hung to his shoulders.

"Very well…going to pass the evening drinking, are you? Rose will take care of your needs, good sirs, when your mugs are empty," he added as the serving wench Maislin had just been upstairs with returned to the public room. "And if you have other needs," he added with an unctuous leer, "she'll be happy to attend to those, as well."

"Come, pritty gurl!" commanded the greasy-haired Fleming, pulling Rose onto his lap and shoving a hand down the loose neckline of her gown.

Opposite him, Maislin's hand tightened on the dagger he wore at his belt, and he half-rose.

"Don't be a fool!" Brys growled in a low voice, reaching a restraining hand out to his squire's shoulder. "We're not getting in a brawl over a tavern wench's favors. Look—she doesn't seem the least bit unwilling," he added, as the woman giggled at the foreigner's pawing.

Maislin set his jaw, but to Brys's relief, did nothing further. Poor Maislin—minutes ago he had been a strutting cock, and now he meant nothing more than a well-earned penny clinking against others in the woman's pocket.

"Welcome t' Lunnon-town, me fine sirs," Rose cooed to the avid-eyed men-at-arms. "Ye're Flanders born, are ye not? Tell Rose why ye've come to the city," she coaxed. Then, unseen by her new audience, she winked in Brys and Maislin's direction.

Why, Maislin must have been bragging to the tavern wench about his exploits in Brys's service, damn his foolish hide! *Maislin, I'm going to wring your neck at my next opportunity, you thick-brained oaf,* Brys silently vowed. But first, he'd take advantage of what he could overhear.

"Ve serve Matilda," one of the Flemings was boasting, tapping his massive chest.

"What, the empress herself?"

"No, foolish gurl—*Queen* Matilda, vife of King Stephen."

"But I thought she was holed up in the southeast? I'm hearin' the empress owns the city now."

The two Flemings guffawed. "Soon, no. The qveen comes to meet wit' that German Matilda. If she does not gif' the qveen what she wants, there vill be trouble here. You too pretty to see such trouble. Come back sout' wit' Jan, yes?"

Maislin bristled at the words. "As if she'd go with the likes o' them! And the empress isn't German—she's King Henry's true daughter! I ought to go acquaint that Flemish bastard with the facts—"

"Do so, and you'll be looking for another lord, you mutton-head," Brys snapped, still keeping his voice low.

"No, I don't think so," Rose was saying, "but thanks just the same. A plague on *all* rulers, *I* say." Now the look Rose leveled at Brys over the seated Flemings' heads was weary. "No matter what they do, it all means trouble to the ord'nry folk."

They listened awhile longer, but learned nothing more that could be useful. When it looked as if Rose was going to go upstairs with the Fleming who'd called himself Jan, Brys decided it was time to leave. He didn't want to watch his squire's anguished face any longer.

As they strode into the deepening shadows of a summer twilight and went to reclaim their horses from the youth they'd paid to guard them, Brys said, "Look you, we were in the right place at the right time, and because we didn't waste our time brawling, we learned something useful. Therefore, we won't be making a useless journey to Kent on the morrow."

"What will we be doing instead?"

"Learning where Stephen's queen is staying while she waits for an audience with the empress."

"Then we'll go and attend her?" Maislin's brow was

furrowed with concentration, and he had apparently already forgotten about Rose's faithlessness.

"Yes...we'll offer to carry a letter to Bristol. But tonight we're going to go and warn the empress that trouble may be brewing in London," Brys said as he swung up into the saddle.

"Tonight." Maislin's tone was neutral, but his crestfallen face told another story. Having drunk his fill and tupped a wench, Maislin was clearly ready to head for Brys's nearby London house with its clean beds and excellent meals, not back to Westminster at this late hour.

"But my lord," he protested, even though he was already reining his horse in the direction of London Bridge, "whether we go on horseback or take a boat, by the time we reach Westminster, the empress will be abed."

"Then we'll just have to wake her," Brys said, imagining just how ill Matilda would take such effrontery. "Hours may count, so the empress needs to know as quickly as possible. We'll have to be well away before 'tis fully light, too. I don't dare be caught at Westminster rubbing elbows with Stephen's rival by Stephen's queen."

Maislin sighed. "My lord, why do you do it?"

"Do what, Maislin?" Brys asked. "I thought I just explained why we were going to Westminster now."

"Nay, not that. I understand your purpose well enough, even if 'tis my opinion it could all wait upon the morrow. I meant serving the Empress Matilda."

"My father vowed an oath of fealty to Henry himself, saying he would support Henry's daughter as queen."

"So did many men, including Stephen. It didn't bind

him. And you are not your father—what bound the father need not bind the son.''

''Do you wish that I would switch my allegiance to Stephen, Maislin?'' Brys asked, studying his squire as they clattered across the bridge from Southwark into the city of London. Did his squire regret serving him, and wish to turn his coat?

''Nay, my lord! I but wish to understand what led you to your choice!'' Maislin said, and looked so distressed that Brys knew he was sincere.

Brys looked away. ''My father said that oaths matter,'' he said aloud, regretting that he couldn't explain to his squire the real reason he served Matilda. He couldn't tell Maislin something even his sisters did not know—that he was really only their half brother.

His mother had been the old king's mistress—one of many that the lecherous Henry had enjoyed, but unlike the rest of them, the lady had insisted on keeping their liaison secret. When the inevitable happened and she became pregnant, she asked to be given a noble husband. Henry had chosen the Baron of Balleroy.

Not being claimed—branded—a royal bastard had been both a blessing and a curse, Brys reflected. While he could not boast a high title such as Earl of Gloucester, as the king's oldest natural son, Robert, could, he had a *choice*. He could *choose* to serve Henry's daughter Matilda, not be forced to because his parentage would have made any other allegiance suspect.

And because Henry's cast-off mistress had been given in marriage long before the birth of her babe, Brys had been given the gift of *legitimacy*. As Balleroy's supposedly true-born son, he had inherited the barony when his ''father'' died. He was grateful for that—most days, at least.

He would have traded his barony and all the privileges being a nobleman entailed, however, for at least being loved by the baron.

Brys remembered the day he had been bold enough to ask his "father" why he was so harsh and cold toward him. He had been only seven, and about to go off to another Norman nobleman's castle to be fostered, as was the custom. Evidently the question had convinced the baron that Brys was old enough to know his true parentage, for he had called Brys into the Balleroy Castle chapel and told him that King Henry was the man who had sired him upon his mother, not he, the Baron of Balleroy. Then he made him swear an oath on some saint's dried-up fingerbone that Brys would never tell his three sisters the truth. For the good of Balleroy, he'd said.

Exposing Brys's bastardy would make his eldest daughter, Avelaine, an heiress, and the baron didn't want her to be the target of every land-hungry knave who'd marry her just for the barony. It took a man to hold the land.

The baron would never explain why he wanted Brys to know the secret, if Brys was to be his heir anyway.

He hated the baron after that. Before that day he had felt sure of himself, secure in his place in the world. Once he left the chapel that day, he felt the secret weighing him down like a millstone about his soul. He had been given a barony he wasn't really entitled to.

His hatred had only multiplied when Ogier had been born.

Brys felt like the cuckoo left in another bird's nest. He was an impostor, yet he would inherit the responsibility for the welfare of his three half sisters and half brother. It would be up to him to see that the girls made good marriages to men who would cherish them as they deserved. He must provide for Ogier, yet his younger brother was the true heir. But since he had not been released from his vow, he was expected to marry and provide an heir for Balleroy.

But how could he wed a lady, knowing he was not who he pretended to be?

Thinking of heirs and heiresses led his thoughts back to the Norman heiress he had left with Matilda. Gisele would be long abed by the time he'd finished his business with Matilda, but mayhap he could at least inquire how she was faring among the wolves.

Chapter Six

By the time the bishop arose, saying another long-winded blessing that signaled the end of the meal, Gisele was more than ready to seek her bed. It had been a long day, and she was not used to unwatered wine. When she saw the empress stepping off the dais, followed by the men who had eaten with her, Gisele arose also. She was about to tell Manette she wanted to go back to their chamber when she had to stop and cover a yawn.

"None of that, new girl," Wilfride, who had seen the aborted yawn, reproved. "You must arouse yourself! Her imperial highness does not like her ladies to be dull! In the evenings we attend her until she retires for the night. Come ladies," she said, gesturing briskly for the rest to follow, and like a ship under full sail, stepped out into the aisle to follow the empress.

"That Wilfride—she thinks because she has been with Matilda since they were girls in Germany, she may lord it over the rest of us!" Manette sniped, as she and Gisele followed behind the rest of the ladies. "Don't worry, you'll have a good time. Since it has been fine outside all day, we will go to the garden, and there will be music, conversation and sweets. Then we will assist the empress to bed, and we are free for the rest of the night!''

''All I want to be free to do is go to sleep,'' Gisele whispered back. ''I rode half the day before arriving at Westminster, you know.'' She longed to close her eyes and just think of all the new sights and faces she had seen today—and perhaps of Brys de Balleroy, she admitted to herself, remembering the way he had looked when he had walked away from her.

''Don't talk like a rustic. You are at court now, and we do not go to bed at the same hour the chickens do! Besides, my uncle wants to meet you.''

She wanted to tell Manette she had *no* desire to meet de Mandeville, but was afraid she would hurt the other girl's feelings. Clearly she felt meeting the Earl of Essex was a treat not to be missed.

A slender youth was already picking out a soft tune on a lute when they reached the garden.

''That's the lutanist Matilda brought with her from the court at Angers, where her husband, Geoffrey Le Bel, resides,'' Manette said as they crossed the velvety green lawn. ''Does he not play divinely?''

Gisele nodded, wondering if the lutanist was another of Manette's lovers. She turned to look about her. Red roses and yellow honeysuckle climbed the gray stone of the walled garden, perfuming the air with a heady mingling of sweet scents. Closer to the ground, closely planted rhododendrons formed a hedge of pink. At the back of the garden, pear and apple trees provided roosts from which nightingales sang their evening songs in counterpoint to the lute music.

There were stone benches set at random, and on one of these, cushions had been provided for the empress.

Here she settled herself, then directed Wilfride and Rilla to fetch little cakes and more wine for everyone. Bishop Henry chose the bench nearest Matilda and began an earnest, low-voiced discussion with her even before most of the others had found their places. Geoffrey de Mandeville sat down next to Robert of Gloucester, the empress's half brother. De Mandeville appeared to be listening to something Robert was saying, but his eyes kept constantly darting back to Matilda.

Good, Gisele thought. *Perhaps he will forget all about his supposed desire to meet me.*

From out of nowhere, seemingly, lackeys appeared with wine and delicate, sweet cakes. Gisele could not imagine eating another morsel after the supper they had just finished, but Manette handed her another cup of wine without even asking if she wanted it.

"Do you come from Rouen, Gisele?" a voice said, and Gisele looked up to see that one of the ladies—Halette?—had seated herself at a bench situated at a right angle from the one which she and Manette occupied.

"No, from the Risle Valley. In fact, l'Aigle Castle sits overlooking the river." Gisele wished the lady had not asked about her home. Instantly she was homesick, remembering how only a fortnight ago, she and Fleurette had sat in the garden at l'Aigle, sewing two of the gowns she was to wear at court. Now her old nurse was dead and the gown, no doubt, adorned the person of some brigand's bedmate. She blinked away the tears that threatened to spill over onto her cheeks.

"Ah, but you miss your home," observed Halette, her eyes full of compassion. "Perhaps you leave behind some sweetheart?"

Quickly, Gisele shook her head.

"Your mother? Your father?"

She *would not* whine to this well-dressed lady-in-waiting about her uncaring father, or the attack that had taken her old nurse from her! "Nay, I am but tired," she began, but was unable to find the words to go on.

"I *am* sorry—I did not mean to make you sad," Halette said kindly. "But this may cheer you—Her Highness has told me we are to go into London on the morrow! Matilda has decided she needs a milk-white palfrey to ride to her coronation, but doubtless we will not only visit the horse fair, but the markets as well. Wait until you see the wonderful markets in the city! I hope we will visit the goldsmiths. There was a gold ring at one of them that caught my eye...."

Gisele allowed the woman's chatter to distract her. Mayhap the next day's expedition into the city would be very enjoyable, even if she had no coin to spend on trinkets. And she wondered how Matilda planned to afford a milk-white palfrey if she had no money for a coronation gown!

Just then, the empress's voice rose above the dulcet tones of the lute. "I have said *no,* my lord bishop! Absolutely not, and there's an end to the matter!"

The lute fell silent. Conversations died. Even in the thickening dusk, Gisele could see that Bishop Henry's face was purple with anger. What boon had he asked for, that the empress had refused so heatedly? Geoffrey de Mandeville extended a hand toward the empress, but she paid it no heed.

Matilda jumped to her feet in a swish of dark-blue skirts, dropping the jeweled goblet as if it were mere wood. It clanged against the bench, the sound echoing off the wall.

"Come, ladies, I am for bed!" she called, and strode

out of the garden, not waiting to see if anyone followed her.

"I wonder what bee has found its way into her bodice?" Manette muttered to Gisele as all seven ladies-in-waiting ran to catch up with their royal mistress.

Gisele had no idea. She was just relieved to have escaped meeting Manette's uncle.

Wilfride had been sitting closest to the empress, and so she caught up with her soonest. Gisele could hear the German lady, her expression solicitous, speaking to Matilda in German, and the empress answering back in that same language.

"Rilla, what are they saying?" Manette demanded inquisitively,

Rilla, looking over her shoulder to speak to Manette, appeared concerned. "It is something about Stephen's son Eustace—Henry's nephew, of course—but I could not hear what."

It seemed a mile or more through the narrow corridors and up a long, narrow, winding staircase before they reached the empress's apartments. By the time they had gotten there, Matilda had evidently regained control of her temper. It was obvious from her set jaw, however, she was still angry. She moved in quick, jerky motions as Wilfride and Rilla helped her to disrobe, raised her arms as Cosette draped a bed robe about her shoulders, then sat in tight-lipped silence while Aubine brushed out her thick black hair. Gisele could not help but notice that the empress still had a handsome figure, despite the birth of three sons, and that hardly any gray streaked the ebony tresses.

Finally, Manette, gesturing that Gisele was to help her, drew back the curtains and pulled back the silken coverlet atop the royal bed. Without further ado Matilda climbed in.

"Leave us," she said. "All but you, Wilfride. You will read to me from that German poetry book while I go to sleep. It is such a comfort to hear the tongue of my girlhood."

Once back in the corridor, Gisele turned to Manette. "I am exhausted, Manette. Please show me how to get back to our chamber—I fear I have seen so many corridors today I would not find it until morning."

Before Manette could answer, however, a figure detached itself from the wall. Wulfram came forward, and Manette uttered a pleased giggle. She did not seem the least surprised.

"I'm afraid I won't be going back there any time soon, Gisele," she said with a shrug of regret that was belied by the excited gleam in her eyes as she reached out a hand to the grinning English youth. "There is the matter of some unfinished business between my lover and me—but I'm sure one of the other ladies will be happy to show you the way. Just leave a candle burning—"

With that, she bounded off down the hall with the flaxen-haired Wulfram, who tossed a sheepishly apologetic look over his shoulder at Gisele.

Irritated and heavy-eyed with drowsiness and wine, Gisele started walking. All the other ladies had disappeared around the corner, no doubt as eager for their beds as she was for hers. Her feet felt like lead and her legs ached, but surely if she hurried, she could catch up.

"Have no fear, demoiselle. *I* will be most pleased to escort you wherever you should desire," said a voice, simultaneously laying a hand firmly on her wrist.

With a shriek of alarm, she whirled. Geoffrey de Mandeville stood there, so near she could smell the wine on his breath. Where had he come from? She could have sworn there had been no one in the corridor but herself, once Manette and Wulfram had run off!

"Be easy, demoiselle. I but meant to offer you assistance," he purred.

"Oh! But there is no need…I have but to hasten and catch up with the others…." She pulled, but his light grip on her forearm was inexorably strong.

"That is unnecessary," de Mandeville murmured. "I have said I would escort you."

"I—we have not been introduced, sir…." she protested, wanting to be away from de Mandeville's hypnotic black eyes.

"Ah…a small inconvenience, isn't it? But I'm certain my niece, the beauteous Manette, will have told you know who I am—Lord Geoffrey de Mandeville, Earl of Essex and Constable of the Tower."

"Y-yes…" Desperately, Gisele peered down the shadowy corridor, wishing that someone—anyone— would come along. She would not mind walking with de Mandeville so much if she was not alone with him.

"And you are Lady Gisele de l'Aigle, I am told. I could not take my eyes from you, during the meal," the earl added, in a knowing, oily voice. "You knew that, did you not?"

"I…" She did her best to look astonished, thinking to shame him into realizing the ridiculousness of his words. "I thought you looked at something beyond *me*, my lord. I am but one of the empress's attendants, younger by a year or two than your niece."

"Young, yes, but you need not be so modest. You

are very beautiful, you know,'' he said, smiling down at her. ''And an heiress.''

Gisele felt a shiver of apprehension. How had he learned that? Manette had been with her ever since Gisele had been shown to their chamber, so his niece could not have informed him.

The empress must have told him while they sat next to one another at supper. It was the only explanation. That certainty, added to the wine she had drunk, sent nausea roiling in Gisele's stomach as tales of heiresses, wed against their will, surfaced from memory. Was de Mandeville unmarried, and seeking a landed wife? Even if he *was* married, her isolation made the moment no less dangerous.

They had reached an intersecting corridor. ''I fear I am much too tired for flattery, my lord. I would have you take me to my chamber without further delay.''

''Nothing would give me further pleasure, sweet lady,'' he said, snaking an arm around her waist and pulling her none too gently closer to him. ''But come—you were going the wrong way. You would never have found your chamber going that way. Don't worry—you are so new to court, it is natural you would get lost. My niece is a naughty wench for leaving you to your own devices.''

He pulled her down the other, darker corridor, willy-nilly, and for a few moments she did not resist. However much she had instinctively disliked him, it was entirely possible he was right—she *could* have been going the wrong way. But then, as each step took her farther through corridors and turnings that looked totally unfamiliar, she began to hesitate, murmuring, ''My lord, are you sure you're going the right direction?''

"Just a little farther, my lady, you'll see—" he kept promising, and then at last he stopped in front of a door.

"Here we are, my sweet."

"But you're mistaken—this is *not* my chamber, my lord!"

"Ah, but it will be for this night, little Gisele, and then, who knows? You may see the advantages—"

"*Unhand me,* my lord!" she cried, struggling to pull away. She kicked hard at him, aiming for his groin and missing, but connecting solidly enough with his shin that surprise and pain made him lose his grip.

"Tricksome wench!" he shouted, as Gisele picked up her skirts and began to run back in the direction they had come. "I'll make you sorry you made me chase you, damn you!"

Each step was agony with her still-painful ankle. She could hear him pounding after her. She had no idea where she was going, and at last, she made a wrong turn that led her into a corridor that ended in a wall.

There was a door to the right—perhaps whoever was within would help her! Frantically, her chest heaving, Gisele pounded on the door, but no one answered. Finally, in desperation, she threw herself against it, but to no avail.

She turned at bay, with one weapon left—a puny one, but it would have to do. Reaching downward for the eating dagger that swung from the girdle encircling her waist, she clutched it, pointing it at him.

"Don't come any closer—or I swear I will pierce your black heart. Let me go, and we will not speak of this more, I promise you," she breathed. She started backing away, praying that she would not have to make good her threat.

"You think you could reach my heart with that short

blade before I could twist it out of your wrist?'' de Mandeville purred, taking a step toward her for every two she retreated.

"I doubt you even have a heart, my lord,'' she retorted, hoping her hand wasn't as shaky as she felt. "So I'd content myself with carving your cheeks—perhaps with an *L* on each side for *lecher?*''

"And when I take your little toy knife from you, you spitting cat, I will do some carving of my own,'' he snarled at her, continuing to advance on her as she kept the knife out in front of her, his small black eyes darting from her knife-wielding hand to her face and back again.

Any moment now he would leap out and twist the knife from her grasp....

Chapter Seven

Gisele took another step backward and saw de Mandeville freeze in place, lifting his head as if he heard something. She paused too, and listened—

—And heard the sound of booted feet on the stone floor around the corner, coming toward them.

Salvation! De Mandeville would not dare to continue menacing her if someone else came along, would he? Please, God, let it be someone who would help her, not a lackey who would just scuttle past, pretending not to see the powerful earl and his intended victim!

She heard the steps round the corner and stop as the newcomer took in the scene before him, but she was fascinated by the change in de Mandeville. The earl was straightening from his half-crouching position and replacing his expression of aggressive cunning with one of bland urbanity.

"Good even, my lord," he said with bluff good humor, addressing the figure behind Gisele. "I am surprised to see you—that is, I had heard you were at Westminster earlier today, but I was under the impression you had departed."

"It seems you were mistaken, my lord. Obviously, I am here. Is...aught amiss?"

She whirled as she recognized the voice of Brys de Balleroy, and saw his eyes narrow as they fastened on the eating dagger she still held at the ready.

"Nay, of course not, my lord! I was but attempting to set the damsel's feet on the right path," de Mandeville said, his eyes darting now between de Balleroy and Gisele.

"And she felt it necessary to resist your guidance at knifepoint, my lord?" de Balleroy said, skepticism dripping from his voice. "I'd wager the lady would tell another tale." Gisele did not miss the fact that he had moved his hand to his sword hilt.

"That I would, my lord," Gisele said, looking back at de Mandeville, whose face had slipped its innocuous mask and become contorted with frustrated fury. "But later. For now, I would be well content if you would but remove me from this satyr's presence and see me safely to my chamber."

"With all my heart, Lady Gisele," Brys said, then added with a nod, "My lord, with your permission..." The deferential words were but a mockery of formality and everyone knew it.

De Mandeville's black eyes locked with Gisele's. "You have made an enemy this night, damsel," he said. "I would have been an important friend to have." With that, he reversed his direction and stalked away, his back rigidly erect.

Gisele and de Balleroy stared at the retreating figure, neither speaking until de Mandeville's footsteps had died away.

"I think I can guess what happened, Lady Gisele,"

de Balleroy said in a low voice. "You need tell me nothing—unless he has hurt you?"

Gisele shook her head, feeling her limbs begin to tremble as her fear drained away. "Nay, he didn't—though he would have, had you not chanced to come. Just why *are* you here, my lord? I thought you were leaving the palace this afternoon."

"And so I did, but I happened to hear something the empress needed to be apprised of. And so I have come back—not that it did me any good. Her dragon of a waiting woman—one of those German women—refuses to wake her."

The thought of Wilfride sprouting green fins and a tail, and breathing out fire, made her smile.

"You find it amusing that I will have to cool my heels in these corridors till dawn?" he asked, but a glance at his deep-brown eyes told her he wasn't truly offended. "Never mind, my lady, 'tis time you were abed, at least. Tell me where your chamber is, and I'll— *Now* what, Lady Gisele?"

She was helpless to stop the rueful laughter that shook her shoulders. "My lord, if I *knew* how to reach my chamber, you would not have found me fending off de Mandeville! That was the source of the problem! His niece, who shares a chamber with me, went off and left me to find my own way back from the empress's apartments, and—"

"And de Mandeville just *happened* to be there to offer to help you," he concluded grimly. He hadn't been wrong to think of her as a lamb tossed in among the wolves, though he had not thought she would be in danger the very first night!

"I fear *offering* is not nearly strong enough a word,"

she said, smiling ruefully. "I sensed he was not trustworthy, but he just pulled me along!"

"My lady, I think I can find your chamber, if you
will trust *me*," he said, holding out his arm to her with
perfect chivalry.

"With all my heart, my lord," she said, echoing his
own words with a smile as she took it.

"But do not trust anyone else, Lady Gisele, do you
hear me?"

She just looked at him with those eyes of changeable
brown, jade and gold hue, and nodded solemnly.

Brys talked his way past Wilfride so early that he
fully expected to find the empress still abed.

She was yawning and sleepy-eyed, and still wearing
a fur-trimmed bed gown, but sitting up in a backless
chair. All of her ladies-in-waiting were present, one ap-
plying some sort of unguent to her face, another setting
out her garments for the day, some just bustling around
to no apparent purpose.

Gisele, he noticed, was combing the tangles from
Matilda's heavy mane of raven-black hair. Their eyes
met above the empress's head for a long, measuring
moment. Gisele was first to look down, and Brys
thought he could detect a faint heightening of the Norman damsel's color.

Resolving to ponder that fact later, he began, "Domina, I'm thankful you could see me so early—"

Matilda interrupted, "I do not know what was so important you had to assault me with it before 'twas even
light, my lord." She pulled the fur-trimmed mantle Wilfride had provided more closely about her.

Brys forced himself not to react to the sympathetic
look Gisele shot him at Matilda's complaining tone. In-

stead, he studied the empress who, unbeknownst to her, was his half sister. He wondered if she would feel differently towards him if she knew. Probably not. Her father had made many bastards, after all.

"Your pardon, highness, for my intrusion. I did not intend my visit to be an assault. Merely, I gained some knowledge I felt it was imperative to warn you about."

"Very well, I hope it will not take long," she said with barely concealed impatience. "My ladies and I intend to go into London today and visit the markets and the horse fair."

Brys stifled the urge to tell his royal half sister that her shopping was much less important than the trouble that could potentially be brewing.

"Mayhap I should speak to you alone?" he said, with a meaningful nod toward the empress's ladies, who were clearly listening—except for Gisele, who went on brushing through the night tangles in her mistress's hair.

Matilda snapped her fingers. "Leave us, ladies—except for you, Gisele." She glanced over her shoulder at her newest attendant. "You have a soothing touch, neither too hard nor soft. Besides," she added, as the ladies glided out the door, "you already know my lord de Balleroy." She leaned back into Gisele's brushing, closing her eyes as if she were a cat being stroked.

Briefly and concisely, Brys told the empress what he had overheard in the tavern last night.

When he came to the part where the Flemish mercenary had promised trouble if the empress did not grant Stephen's queen what she had come to request, Matilda totally ignored the point. "If she hopes to gain permission to visit her scurrilous scoundrel of a husband in his prison at Bristol, she's come in vain. Why should I be absent from my sons for a year and a half now and she be granted the comfort of a conjugal visit?''

Brys noted that Matilda fumed about missing her *children,* rather than her husband. Ah well, everyone knew she and Geoffrey, Count of Anjou, despised one another.

''I do not know if that is the request the qu—that Countess Matilda—means to make,'' he said, seeing the empress glare at him for his near gaffe. She hated being reminded that Stephen's wife had been crowned, while she had yet to be. ''But I am concerned by the trouble her mercenaries seem poised to make. Mayhap 'twould be wise to postpone your trip into the city until you hear what it is she wants.''

She dismissed his worry with a regal wave of her hand. ''I am not about to wait upon the usurper's wife's convenience when I must make ready for my coronation! The Londoners have figured out their trust in Stephen was misplaced. They'll not offer me any offense.'' She paused, a finger on her chin. ''Ah, I'll wager I know what she wants! Now it all becomes clear! She used Henry to test me about it only last night!''

''Your Highness?'' Brys prompted, mystified. Was he supposed to know what she meant?

''Bishop Henry is mightily displeased with me,'' she explained in a defiant singsong. ''He asked me to confirm Stephen's son's right to inherit the county of Boulogne. Of course I refused.''

''You refused?'' Brys echoed, incredulous, and then before he could think better of it, added, ''But that county belongs to his mother, not to Stephen.''

Immediately he knew he had gone too far. The empress's jaws clenched and her lips tightened into a thin line.

"You think I have not the right, my lord, but I will not be lessoned by *you!* You may *go,* de Balleroy."

God curse his impulsive tongue! Matilda didn't want to let anyone tell her what to do, not after a lifetime of being ordered around, first by her father King Henry, then by her aged husband, the Holy Roman Emperor, then by Count Geoffrey, who had still been a stripling when she had been forced to marry him. And suggesting that fairness was owed to anyone connected to Stephen was the one thing sure to make her stop listening. Sighing, Brys knelt and bowed his head.

"Domina, I humbly crave your pardon. My only priority is to serve you. Please do not dismiss me so hastily that you do not fully hear my concern." He was aware that Matilda's eyes still shot daggers at him, but concentrated instead on Gisele's deft, slender fingers nimbly braiding the empress's hair.

"And what would you have me hear?" Matilda demanded.

He took a deep breath and looked the empress in the eye again. "As I said, I pray you would reconsider going into London, at least until the countess and her hired Flemish troublemakers have departed. If there are things you must buy, send some of your ladies to purchase them, Your Highness." Involuntarily, his eyes went to Gisele, who immediately cast her eyes downward and pretended great absorption in the task of binding the end of the braid.

Matilda saw the direction of Brys's gaze, though, and drew back so she could view Gisele's reaction. "Ohho, so that's the way the wind blows! I suppose you would like the task of escorting one of my ladies in particular, eh?"

Curse Matilda! "No, Domina, I...you mistake me.

My intention was to—'' And then he remembered that Gisele knew nothing of his double role, and that it was probably better for all of them that she continued in ignorance. ''I had other plans. Perhaps it would be best if we were totally private?'' He winced inwardly as he spoke, knowing his words would feel like a verbal slap to Gisele.

Just as he had feared, Gisele stiffened, her eyes hurt. She opened her mouth as if to argue, but shut it again just as quickly.

''Wait just outside, Gisele.''

''Yes, Domina.'' Gathering her skirts, Gisele made her obeisance and left the chamber.

Welladay, perhaps it was better that she hate him. Hadn't she said she wanted to maintain her independence at court, not belonging to any man? And even if she someday changed her mind and decided to give her heart to some lucky knave, it was better that she harbor no tender feelings for one who was just as much a usurper to his title as King Stephen!

If Matilda was aware of the tension remaining in the atmosphere, she said nothing of it, just waited until Brys spoke.

''Domina, I planned to call on Countess Matilda today, once I learn where she lodges. Perhaps I can learn what she plans to do, when she hears your refusal in regard to her son's inheritance.''

''And if she wants you to carry a letter to Stephen in Bristol?''

''I will of course be happy to comply, Your Highness. After I have made known to you its contents, of course.'' Surely riding clear to Bristol would cool his desire for Lady Gisele de l'Aigle.

Matilda gave him a cool smile. ''Your tongue may

occasionally be clumsy, but I believe in and rely on your loyalty, Brys.'' She rose.

The audience was clearly over. ''I thank Your Highness for your trust in me,'' Brys said, rising also.

''Send Gisele back to me. I would finish dressing and go to Mass.''

He stepped outside, immediately spotting Gisele standing by the window embrasure, her back to him.

''Lady Gisele,'' he began, ''please forgive my seeming rudeness. Believe me, there are things you are better off not knowing—for your own safety, as well as m—''

She whirled about, her eyes flashing golden sparks. ''In a moment you will say I am not to worry my 'pretty little head' about matters that do not concern me, won't you? But you would not *dare* speak so to the *woman* in there, would you?'' she demanded, stabbing a finger towards Matilda's chamber. ''A plague on you and your secrecy, my lord! You may keep your precious secrets—I care not!'' She turned and started back toward the chamber.

''Hold, Lady Gisele—'' But she had already disappeared inside the door.

Chapter Eight

Consciously maintaining a serene expression, Gisele was still fuming inside as she accompanied the empress and her other attendants to the hall to break their fast after Mass. *The self-important popinjay!* What cared she what Brys de Balleroy did with his spare time? Maybe he was even the empress's lover, and if that was true, she could not care less!

"Make haste to eat, ladies," Matilda directed as they tore off chunks of freshly baked manchet bread and sipped watered wine. "We will journey upstream to London as soon as we have filled our bellies!"

"This is going to be such fun!" crowed Manette, sitting beside Gisele. "Wulfram is one of those going along to carry the empress's purchases, and he has promised to slip aside and buy me a present!"

"How pleasant for you," Gisele murmured noncomitally, eyeing her chambermate's still kiss-swollen lips and the telltale bite mark that showed above the neckline of her gown. She wondered what sort of a present a Saxon servant could afford to buy for a noblewoman.

Gisele had pretended to be asleep last night when Manette had slipped back inside the room after her tryst with Wulfram. She had been much too exhausted to confront Manette just then about leaving her prey to Geoffrey de Mandeville. There had been no opportunity to discuss it with her before attending the empress, either. Manette had slept right through Aubine's summoning knock and had only joined the ladies as they left Mass.

"You're very silent this morn, Gisele. Cat got your tongue?" Manette said, her eyes sly. "Or could you be thinking of my charming uncle?"

There would be no avoiding the subject, then. "I was indeed thinking about your uncle, Manette, but not, I'm afraid, in the way you had hoped. I...I did not come to court to find a lover," she said, trying her best to be diplomatic.

"Ah, but one sometimes finds a treasure where one least expects," purred Manette. "Take advantage of your good fortune."

Obviously Manette had not spoken with her uncle this morning, or she would have known Geoffrey de Mandeville had not succeeded in his forceful attempt to seduce Gisele last night. Gisele could see she would have to be more plainspoken.

"Manette, your uncle is old enough to have sired me—"

"Pooh, what of that? It only means he has years enough to be a skillfull lover!"

Was nothing but bed sport important to Geoffrey de Mandeville's niece? Her temper, already ignited at de Balleroy's secretiveness, flared anew. "Manette, I will not welcome any further...*attentions* from him, and you may tell him so!"

The other girl's eyes narrowed, and spots of pink

flared on her cheeks. "So, you think you are too good for my uncle, you upstart from Normandy?"

Gisele's heart sank. In less than a full day's time, she had made two enemies, and she certainly didn't want to have to share a chamber with one of them. "Manette, please. Let us agree to disagree on the subject of your uncle. I'm sorry, but 'tis best I am honest, is it not?"

Manette kept her face averted for the longest time. "Even the haughtiest vixen is eventually laid low," she snapped, and the look in her eyes chilled Gisele all the way to her soul.

She would have to step carefully from now on, Gisele thought, and manage somehow never to be alone at court. But what of their shared chamber? Was it no longer a safe haven? Would Manette stoop so low as to give her uncle the key and deliberately stay away? Perhaps she should ask Talford if she could change chambers. Even if she had to sleep on the rushes while another pair of ladies slept on the bed, 'twould be safer than remaining with Manette de Mandeville!

Why had she thought life at court would be such a paradise? Might it have been better to wed one of the Norman lordlings at home, rather than leave l'Aigle for this nest of vipers?

"We go, ladies," announced Matilda, rising from her carved-back chair.

Obediently, Gisele fell into line with the rest of the ladies, staying as far from Manette as she could be without being obvious.

"Domina!" called a voice, just as they reached the exit from the hall that led to the dock.

Gisele looked back to see the chamberlain hastening toward them, his arm upraised, his short legs propelling him with awkward rapidity beneath his calf-length gown.

"What is it, Talford?"

"Domina—"

"Quickly, Talford," Matilda ordered over her shoulder with barely leashed impatience. "We are eager to depart for London."

"But Empress, the Countess of Boulogne has arrived. She awaits you in the presence chamber, and bids me tell you she humbly craves an audience."

Matilda swore a most unregal oath. "Damn the woman! Matilda of Boulogne never 'humbly' does anything! We've a good mind to leave her in the presence chamber cooling her heels while we slip out the door and proceed to London as planned! We have no desire to hear anything she has to whine about!"

"Domina," Talford said, worry creasing his already-wrinkled forehead, "it might be well to hear her out. She has come a long way...."

Matilda's face darkened. "I don't care if she journeyed from Cathay—I do not wish to see her!" she said, clearly too upset to remember to use the royal *we*. She paused, and Gisele could see prudence warring with self-will on her face.

Matilda sighed at last. "All right, Talford. Precede me and tell her we will give her a few minutes of our precious time, out of courtesy—but nothing more!"

Talford sped away, his bandy legs churning beneath him.

"Never mind, Your Highness," Wilfride soothed. "It is early yet. There will be plenty of time to go into the city even after Your Highness has spoken with the countess."

"We'll see," Matilda said, her tone dubious. "Stephen's wife never says something in six words when she can say it in an hour. She'll still be here at supper time if we allow it—which we will not! Pray busy yourselves with your sewing, ladies. If we are attended by all of you, she will but talk the longer!''

It was only an hour later that the empress rejoined them, grim satisfaction painted on her face.

'''Twas just as we suspected,'' Matilda announced in response to a timid question from Lady Rilla. ''She came to beg for her son to inherit Boulogne, just as the bishop did last night. The gall, to ask me to give away part of our lands when her husband has taken our crown! And she thought she could move me with the threat of her cursed Flemish mercenaries!''

Gisele had no idea what these Flemish mercenaries could do, but clearly the empress did not consider them cause to worry.

''Well, then, ladies! Shall we depart? I had hoped to be in the city by now, but no matter!''

As if in answer, thunder cracked almost directly overhead, and seconds later, rain drummed on the lead roof above their heads.

'''Tis only a summer shower. 'Twill soon pass!'' Matilda announced confidently. ''We may as well wait it out in dry comfort here, however. There's no joy in being on the Thames with water dripping down the backs of our necks, eh? The canopy shelter always leaks.''

But it did not stop raining. The ladies could see lightning flashing in the high clerestory windows, and thunder continued to rumble in counterpoint to the driving rain. Soon it was evident they would have to remain indoors at Westminster that day.

"We can go tomorrow, Domina," the ladies consoled their mistress.

"Tomorrow there will be no horse fair! I will have to wait another week to find a white palfrey!" Matilda grumbled, taking the rain as a personal affront.

Brys and Maislin located the queen's camp below Southwark and were standing in the entrance of her commander's large tent, sheltering from the downpour, when Matilda of Boulogne returned from her visit to Westminster. She was accompanied by a small escort of mounted men-at-arms.

"Brys! What a pleasant surprise!" the countess called, sheltering her face from the rain as she dismounted her palfrey. "And Maislin, too! 'Tis always good to see you!"

Matilda of Boulogne was a much smaller woman than Matilda, fair where the empress was raven-haired, and several years younger. Her features were delicately pretty, but as with the empress, worry had etched lines in the creamy perfection of her face.

Brys backed up, allowing the queen room to enter the tent, then went down on one knee, taking the hand Matilda of Boulogne offered and kissing it.

"Dear Brys, dare I hope you have brought a letter from my Stephen?" Matilda of Boulogne asked. Pearls of rain decorated her mantle and veil.

Brys wished he could say yes, and make the countess happy. Though her husband was a scoundrel and a crown stealer, the woman before him did not deserve the worry she was experiencing. "Nay, Your Highness," he said. "I have not been to Bristol since I brought you that last letter, but at Tichenden, checking to see that all is well there. But I thought perhaps I could carry a letter now from you to your lord?''

Matilda of Boulogne's face, briefly crestfallen, became animated. "Excellent! I will go this moment to my tent and write it! I cannot wait to tell my lord what we will be doing to teach that other Matilda a lesson this night!" She started to leave the tent, then paused. "Oh! Have you met William of Ypres, the captain of my mercenaries, Brys?'' she asked, nodding toward the man who had helped her dismount and followed her into the tent. "William, see that my lord de Balleroy and his squire are given refreshments.'' She added, over her shoulder as he went back out into the gradually lessening rain, "Tell Brys about our plans, Will! Perhaps he will want to delay his departure a couple of days and join in the fun!''

Brys straightened and studied the short, sharp-featured man who was infamous, even among mercenaries. "And what would those plans be?''

The Flemish mercenary captain grinned a wolf's cold-eyed grin. "Ve raid Southwark this night! Ve vill burn and pillage—aye, maybe even rape—until de Londoners repent of allowing Matilda entrance into de city! Join us, my lord! Even nobles can enjoy a bit of plundering from time to time, eh? Especially in such a good cause as dis?''

Brys knew he had to reply convincingly, or his loyalty might be suspect. He forced himself to grin back. "Oh, indeed! What joy 'twill be to commit mayhem in the king's name! If only the rain does not keep us from burning the stews and taverns! Do not fear, I wouldn't miss it for the world!''

And he would be there—just long enough to be seen by William d'Ypres. He would *appear* to be participating in the destruction, while actually doing none, then disappear in the confusion and go off to warn the empress. Matilda would have to realize how volatile the situation was becoming, for, once the Flemings had burned Southwark down, what was to keep them on the southern side of the Thames? And if they attacked London, Westminster would certainly be next.

All at once he realized that if Westminster should be overrun, it was Lady Gisele, rather than the empress, that he was most worried about. Matilda had loyal nobles who would protect her, and if worse came to worst she would merely be used to ransom Stephen, but who would care about one lately come Norman noblewoman?

Dusk was closing in, but still the empress was loath to leave her garden, despite her ladies' murmurs about the wet hems of their gowns.

"Bah! What is a little wet grass, when we have been cooped up inside all day? Never fear, it promises to be fair tomorrow and we shall make our expedition into the city, and have that much more enjoyment for the waiting!" She paused, looking thoughtful. "I wonder where my friend the bishop is keeping himself? Have you seen His Grace of Winchester, Geoffrey?"

Gisele kept her eyes on her sewing as the earl cleared his throat to speak. She had resigned herself to the necessity of occupying the same palace as he, but she did not want to attract his attention.

"Nay, Domina, that I have not. I fear he still pouts."

The empress was silent for a moment, but when she spoke, her voice was unruffled. "He'll be back, when he sees we will not be swayed by his moods!

Hmm…what is that smell out of the east? I wonder what can be going on?''

"'Tis smoke you smell, Empress," said a new voice from the entrance of the walled garden, a voice which caused Gisele's heart to skip a beat, then gallop. She looked up and beheld Brys de Balleroy, standing there in his hauberk, a dark smudge crossing his lean cheek.

"There are a dozen buildings on fire in Southwark."

"Brys, what are you saying? Fires in Southwark? Who set them?''

"The Flemings, Domina. At the direction of Stephen's countess."

"What?"

Gisele could see the color drain from the empress's face.

"How dare she? I must see! Come with me to the tower in the abbey, all of you!''

Minutes later, they had climbed to the highest vantage point in Westminster Abbey, and stood panting, staring out the square opening in the tower that faced the northeast. From there they could clearly see spots of orange-red glowing in the gathering darkness across the Thames in the direction of Southwark.

"I came from there as fast as my horse would carry me," Brys said. "They are looting what they are not burning, raping any woman unlucky enough to cross their path—''

"This is an outrage! The foolish woman—what can she hope to gain?" Matilda asked. "'Twill make the Londoners that much more determined to support *me,* their rightful queen!''

Gisele could see that Brys's face was troubled.

"I hope so, Empress," he said.

"You sound doubtful!''

Brys sighed. "Londoners are a fickle lot. Who can say what this will make them do?"

"You are a gloomy fellow, to be sure, de Balleroy," de Mandeville said with a sneer from his position at Matilda's side.

"Indeed, Brys! Nay, 'twas fortunate we did not go to the city today. The timing could not be arranged more excellently! Tomorrow when we go, we will be cheered as saviors," Matilda declared. "This night's work will show them who their true monarch is!"

Brys's face was stony. "Domina, now more than ever, I must renew my urging that you do not go to London—at least until the citizens' emotions have a chance to cool!"

"Nonsense. You talk like an old woman."

Gisele was watching close enough to see Brys's lips thin at the taunt, and knew a moment's sympathy for him. He was trying to advise Matilda for her own good, and she was too headstrong to listen.

"Now then," the empress said briskly, "did you obtain that item we discussed this morning?"

More secrecy.

"Yes, Empress." He reached inside the neck of his hauberk and the quilted gambeson beneath it and brought out a small oiled-leather folder, which he handed to her.

"It's gotten too dark to read it here. Come within, Brys, to my chamber. 'Twill be naught but sentimental tripe, I make no doubt, but you may read it to me before my ladies prepare me for bed."

Brys inclined his head in obedience, and fell in step with the empress. But when Geoffrey de Mandeville started to follow, too, she stopped him.

"Good even, my lord de Mandeville. If you see the

bishop, tell him we are eager to see him on the morrow when we we return from the city.''

The earl, obviously discomfitted by his dismissal, could do naught but bow in acceptance.

''Ladies, come and wait outside the door. This won't take long.''

Chapter Nine

"Thank you, ladies. I would sleep now. Seek your own beds, for the royal barge takes us early to the city."

Mindful of de Mandeville's ambush last night, Gisele was careful to leave with the other ladies. But when she left the empress's chamber, it was Brys de Balleroy, not de Mandeville, who detached himself from the opposite wall in the corridor.

"My lady Gisele, I will see you to your chamber." It was not a question, and in any case she did not wish the other ladies to see her arguing like a Billingsgate fishwife with de Balleroy. As it was, they were giving him sidelong glances and tittering behind their hands, and Gisele knew she would be teased on the morrow about her "swain."

"My lord, I am surprised to see you lingering about," she said lightly. "I thought after you and the empress discussed your...*business together*—" she raised a brow ironically "—you would be gone, or at least seek your bed."

"Nay, I thought it best to make sure that you reached your chamber safely again."

The fact that he had been standing here, waiting in

the discomfort of his hauberk for an hour or so, out of a concern for her well-being, so surprised and touched her that her mouth fell open. "My lord, 'twas kind of you, but as you saw, there was no need. The other ladies had promised to see me to my chamber."

"Ah, but you do not know your belongings have been moved to another chamber," he said, as they began to walk down the corridor. "I took the liberty of speaking to Talford this morning about what happened. While I was waiting for you to finish your duties with the empress, he came and told me he had arranged the change."

She stopped stock-still, as vexation and shame promptly replaced gratitude within her. So he apparently thought she could not take care of herself?

"My lord de Balleroy, you have taken too much upon yourself—" she began.

He held up a hand. "Lady Gisele, I am aware that the lady who shares your chamber is none other than de Mandeville's niece and ward. I am also aware that she is a faithless jade who wouldn't lift a finger to help you if her uncle told her to stay away. Now that the earl has indicated a lecherous interest in you, Talford and I thought it best to provide you with safer quarters—unless, of course, you're willing for de Mandeville to have his way with you?"

De Balleroy's narrowed brown eyes glittered in the torchlight, his face just inches from hers.

"Of course not," she replied stiffly. He was too close, so close she could clearly see the smudge of soot that still decorated his cheek. She wanted to step back, but she was damned if she'd let him know how his nearness affected her. "I...where is this new chamber? I do not share it with anyone?"

"'Tis just up these stairs and at the far end of the corridor," he said, putting a foot on the first step of the staircase they had stopped beside, "and 'tis very small. But yes, you have it all to yourself, though if you should want company, Lady Cosette and Lady Aubine's chamber is nearby, just beyond yours."

She said nothing as they climbed the twisting stairs and walked down the corridor until he stopped in front of an oaken door.

"Here it is," he said, pushing it open and standing aside so that she might see.

The chamber was indeed tiny, about half the size of the one that she had shared with Manette, but it was certainly roomy enough if she was the only one to occupy it. And the bed, while narrow, possessed clean linens and looked comfortable enough. A brazier stood ready in case the weather was chilly. A wooden chest sat at the foot of the bed. Finally, Giscle was pleased to note that the door had a heavy bolt that could be shot from the inside.

"Talford has already placed your belongings in the chest. If the room does not please you, of course you may return to the one you shared with Lady Manette," he said behind her.

Hadn't she worried that Manette's treacherous nature would make sharing a chamber with her dangerous? As much as she wanted to be self-sufficient, to owe nothing to any man, she had to admit de Balleroy had done her a great service, with the chamberlain's help. She owed him thanks.

She had half turned to make them and apologize for her prickliness when she realized that de Balleroy had started to walk away toward the stairs.

"Wait, Lord Brys!" she called, and saw him pause and look over his shoulder at her.

"I…" She gathered her skirts and took a step or two in his direction. "I will take the chamber, and thank you. I… It was very good of you to trouble yourself for me—especially after the shrewish way I spoke to you this morn. I doubt not I shall feel much safer here."

His lips curved upward and he walked back to her. "Shall you? Even if I tell you my chamber is just at the head of the stairs?" He grinned as she started backward. "Do not worry, damsel. It's rare enough that I shall be there," he said. "And you are welcome, Lady Gisele. I was happy to render such a trifling service."

She told herself it was foolish to feel so giddy just because a well-favored man smiled at her, but then she sensed that he was about to bid her good night and walk away. "Do you…will you be here on the morrow, or does your business take you from London?" she asked, despising herself for sounding like a silly milkmaid.

His brow rose at the question. "We shall see, Lady Gisele, we shall see," he murmured, and before she was aware of what he was about to do, he had laid his fingers along her cheekbone and lowered his head to kiss her.

She felt his lips touch hers like a whisper; then, as she hesitated a heartbeat too long, he placed gentle hands on either side of her face, holding her there while he deepened the kiss, lingering like a thirsty man might linger at a deep well.

At last he pulled away, and she opened her eyes quickly enough to see the spark of surprise in his before it faded. "Good night, damsel," he said in a low, caressing voice.

* * *

They rode through the streets the next day on horses which the Earl of Essex had arranged to have ready for them where they landed.

London was a city of scents, Gisele decided. At the wharves, the pungent odor of fish and the fainter tang of saltwater mingled with exotic spices being unloaded in casks from the Orient and Outremer—mace, cinnamon, ginger and peppercorns. Gisele caught whiffs of smoke when the wind came across the Thames from Southwark, and the stench of rotting garbage, too, but she was determined not to pay attention to those.

It was a city of sounds, also—the cries of the chestnut, oyster and cherry vendors, the babel of voices speaking French and English, Italian and even Arabic, and the endless bells from the churches.

"That's St. Paul's," Cosette told her in her knowledgeable way, pointing in the direction of the chiming. "And that, St. John's, and the shrill one over there, St. Brides. Ah...and there's Mary-le-Bow, last but not least."

They stopped first at the perfumers' stalls, and Matilda bought ambergris and musk in stoppered clay jars, then went on to the benches of the leather workers, where boots of Spanish kid caught the empress's eyes, but she remained to pick out pairs of shoes for herself in half a dozen colors. "Send the bill to the palace, where the council will see it paid by my subjects," she told the shoemaker grandly, just as she had told the perfumers. "I am certain the Londoners would not have me going barefoot to my coronation."

"Yes, Domina," the shoemaker said, bowing low, but when he straightened, only Gisele noticed the way the shoemaker glared and spat at the empress's back. It made her uneasy, and aware that the shoemaker was not the only one pointing and frowning as Matilda claimed seemingly every item she laid her eyes upon. Most of the onlookers would never be able to buy even one of those things, even after a lifetime of hard work.

Didn't the empress realize how important it was to make a good impression on her citizens who had so recently been loyal to Stephen? Didn't she realize that the one word they would now associate with her was *greed?* Why wasn't she going out of her way to *meet* her subjects, and let them see she was human just as they were?

Then Gisele felt guilty for her critical thoughts. For all the empress's self-involvement, Matilda had been very good to her. And perhaps it was normal to want so many things after all she had been through.

Word of the empress's presence had evidently spread, for as they rode along, more and more people gathered and stared at Matilda and her entourage. Few of them smiled or seemed happy that the empress had come to the city. Gisele heard murmurings in English. She wished someone would translate.

Oblivious to the mutters of the crowd, Matilda declared herself hungry, halting her party at a vendor of roast chestnuts. She purchased paper cones of the savory nuts for herself and her ladies. Then she flagged down urchins selling meat pasties and bought a score, sending Wulfram and Manette to a nearby vintner's booth to buy Lombardy wine to wash down their impromtu midday meal.

At Chepeside, they lingered for over an hour at the drapers' stalls while the empress considered linen from Flanders, silks from Italy, and even furs from Scandinavia. Dark-eyed Levantine traders approached her with bolt after bolt of brocades and cottons, and she delightedly fingered all of them.

Two or three of the ladies were purchasing cloth, too, planning their own coronation wear. Candles at Westminster would burn well into the night and eyes would be strained as cloth was cut and sewn into gowns, that was sure!

How lovely to be able to purchase even the humblest of these bolts, Gisele thought, longingly stroking a particularly lovely length of dark-green silk shot through with silver threads. She then reluctantly put it down again and walked away so she wouldn't be tempted. She would have to have another gown or two made eventually, but it would have to be something less exotic, for she had only a few silver pennies in the pouch at her girdle.

"Lady, thees ees for you," the swarthy-faced Venetian silk merchant said, holding out the folded silver-shot green silk toward her.

"But I said I could not afford it," she replied, thinking the Venetian had misunderstood her intent. "No, it is too costly." She shook her head and backed away to emphasize her point.

"But *signorina,* eet is bought for you," the trader insisted. "Here, take."

Had Matilda seen her yearning for the cloth, and made a present of it? Once again feeling guilty for having thought ill of Matilda earlier, she looked around her until she had spotted the empress, and went over to her.

"Domina, with all my heart I thank you," she began, but stopped when she saw Matilda's puzzled face. "You...you didn't purchase this for me?"

"No, my dear. Perhaps you have a secret admirer?" Matilda chuckled. "You should keep it—the hue suits you, you know...." she said vaguely, before she was distracted by a cloak of royal-purple from Crete.

De Mandeville? Gisele thought with a shudder of distaste, knowing that if it was the earl who had bought the cloth for her, she would have to refuse it. She could never be able to enjoy wearing anything made of it without wondering when de Mandeville would come to claim his due.

But hadn't the earl remained behind at the docks, saying he had some business to conduct? Had he perhaps rejoined them when she hadn't been looking? Looking about her, however, Gisele didn't see him skulking about with his satyr's smirk—but she did have the oddest feeling of being watched by *someone*.

Whirling around suddenly, Gisele was just in time to spot a shadow disappearing behind the corner of a carpet maker's shop.

She started forward, then stopped as the empress announced her wish to proceed on to Goldsmiths' Lane. She dared not become separated from the empress's party, especially since the crowd's mood was so hostile, so she was forced to place the folded cloth in her saddlebag and mount up.

Once inside the most prosperous-looking of the goldsmiths shops, Matilda indulged in an orgy of present buying. "This is for young Henry, who will be eight this year," she proclaimed with a mother's pride as she picked out a gold cloakpin with a ruby set in it. "And this for his brother, little Geoffrey," she added, picked up a slightly less ornate version for her middle son. "William is, of course, too young to appreciate such finery, though that gold-fitted cup on the shelf, there, will do very well." The empress sighed as the goldsmith fetched it down for her inspection. "I suppose I should buy something for my husband, too, or he will sulk," she mused aloud. "Geoffrey Le Bel is the only man I ever met who can express sulking in a letter! Oh, but this I must have for *me*," she cooed, spying a gold ring of ornate filigree work around an enormous fresh-water pearl.

All around her, the other ladies in waiting were ooh-ing and aahing over similar golden treasures, but Gisele's attention had been captured by a tray of Celtic silverwork held out by one of the goldsmith's apprentices.

Wouldn't it be wonderful to have a silver pendant of this elegant Celtic scrollwork to set off the silver threads in her as-yet unmade green gown! *If only...* It was impossible not to be envious as she spied Manette across the shop, buying a heavy gold torque for her swanlike neck, out of funds given her by her indulgent uncle, no doubt.

From his vantage point amid the crowd watching through the open doorway, Brys saw Gisele touching the silver Irish necklace, and the fleeting wistfulness in her eyes before she resolutely put the piece back in the apprentice's tray. Poor little noble damsel. For all that she was the heiress of the Comte de L'Aigle, her worth was in land, not in ready coin, which made her little better than a beggar when it came to making purchases. He had a purse given to him by the Countess of Boulogne, though, and since he wouldn't feel right about spending it on himself, who better to spend it on than Gisele?

He knew that if Gisele looked out at the crowd, she'd never recognize him, standing there disguised as a bearded seller of hot pork pies.

''The German whore,'' muttered a Londoner by his side. ''Look at her, buying a king's ransom in gold, whilst our *king* rots in a Bristol dungeon!''

Stephen's cell was actually quite a comfortable one, well above ground level, with a brazier kept well-supplied with hot coals when the weather was chilly, but Brys dared not argue him, nor point out that Matilda was as Norman as Stephen. Nor had anyone any proof that she had ever been unfaithful.

Brys had been following the empress's party at a distance ever since they'd stepped off the royal barge. He'd been worried about how Matilda would be received in London after the events of the night before, and that worry only increased as he saw her making purchase after purchase and spending no time getting to know the people over whom she wished to reign.

Brys was supposed to be out assessing the mood of the citizens for the other Matilda, the countess of Boulogne. He'd donned this disguise to do so, because he hadn't wanted to be spotted by anyone in the empress's party—especially Gisele, who did not know about the dangerous double role he was playing. Even in disguise, he would be free to come to the empress's aid if worse came to worst.

Stephen's Matilda would certainly be happy with his report. He'd heard the Londoners muttering how they'd been wrong to let the empress stay at Westminster and plan her coronation—the destruction in Southwark by rival forces was proof it had been wrong! As he followed the shopping expedition around the city, the murmurs had become more frequent and open. Rumors were passed that the Flemings intended to cross the Thames into London itself and repeat their burning and looting if the city continued to welcome the empress.

Perhaps it was not too late to rescind their welcome to the empress, they said, and apologize to Matilda of Boulogne, who was only upholding her husband's rights! Surely, if they did, the Fleming marauders would go away!

Just then the empress and her ladies came streaming out, only to go next door into another goldsmith's shop. Gisele hadn't seen him; she had been too intent on something Lady Aubine was saying to her as the latter held up a set of Paternoster beads of garnets and jet.

He stepped into the first goldsmith's shop briefly, and after persuading the suspicious goldsmith that he was not *really* as poor as he looked, but had several gold marks in his wallet, made a purchase.

When he came out, the empress's party was still within the second shop, but the crowd was getting ugly. Hotheads among the group were prying at loose cobbles or picking up horse droppings. He heard the chilling chant, *"Stone her."*

A vision of Gisele, not Matilda, being struck in the forehead by a cobble, sent him hastening down the narrow passage between the buildings and into the second shop's rear entrance. He wished he had not sent Maislin on to Bristol this very morning with the letter to Stephen from his wife. It would have been good to have his giant of a squire at his side if all hell broke loose and they had to fight their way to Matilda's side. But perhaps if he could persuade the empress it was time to leave *now*...

Matilda had belatedly started to realize just what sort of bills she was running up, bills that would only inflame the London representatives who had already been loath to buy her new coronation robes, let alone the mound of purchases that Wulfram and the other lackeys were struggling to carry. She was therefore ready to listen as Brys told her of the growing temper of the crowd.

Ignoring Gisele's shocked face as she heard Brys's voice issuing from this stranger's face, and the titters of the ladies as they, too, recognized him, Brys hustled them out the back door of the goldsmith's shop. He'd worry about the horses, tethered out front, once he made sure Gisele—and her royal mistress—were out of danger.

Chapter Ten

"Withdraw from London? 'Tis out of the question, my lord," Matilda said shortly. "We are not about to retreat just before we are to be *crowned*. My coronation is just a few days away. As it is, I shall have to send Talford to obtain the white horse I did not get to buy."

Her tone and face, Gisele could see from her seat on the barge, were obdurate.

Brys could be just as stubborn, and he was beginning to sound as if he were losing his patience. "Can't you see, Domina, 'tis too dangerous for you here just now! Your withdrawal would not be permanent—just until our forces succeed in driving off the Flemish mercenaries. Surely Your Highness will reconsider, for the sake of those who fight for you, if not for your own safety? All our hopes are lost if you are taken, Empress."

Brys spoke such eminent good sense that Gisele wanted to throttle her royal mistress for refusing to listen. Back at the goldsmith's shop, Gisele had seen the empress glance outside while Brys was telling her of the crowd's threats. Hadn't Matilda *seen* the ugly glares aimed at her?

The royal party had been lucky to escape on foot out the back exit and through narrow side streets back to the docks without being seen by the mob, but the empress treated their hasty retreat as a mere inconvenience.

"Domina, at least call a meeting of the council to discuss the matter," Brys pleaded, as the barge drew near to Westminster.

Gisele could see from the furrows in his brow and the jutting of his jaw that de Balleroy's supply of tact was growing low.

"Quite impossible," Matilda snapped. "We have a fitting of our coronation robes now. And then 'twill be supper time."

The barge was bumping the dock now, and Brys said nothing further, just nimbly jumped to the wooden platform and assisted the empress to disembark, then all her ladies.

Matilda and the rest of her ladies proceeded into the palace, all but Gisele, who, still holding her folded silk, felt constrained to remain.

"I... No one has thanked you for your timely intervention in the city today...." she began. "I'm most grateful, my lord. Events might well have fallen out differently, had you not been there. Why—"

But he cut off her question. "Your thanks more than makes up for her lack of them, Lady Gisele," he said, nodding in the direction Matilda had gone.

She smiled at him, not knowing what else to say, and then would have left to follow the others, but de Balleroy restrained her with a gentle hand to her wrist.

"Lady Gisele, remain with me awhile, if you would be so good," he said. "I would talk with you, and the empress won't need you until at least after supper. We could stroll in the garden. There should be no one about at this hour.''

Wary, she nodded, saying, ''Perhaps we can sit somewhere in it and talk? After all that walking today, my ankle is reminding me it's still recovering.''

She watched as he pulled off the fake beard and rubbed at the reddened spots where the paste had glued the beard to his cheeks and chin. Now he looked like Brys de Balleroy again.

He did not seem in a hurry to speak, however, once they were among the fragrant beds of roses, lilies, foxgloves and rhododendrons. They had stopped by a stone bench, and he pulled her gently down next to him. A thrush in one of the fruit trees sang its melodious ''did-he-do-it? He-did-he-did-he-did,'' song; bees buzzed among the flowers in counterpoint.

Finally, she broke the silence between them. ''You have not answered my question, my lord. How did it happen that you appeared, disguised, just in the nick of time to save us from the mob? Were you spying upon us the whole time? If so, why, may I ask?''

He ducked his head with a rueful smile. ''And if I say 'No, you may not ask?'''

It was a teasing challenge. She raised her chin and said, ''You may not answer, my lord, but I will ask nonetheless.''

He patted the hand that rested lightly on his arm. ''Let us just say that having observed the mood of the people when I was away from the palace, I thought it best to keep an eye on the empress and her ladies while you were in the city. I went disguised because I did not wish to spoil the fun, had my fears been groundless.''

''But they were not.''

"Nay. I fear that matters will only worsen, not get better." With his free hand, he rubbed his chin.

"It frustrates you mightily that the empress won't listen to you, doesn't it?"

He stopped, and gazed down into her face. "Those eyes see only too clearly," he murmured, brushing his fingertips light as a butterfly across the lashes of her left eye.

"Yes, I wish with all my heart I could persuade the fool woman to retreat to safety, at least until Robert of Gloucester can capture d'Ypres and gain better control around the city."

She was startled by his vehemence. "You think there is real danger to the empress," she said, feeling a shiver of fear race down her spine. She laid down the cloth on the bench beside her.

He nodded. "But Her Highness is so hell-bent upon her crowning, she little sees the danger—or that without winning the hearts of those she would rule, wearing the crown means naught."

"She is fortunate she has *your* heart," she told him, moved at his obvious sincerity. "And your eyes."

Again, he turned his sunlit brown eyes upon hers, gazing until it seemed he could see into her soul. "The empress has my *fealty*," he corrected her. "I would give my life to save her, should she require it, for I meant the oath of loyalty I swore on holy relics. But my heart is still mine to give."

That, too, sounded strangely like a challenge. While she was still pondering his words and wondering how to reply to them, she changed the subject slightly. "While we were at the drapers' stalls, a curious thing happened, my lord. I had been looking at this length of fabric—'' she pointed to the folded cloth lying beside her ''—and the next thing I knew it was mine.''

''Matilda can be very generous to those she likes—'' de Balleroy began, but she cut him off.

''No one, including the empress, seems to know who purchased the fabric for me, my lord. At first, I feared Geoffrey de Mandeville might be skulking about, but I never saw him. You showed up not too long afterward. Was it you? Had you been watching? Did you see me pick up the cloth and guess that I had liked it?''

He looked down at his hands, which had been idly toying with a fold of his cloak, then up at her. ''And if 'twas I who saw your wistful face as you picked it up, only to put it back down again with sadness in your eyes?''

''You saw much from your hidden vantage point,'' she muttered, dismayed that her face had mirrored her feelings so nakedly.

''Such a color would become you well, my lady.'' His voice was husky. ''Especially with this at your throat,'' he added, reaching inside the pouch at his belt and bringing out the very same Celtic silver necklace she had been wishing for inside the goldsmith's shop.

She gasped, staring at the necklace but not taking it from his hand. ''My lord de Balleroy, how did you— I cannot possibly—''

''Brys,'' he corrected her, smiling at her flustered state. He reached out and laid his fingers against her throat and cheek. ''Lady Gisele, I would die to protect you, too, not because of fealty, but because I would give my heart to you. Would you would accept it, beautiful lady?''

Before she could answer, his lips were on hers, drugging her with their sweetness, making it impossible to think clearly, to resist when he pulled her more closely into his embrace and his lips strayed down her neck. Her emotions whirled and skidded as she tried to find the words, *the strength,* to refuse his amazing gift. Each time she opened her mouth to call a halt, his lips returned to hers, until at last she forgot she had any will but his. At some point she heard a metallic *clink* as the silver necklace fell from his fingers onto the stone bench at his side.

"Brys, I..."

In a haze of awakening desire, she felt him lift her onto his lap, one arm around her back, the fingers of that hand stroking and bunching her skirts over her upper leg, while his other hand cupped her breast, making her cry out in ecstasy at the shocking pleasure of his touch. Instantly she discovered he could produce even more joy by circling her hardening nipple with his thumb.

Brys's breathing had grown ragged, and the pupils of his eyes had grown so large the eyes appeared black before he pressed his feverish forehead against hers.

Just then the supper horn blew, startling her from her passion-fogged state.

Brys groaned. "Come away with me, my sweet lady," he said.

"To your chamber? But I am expected at supper..."

"Aye, to my chamber. And then to my keep at Tichenden, and eventually to Normandy, where I vow I will keep you safe always, Gisele..."

Her brain was no longer so clouded with desire that she missed the fact that while he had spoken of protecting her and giving his heart to her, nowhere in his invitation to passion had he included the words *love* and *marriage.*

Just as he was about to kiss her again, she pulled back. "Come with you to Tichenden? As what, my lord? Your leman? And am I to go back eventually to Normandy with you, where my father lives, as *your mistress?*"

"Nay, Gisele—"

She jumped up from the bench, hot with anger. "I told you I did not come to court to become some man's possession, even in the honorable state of marriage! But you do not even offer me *that,* do you? You would make me a mere plaything," she accused in scathing tones. "Yet you do not even trust me. You are a man of secrets, Lord Brys—none of which I am good enough to share."

She saw the point had gone home when he visibly flinched. "Not at all, sweet lady, you did not let me finish...." Brys reached out to her, but she backed away, the spell thoroughly broken now.

"I must get to the hall." Gathering her skirts in one trembling hand, Gisele turned around and began running out of the garden.

Her throbbing ankle slowed her down, though, and Brys caught her in a few strides.

She had thought he would just let her go, and when his arm snaked around her waist, she was frightened for a moment. Unwilling to accept her refusal, did he mean to force her?

"Unhand me, my lord," she snapped, injecting ice into her voice so she would not reveal her fear. But once she looked into his eyes and saw only concern and tenderness in their brown depths, she relaxed slightly.

"All right, if you will not go with me out of love, then let me take you away from court for your own good," he told her.

''For my own good?'' she echoed, mystified.

Brys nodded. ''I fear for you, Lady Gisele, just as I fear for Matilda, but she has other liegemen who will watch out for her. The city is about to boil over, thanks to the countess of Boulogne and her Flemings—and those Londoners who were never for the empress anyway. And when it boils over, they will head for Westminster, Lady Gisele.''

''Who are you, my lord, that you are so familiar with what they will do? Whose side are you on, really?'' she demanded.

''If you will come with me, I will explain, I promise. But never doubt I am the empress's liegeman. I... I would not have you in their path, lady. I...I care too much for you. If you will not stay with me, let me take you home to Normandy, to l'Aigle.''

Go home to her father, who cared only that she marry and give him a male heir for l'Aigle? She could imagine the count's cold smile when he saw her, his sneer at her failure. But she couldn't confess this to Brys, and see his earnestness turn to pity that she had nowhere to go.

''That would be impossible, my lord.''

He must have thought her still suspicious of his motives, for he said solemnly, ''Lady Gisele, I swear by all that's holy I will take you straightway to your father, as much a maiden as when you left him.''

She was startled that he put it so bluntly. ''Nay, my lord, you mistake me. 'Tis not that I distrust you, but that I do not wish to leave the empress. She will need her ladies, if there is trouble coming.''

Brys took a step back, his eyes shuttered now. He bowed. ''I have no choice but to admire your loyalty and accept your decision,'' he said. ''But I would have you know I will always be there if you need me, Lady Gisele.''

She nodded, still tingling from his touch, her body still yearing for his. She wanted to give in, to cry, *Take me, my lord! To your chamber, to the ends of the earth, if you wish!* But she said only, "I thank you, Lord Brys. I will keep it in mind."

She started to leave the garden again, only to have him call out to her, holding out the necklace upon the folded cloth.

"You forgot these, Lady Gisele. It would give me pleasure for you to have them, regardless of how you feel about me."

She stared at the two gifts. *Can't you see I want you as much as you want me? That I fear I might even...love you?* "I...I will take the silk, and thank you, my lord." She shouldn't, she knew, but she could not summon the resolve to refuse it, knowing she needed a second gown and that the silver-shot green would make her look and feel beautiful as no color had ever done before. "But I cannot take the necklace. 'Tis a gift a man should give a wife—or to his betrothed."

And you have not asked me to be your wife, only your lover.

Chapter Eleven

It seemed that the supper horn had blown hours ago. If only she had time to go to her chamber, drop off the cloth and splash some cool water on her flushed face! But the empress frowned on anyone coming to table after she had made her grand entrance, and so Gisele hastened toward the great hall instead of up the stairs.

She skidded to a stop just inside the hall as she realized that Matilda's chaplain was already in the middle of grace. His praying, however, didn't stop the curious from looking from under their lashes at the latecomer.

"How pleasant that you could join us, Lady Gisele," the empress commented tartly, after the prayer was finished.

Gisele bowed in the queen's direction, feeling herself blushing anew. "I'm sorry to be late, Your Highness," she murmured, bracing herself for a stern rebuke.

But Matilda seemed more inclined to toy with her than reprove her. "And did you discover the identity of your gift giver?" the empress inquired with arch gaiety, indicating the folded cloth that Gisele still clutched in her hand.

Chuckles and guffaws arose from the nearby trestle tables.

Gisele wished at that moment that she'd perished in the forest next to Fleurette, or at least never picked up the damned cloth! Miserably aware of every eye upon her, and wondering if Brys had slipped in behind her and was watching her being made sport of, Gisele hesitated, then stammered, "Yes—no—that is…"

"Why, it's obvious that she did," hissed a voice from the ladies' table, a voice that Gisele identified as Manette's. "Just look at those kiss-swollen lips! And those overbright eyes! I'd venture to say she has been off somewhere demonstrating her gratitude in no uncertain terms!"

Aghast, Gisele darted a glance at the head table, but Matilda was already accepting the first choice dish from her servitor and apparently hadn't heard Manette's remark, much to the latter's disappointment.

Keeping her head down, Gisele slid into the empty place next to Halette.

"Sheathe your claws, Manette," that lady called down the table; then, said to Gisele, "Never mind, dear. I think that's lovely that my lord de Balleroy is courting you. 'Twould be an excellent match—and such a handsome man!"

"But he isn't—that is, I'm not—" But all she could think about at that moment was the feel of Brys's lips on hers, and the heat of his hand as he had cupped her breast, and she reddened all over again.

"Oh, yes he is, and you are, so don't try to deny it!" crowed Lady Aubine from across the table.

"Yes, don't try to deny it," chimed in Emmeline, a knowing smile on her thin lips. "Your cheeks tell the truth! So…*he* gave you the silk?"

"The question is, what did Gisele have to give in return?" Manette asked, loud enough to be heard by the tables behind and in front of them.

"*Ladies!* Dat vill be quite enough of dat unseemly talk!" Wilfride announced, her German accent thicker in her outrage.

Everyone ducked their heads, pretending great interest in the soup that was being ladled into their bowls, for no one wanted to be taken aside by the chief of Matilda's ladies. Gisele was left in peace at last. But her head was already throbbing, and the soup, and everything served after it, tasted like wood shavings.

Supper seemed interminable to Gisele. Once she had given up on eating, she passed the time by looking about the hall to see who was present. Brys de Balleroy, clearly, was not. Had he quit Westminster in disgust, after he found he could not so easily seduce her? Or did he have more of his mysterious business to conduct?

Her heart ached as she wondered whether she had been right to refuse his love. Would sticking to her ideals cause her to end up an embittered old virgin such as Lady Wilfride?

Ominously, Henry, Bishop of Winchester, was still absent from his place next to the empress. Had the bishop changed his coat yet again, and gone back to his brother, King Stephen? Was Brys correct that Matilda's support was eroding to the point where she and her court were in grave danger?

Geoffrey de Mandeville was there, but seemed lost in his thoughts. At least he made no attempt to capture her gaze. Perhaps he was already after other, more willing prey.

Gisele was not the only person who noticed de Mandeville's abstraction. She saw Matilda lay a hand on the

earl's sleeve and make some remark to him. At once, a
mask of smiling urbanity replaced his pensive expression, and he responded, apparently with some compliment, for the empress preened.

When at last Matilda arose and announced that she
would not sit in her garden tonight, Gisele breathed a
sigh of relief. She could not bear to return so soon to
the place where she had come so close to surrendering
herself to Brys de Balleroy! Perhaps she could even go
to bed early.

"Ladies, I believe I will go into the abbey and pray,
as I have much on my mind," she announced as Gisele
and the rest waited for her at the foot of the dais. "You
are dismissed—all except for you, Lady Gisele, who are
to accompany me to the abbey, and you, ladies Wilfride
and Rilla, who will please be so good as to await us in
the royal chamber. We shall not be long."

Gisele stifled a sigh of disappointment as she nodded
submissively and fell into step behind the empress. This
was evidently her penance for being late.

Out of the corner of her eye, she noticed de Mandeville going to the back of the hall, his hand raised in
greeting to a man standing there—a prosperous burgher
by his dress.

Contrary to what she had promised Wilfride and
Rilla, Matilda was long at her prayers, and Gisele was
smothering yawns as she stood in the royal chamber
and assisted the other ladies to prepare Matilda for bed.
They were just about finished when the empress started
and cried, "Lady Gisele! I left my prayer book in the
abbey! You must go and fetch it for me!"

"Domina, surely it will be all right there until morning,'' Lady Rilla assured her, with a sympathetic glance at Gisele.

"Nonsense! It has a jeweled cover, and was given to my father, and blessed for him by the pope himself! I do not want to chance it being stolen.''

Gisele's heart sank, even as she arose. "I will be happy to go get it for you, Your Highness.''

But Matilda had thought more of what her demand would mean. "Ah, but I am ready to sleep, and it will take you too long to walk down to the abbey and back up here again. 'Twill be sufficient that you go and fetch the prayer book, Lady Gisele. Just keep it safe with you until you attend me in the morning.''

Over the empress's bent head, Rilla rolled her eyes, as if to say, *Ah, the whims of monarchs!*

"I will, Your Highness. Might I borrow a candle?'' Matilda didn't seem to realize her order meant a long walk down several dimly lit passages, as well as a short passage in the night air between the palace and the abbey. Gisele was half tempted to rebel and leave the prayer book there until just before she attended Matilda in the morning, but she couldn't be sure of waking early enough.

The empress inclined her head regally, granting the boon.

The abbey was an awe-inspiring cavern of flickering candles and broad-cast shadows at this late hour, with the sputtering of every candle magnified in the stillness. She could feel her heart pounding in her ears. It seemed a sacrilege to disturb the shadowy peace of the place, so, walking as quietly down the middle aisle as she could, Gisele reached the spot where Matilda had been kneeling. She picked up the prayer book and began to retrace her steps. Hearing soft voices in one of the side chapels, she assumed it was two priests. Possibly they were preparing for Mass on the morrow.

But as she was passing behind a massive stone pillar, a pair of figures came out of the side chapel. It was Geoffrey de Mandeville and the burgher.

Quickly she shrank behind the wide pillar. It had been their voices she had heard in the side chapel, and while they were still keeping their voices down, it was obvious from earl's wrathful expression that they were in the midst of a disagreement.

They had not seen her. And since the Earl of Essex was the last person she wanted to encounter, she stepped back into the shadows and hoped he would exit without spotting her.

All at once, the burgher raised his fist and shouted, "And I tell you it shall not be! I will expose you, my lord earl, for the viper you are! If you think you can sell London to the highest bidder—"

"You'll expose me?" de Mandeville snarled. "How nice of you to warn me, Osgood! But I don't think you'll be exposing *anyone*…" Then, quick as the viper he had been called, the nobleman pulled a long-bladed dagger from inside his sleeve and stabbed the burgher in the chest.

The burgher screamed and tried to twist away from de Mandeville, but he had been mortally wounded, and as Gisele stared in horror, de Mandeville pulled out the knife and with a slashing motion, cut the burgher's throat. The screaming abruptly ceased. Then, de Mandeville cooly wiped the blade of his dagger on the burgher's gown.

Gisele's first, terrified gasp had been drowned out by the burgher's scream, but now her nerveless fingers let go of the prayer book. It dropped to the stone floor with a soft but all too audible thud.

Once more, she shrank behind the pillar, praying de Mandeville would be too intent on making his own escape to have noticed the sound.

But he had. *"Who's there?"* de Mandeville demanded. "I know you're there—you may as well come out! *Who's there, damn your hide!"*

She heard the thudding sounds of booted feet approaching her hiding place, and knew she had no choice but to run. De Mandeville would want no witnesses to this murder, done right in the middle of the abbey!

Picking up her skirts in one hand, Gisele ran, expecting at any moment to feel him grabbing her arm, and the cold steel of his dagger blade burying itself between her shoulder blades.

"Come back here, wench! You can't hope to outrun me!" the earl called after her. "Come back, and maybe…maybe I'll let you live—for a price!" He laughed evilly, the sound echoing off the high beamed ceiling of the church—but there was a deadly edge of desperation to that laugh.

Needles of pain shot up from her ankle, but she dared not pay attention. There—ahead of her! The doorway! If she could make it across the courtyard and into the hall, surely there would be someone who would help her! At least de Mandeville, powerful and ruthless as he was, wouldn't dare to murder her in front of witnesses! But he was gaining on her. She could almost feel his hot panting breath on the back of her neck— *Jésu, save me!*

As if in answer to her prayer, she heard a heavy thud behind her. Chancing a glance over her shoulder, she saw that de Mandeville had apparently stumbled on the steps that led down into the courtyard, and fallen head over heels onto the cobbles.

It didn't give her much of an advantage, but the tiny infusion of hope was enough to give wings to her feet. She gained the hall, her eyes darting wildly about her for some wakeful person who could aid her.

The hall, though, was full of snoring servingmen, and Gisele, dodging sleeping forms on benches and lying amidst the rushes, reconsidered. Even if she could waken one of them quickly, how could he do more than forestall her doom? De Mandeville might only shift from killing her outright to accusing *her* of murdering the burgher. It had been obvious at supper tonight that de Mandeville was still very much in the empress's favor. She couldn't count on her royal mistress to believe in her innocence against the skillful lies of her favorite courtier.

No, her only hope lay in reaching the sanctuary of her room. She didn't think he had identified her from the back, and if she could reach the stairway before de Mandeville gained the hall, he might not know where to find his quarry.

But even with fear spurring her on, she was running out of air and endurance. Her lungs burned within her, and her legs, numbed by terror, felt like jelly.

"Stop her! That running wench, there! She's a murderess!" came the shout in back of her. De Mandeville had reached the hall, and it was just a matter of a few strides before he caught her!

But his cry had worked against him, for it had awakened most of the sleepers. Bodies struggled upright from benches and the rushes and blocked his path, slowing de Mandeville as he dodged around them. She heard him rain curses at them, then he cried out in alarm.

She saw that he had tripped over one of the sleepy servants and fallen. She just might make it! The thought spurred her on, and she fairly flew up the winding staircase. One floor, then two! Just as she reached the third floor, the floor her chamber was located on, pounding footsteps echoing up the stairs told her that her pursuer was once again on his feet.

She'd never reach her own chamber—it was nearly at the end of the corridor. But Brys de Balleroy's chamber was right at the top of the stairs. Pray God he hadn't locked his door, if he had left Westminster…

Chapter Twelve

"My lord earl! Is aught amiss? What are you shouting about?" The voice drifted up the stairwell just as Gisele tried the door and found it unlocked.

Stealthily, she pushed it open, praying the hinge wouldn't squeak and give away the location of her sanctuary. It didn't, and she crept inside, closing the door and shooting the bolt with the same quiet care.

The flickering hour candle revealed that Brys de Balleroy *was* there, lying on his back, deeply asleep.

The linen was pushed down to his waist, but Gisele knew she didn't have time just then to stare at the magnificence of his well-muscled masculine body. Instead she turned back to listen at the door for what answer de Mandeville would give Talford the chamberlain.

"Get out of my way, fellow!" The cry was muffled by the door, but clear enough. "I...I'm chasing a murderess! I just saw a man being killed in the abbey, and the wicked wench fled up these stairs!"

"But...you say a *woman* killed this man? Are you certain? Why would a woman kill a man, and in the abbey, of all places?" the chamberlain cried. "'Tis sacrilege!"

Evidently Talford, in his amazement, was holding on to de Mandeville, for the earl retorted, ''Let me go, you old fool! How do I know why she killed him? Of course it's sacrilege, but if you slow me down, she'll get away!''

''Do you know who it was?''

''Lady Gisele de l'Aigle,'' came the grim, impatient answer. ''She was wearing a purplish-red sort of gown. Come with me, and you can help apprehend her!''

Gisele's heart froze within her. So he *had* seen enough of her to know her!

''Where is the murderess's chamber?''

''Why, let me think…'tis on the third floor, the one farthest down the hall, I believe….''

''Come on. We'll break the door down, if need be!'' de Mandeville shouted, already pounding up the stairs.

Gisele turned back to the shadowy form on the bed. Brys's regular breathing told her he was asleep, though she marveled at how he could sleep through all the noise. Even with the muffling effect of the thick wooden door, the loudness of the footsteps, the voices, and now the sound of a door being forced down the corridor— *her* door—would have startled *her* awake, even in here.

Gisele thought quickly. De Mandeville's certainty that it was she he had seen, and that he would find her in her room, might actually give her the added time she needed to make it look as if she could not possibly have been the one in the chapel, at least to Talford.

God forgive me for what I am about to do. Quickly, with trembling fingers, she undid the girdle about her waist and allowed it to fall to the rushes, then pulled the gown itself off over her head.

''Whaaa—who's there?'' murmured a sleepy, husky voice. Brys's voice.

The gown had to be hidden, she thought, for de Mandeville might still convince the chamberlain she was the murderess if he caught sight of its telltale mulberry hue. She hurled it under the bed.

Brys was sitting up on the bed now, rubbing his knuckles over his eyes. "Gisele? What are you doing here?" Then, as she pulled off her chemise and let it drop to the rushes, he breathed, "Gisele, what are you doing?"

I'll tell him the truth later, I swear by all that's holy, she promised within herself, as she stood before him, naked as the day she had been born. Then, before she could lose her nerve, she went forward, sitting down on the bed beside him.

Brys was sure the apparition before him was but an extension of his dream. He had been dreaming of Gisele, dreaming of her coming to his bed, and now here she was. But surely no fantasy Gisele would be breathing as hard as this one was. And when she sat on the edge of the bed beside him, and he reached out and touched her, her skin was warm and damp with perspiration. Oh, she was real enough, or this dream was more realistic than any he'd ever had before.

"Gisele…what are you doing here, sweetheart?" he repeated again, sliding an arm around her waist and feeling her trembling.

"I…I was wrong, Brys," she whispered, her voice and expression urgent. "Earlier, I mean…when I refused you. I want you, Brys. I want you to make love to me—right now!" Then she stretched out on her side against him, and the feel of her breast against the side of his chest nearly drove all rational thought from his brain right then.

Saints, if this was a dream, let me not wake up until I have taken her! But aloud he said, "Ah, sweetheart, I'm so glad you've changed your mind! You won't be sorry, that I promise, sweeting. But surely there is no need for haste…I have some wine on the table next to the bed. Would you like some?"

She was nervous, he could tell. Certain that she was a virgin, Brys wanted to calm her, to relax her, so that this first lovemaking might be as glorious as he knew it could be between them. And he wanted to calm himself, too. His blood had heated so much at the sight of her naked body that he feared he could unintentionally hurt her in his haste.

Dimly, Brys was aware of some commotion beyond his chamber, but it had no meaning for him. Nothing and no one had any significance for him but this very enticing female whose bare body touched his from breast to thigh.

"No, Brys! I—I don't want any wine! I want you to make love to me—*now,* Brys! I'll die if you don't make love to me this very minute!" Snaking an arm around his neck, she half raised up until her parted lips met his. And he was lost.

When he could breathe again, he said, "Gisele de l'Aigle, you are as impulsive as you are stubborn, but if it's lovemaking you want, that's what I'll give you, sweeting." The only question was how long he would be able to last with her wiggling against him like that. He could feel his manhood, hard and throbbing, demanding that he bury it in her softness.…

Maybe she *wanted* him to take her hard and fast the first time. Then he could show her all the delights of slow, sweet loving the rest of the night! He couldn't imagine what had gotten into Gisele that she was in such a fever to give herself to him, but thank the saints for it, whatever it was!

He gave himself up to the luxury of a deep kiss, his tongue dancing with hers even as his hand was acquainting itself with her breasts, reveling in the lack of clothing between them, in the way they filled his questing hands. But he couldn't stop there! His hand strayed lower, lower, over her taut belly, and into the nest of curls between her legs, parting her legs, searching out the center of her femininity...

And then all of a sudden there was a pounding at the door. Brys felt Gisele stiffen beneath him, burying her face in the crook of his neck.

"Who is it? Go away—'tis the middle of the night!" Brys shouted in the direction of the door. Surely it was just some drunken courtier whose sense of direction had been drowned by wine....

"'Tis the Earl of Essex! Open up, de Balleroy! 'Tis vitally important."

Geoffrey de Mandeville, pounding on *his* door? It wasn't as if they were friends. *He* didn't trust the earl any farther than he could throw him, and he was certain de Mandeville had sensed that.

"My lord—" Then he remembered the threat of revolt by the Londoners, and thought better of telling the devious earl to go to blazes. "What is it? Is the palace under attack?" he called through the door.

"Nay! We are searching all the chambers on this floor," came the reply. "I have reason to believe a murderess is hiding in one of the rooms!"

Brys wrenched his head back to stare at Gisele, who was sitting up against the headboard, the sheet clutched over her breasts, her eyes wide and staring.

"A murderess?" he demanded, keeping his eyes upon Gisele. "What nonsense is this?"

"De Balleroy, open up, damn you, or I'll break it down!" the earl bellowed through the door, obviously angry now. "A man was murdered just minutes ago, right in the abbey! I saw it! And I believe 'twas Lady Gisele de l'Aigle who stabbed him in the heart, *and* slit the poor bastard's throat!"

Gisele was shaking her head violently, her lips forming the words *No, no, no! It wasn't me!*, her eyes glistening with unshed tears.

"My lord, 'tis I, Talford. Open, I pray you! The earl means what he says about breaking the door down!"

"There's no need to do that, my lord, I'm going to open the door," he said, in a voice that was calmer than he felt, snatching up the coverlet that had gotten pushed to the end of the bed and wrapping it around his waist. But he took a moment, before leaving the side of the bed, to look back at Gisele's imploring face.

Sudden understanding of her impulsive giving of herself flooded his brain, chilling the heat of his ardor, even as he slid back the bolt and pulled open the heavy oaken door.

De Mandeville, followed by the chamberlain, spilled inside, blinding both Brys and Gisele with the torch he snatched from Talford. But he stopped dead as he spied Gisele shrinking against the headboard, a terrified expression on her face, the linen sheet clutched to her neck. Brys saw his gaze drop to the chemise lying on the rushes beside the bed, and knew that de Mandeville knew she was naked beneath the linen.

"I believe you owe the lady an apology, my lord," Brys drawled, as his eyes accommodated to the bright light. "It must have been some other woman. As you see, Lady Gisele could not possibly have been murdering anyone. You said the fellow was killed just minutes ago? Lady Gisele was with me during that time…occupied in a much more *pleasant* way, I promise you.''

De Mandeville glared, first at Brys, then at Gisele, then back at Brys. His jaw clenched so tight that Brys fully expected to hear his teeth crack.

Talford, in contrast, was pink with embarrassment. ''I beg your pardon, my lord, my lady. Obviously my l—that is, *we* were mistaken. If you'll excuse us, we will trouble you no fur—''

''Now wait just a minute,'' de Mandeville growled. ''I'm not about to let these two get off so easily! I still think 'twas Lady Gisele who murdered that poor man, and when I leave this chamber it will only be to take her to the dungeon, where an evil woman such as she belongs!''

''She's *not going anywhere with you, my lord,*'' Brys growled, even as he reached for his sword, standing in its scabbard in the corner.

De Mandeville went very still. ''Have a care, de Balleroy. Perhaps I will have you arrested as an accomplice.'' His eyes locked with Brys's, and for a moment the only sound in the chamber was the harsh, ragged rasp of their breathing.

Then Talford broke the silence. ''Perhaps the empress should be summoned to decide the matter, my lord, as Lady Gisele is her attendant.''

''Very well. Go fetch her,'' de Mandeville growled without taking his eyes off Brys.

But Talford could be stubborn, despite his inferior status. ''Nay, my lord, I think 'tis best you summon her. I will remain here to assure that neither my lord de Balleroy nor Lady Gisele leave the chamber.''

The earl looked as if he'd like to argue, but finally nodded and turned on his heel, muttering, ''See that you guard them well. I shall hold you responsible.''

The presence of the chamberlain made speech impossible—which was deliberate, Brys realized. Talford might be thinking that as long as he was in the room, the lord and lady couldn't confer to make sure they were telling the same story. Or perhaps the anxious-looking chamberlain believed that the lady was innocent, and was wise enough to realize that by preventing them from speaking privily together, he was making their testimony that much more believable. But it made Brys feel helpless to do nothing but wait, wondering what had really happened while Gisele crouched, white-faced and frightened, in his bed.

''Might we step outside so that Lady Gisele could dress, Talford?'' he asked. Surely Gisele would feel more composed, facing her royal mistress wearing more than a sheet.

''*No!*'' Gisele exclaimed, just as Talford said, ''I do not believe she should do that, my lord.''

Brys was surprised—not at Talford, who might not have felt he should leave her alone, even long enough to put on her gown. Perhaps he thought this was one more act of preserving proof that Gisele's story was true. But why didn't *Gisele* want to don her clothing? Was she so demoralized by de Mandeville's accusation that she didn't feel able to move?

Brys didn't believe Gisele had actually murdered the man. Even if she had been violent and temperamental of nature—which she most certainly was not—murder was usually a man's crime, especially with a knife. It took strength and power to stab a man, then cut his throat. But what had Gisele been doing in the abbey, and who was the man she had supposedly murdered?

About half an hour later, the Earl of Essex returned with the empress in tow. Matilda had dressed hastily in a full-length fur-trimmed robe. Her raven-hued hair was loose down her back, making her look suddenly younger than she had when he had seen her earlier in the day, clad in queenly apparel.

Her eyes raked over Brys, standing there wrapped up in his coverlet, and then over Gisele, still huddled against the headboard, covered only by the bed linen.

"There she is, Your Highness," snarled de Mandeville, extending his arm to point at Gisele. "There's the woman I saw stab that poor man in the abbey."

"Oh, so now you are *certain,* my lord?" Brys said, taking a step toward him. "'Twas not so when you went to summon her highness—"

The empress put out a peremptory hand. "There are guards going to the abbey even now, to find this supposed corpse. Lady Gisele, what is your side of this tale?" Her face was unreadable as she waited for Gisele's answer.

"Domina, Lady Gisele was with me," Brys said. "She could not have killed the man in the abbey as Lord Geoffrey claims."

"I asked the question of *Lady Gisele,* my lord!" Matilda snapped.

All eyes were on Gisele. "Your highness, 'tis as Brys—my lord de Balleroy—says. I was here in bed with him," she said in a voice that trembled even as her body did, "during the time my lord de Mandeville claims to have seen me murder a man in the abbey."

"Yet when you left my chamber, you were under

orders to fetch my prayer book,'' Matilda said, surprising Brys with this new information. "If you obeyed me, you had cause to be in the abbey." Her tone became less accusatory. "What happened, Gisele? Did this man accost you? Perhaps offer you dishonor, so that you felt compelled to defend yourself?"

Gisele hung her head. "Nay, Your Highness. I never had contact with this man...for I did not—I'm sorry, Domina—I did not obey you. I came here, instead, to be with my lord de Balleroy. I intended to go get your prayer book before I attended you in the morning."

"You disobeyed me and came to lie with my lord de Balleroy?"

"Yes." She seemed about to leave her answer at that, then said, "Your prayer book should still be in the abbey. You will not find it in my chamber or my lord de Balleroy's."

"You never spoke with this man whom my lord de Mandeville says lies dead in the abbey?"

"No, Domina."

"I wonder who he is, and what he was doing there," the empress mused to no one in particular.

Was it Brys's imagination, or did de Mandeville suddenly look uneasy?

"Is Your Highness going to ignore my testimony that I saw this—this woman murder the fellow?" the earl sputtered, red-faced.

The empress drew herself up to her full statuesque height, and since Geoffrey de Mandeville was not over-tall for a man, she was able to look him in the eye.

"Take care, my lord. I am trying to get to the truth of the matter. A man has been murdered in the house of God! And what were *you* doing in the abbey at that hour, that you would see this horrible thing happen?"

The choler drained from de Mandeville's face. He hesitated. "I—I was praying, of course, Your Highness."

Matilda's eyebrow rose. "'Of course'? You never impressed me as being particularly devout, my lord de Mandeville."

He looked down, his jaw clenched, his forehead dotted with beads of sweat. "Piety is a private matter, is it not?"

Perhaps he could make him sweat some more, Brys thought. "Domina," he said, "I'm wondering how my lord of Essex's garment came to be spattered with blood, if he is as innocent as he claims."

De Mandeville's jaw dropped, and even in the dim light Brys could see him blanch as he gazed down at his chest, where the dark-red blood spatter made a wild pattern on the fabric of his robe. Clearly, he had not known it was there.

"I—I…" He swallowed as if he had no spittle left in his mouth, then seemed to regain strength. "But of course my gown is bloody! I cradled a dying man in my arms as his lifeblood poured out of him!"

Brys saw Gisele's eyes kindle and she opened her mouth as if to speak, then seemed to think better of it.

The fact that de Mandeville didn't demand that Gisele show what *she* had been wearing was almost tantamount to a confession, Brys thought. *He didn't ask because he knew Gisele's gown was free of bloodstains.* Had the empress realized that?

Matilda's gaze was darting back and forth, studying Brys, the earl and Gisele in turn, but when she spoke, she gave no indication of what she thought of the blood on de Mandeville's gown and his explanation for it.

"Indeed, my lord. Piety is a private matter, and so is

murder, but *murder* does not remain so. There will be a full investigation in the morning, after the captain of the guard has had a chance to investigate the matter. You are to be present.''

''I will be happy to do so, Your Highness,'' de Mandeville said stiffly. ''And Lady Gisele?''

''—Was apparently otherwise occupied,'' the empress said, nodding at her, still sitting on the rumpled bed. ''You may go, my lord, but I will expect to see you later this morning,'' she said, turning her back on de Mandeville, who stared at her for a moment, his face incredulous with frustrated rage. Then he stomped out of the chamber, slamming the door behind him. Talford remained.

''And now, as to you two...'' Matilda said, focusing on Brys and Gisele.

Brys stepped over to the bed, and placed a protective hand on Gisele's shoulder. He was hurt that she had come to him for sanctuary, not purely for love, but he knew she was no murderer.

''Lady Gisele, your father did not send you to me for your honor to be stolen.''

Gisele's eyes were downcast again. ''No, Domina.''

''And *you,* my lord. I'm surprised at you, seducing an innocent damsel such as Gisele.''

''I...I did not mean her any dishonor, empress. I...I care deeply for the lady.'' Before they had been interrupted, Brys thought, he might have said he loved her. Now he didn't know how he felt about her, wouldn't know until he had had a chance to talk privately with her and discover why she had used this ploy to protect herself from de Mandeville's accusation.

''It is well. You should have some regard for the lady you will wed.''

"Wed?" The word erupted from Brys's and Gisele's throats simultaneously.

The empress nodded. "But of course you will marry. Lady Gisele de L'Aigle, who came to my court an innocent maiden, has been found in your bed, my lord. You have compromised her honor. You will wed her this very night, as soon as the lady can be made ready for her wedding."

"But the abbey, Domina—" sputtered Talford, while Brys and Gisele were still staring at one another, thunderstruck.

"Naturally, the abbey is not usable at the present time, but my chapel will be perfectly adequate. Go and wake my chaplain, Talford, and tell him his services will be required within the hour."

The chamberlain bowed and left the chamber.

"But—" Gisele began, but Matilda cut her off.

"Neither of you are precontracted, are you?"

Brys and Gisele shook their heads.

"You will marry my lord de Balleroy, Lady Gisele. You obviously have some affection for him, or you would not be in his bed, eh? Many wives begin with much less acquaintance or regard for their lords. And I will not have it said that virgins are seduced at my court without remedy."

Mutely, Gisele nodded. "As Your Highness wishes."

"My lord, you are to step outside while your future wife clothes herself again. Then she will go to her chamber, where some of my other ladies will prepare her for her nuptials. See that you are in the chapel when she comes down. Both of you will need to go to confession with the priest before he marries you, of course. You cannot be wed with the sin of lust on your souls."

Brys nodded his acquiescence, his brain reeling. In

an hour, more or less, he would become the husband of Lady Gisele de L'Aigle. He was not going to be given any opportunity for private speech with her beforehand, so they would marry without him knowing how she truly felt about becoming his wife or why she had sought refuge in his bed.

Chapter Thirteen

One hour later, Gisele found herself standing at the altar of the empress's chapel, shivering in her wedding finery in the chilly predawn air.

"Normally, this wedding would not be taking place until the crying of the banns for three consecutive weeks," the priest announced. "But Her Highness," he added, nodding toward the empress, who stood to the right of the couple, "has convinced me that it is—ahem!—*advisable* to go ahead and unite these two in the Sacrament of Matrimony without delay, so we shall proceed...."

Beside Gisele, Brys de Balleroy seemed like a stranger, his face unreadable in the flickering candlelight. Did he think she had deliberately entrapped him in marriage when all he'd planned on was enjoying a passionate tumble with her? Was he filled with resentment, even hatred, for her now, so that this wedding ceremony would shackle them together in a lifetime of misery? He would never believe now that she had been falling in love with him, despite her desire not to be belong to any man!

Lord, how much simpler it would be if she only dared

accuse de Mandeville of the murder! If she was a man, she could have challenged him to trial by combat, and let God decide who was right. But since she was but a woman, it would be her word against his—and who would listen to a damsel against the word of a powerful nobleman?

If Brys was a stranger, he was a strikingly handsome one, dressed in a tunic of deep forest-green that complimented his auburn hair and brown eyes. The tunic had gold banding around the neck, sleeves and hem, and he wore a longer undergown of a lighter green. The candlelight seemed to confer a halo of gold in the dark-red hair that brushed his collar in the back.

As the priest droned the words of the marriage ceremony, Gisele's mind drifted back to the scene in Brys's chamber. Thank God, the earl had not thought to demand to see the gown she had been wearing! If he'd seen the gown and told the empress this was the color of the gown he'd seen on the woman fleeing the murder scene, Matilda might have paid more attention to the earl's claims. Instead, she had sent Geoffrey de Mandeville away before she ordered Gisele to redress.

'Twas fortunate also that I dropped the prayer book in the abbey, Gisele thought. If she had brought it with her to Brys's chamber, her possession of it might have convinced the empress that Gisele *had* been in the abbey and committed the murder, even though it really proved she could have witnessed her favorite earl doing so!

She imagined her father's reaction when he heard of her marriage. Oh, he'd be pleased that his daughter's husband was a baron with lands in both Normandy and England, and that his allegiance was to the empress. But he wouldn't spare a moment to wonder whether his daughter was happy in her marriage, or whether her new lord loved her.

Fleurette would have cared. Her old nurse was the only one, since Gisele's mother died, who had ever cared about Gisele's happiness. Her old nurse would have liked Brys de Balleroy, Gisele suddenly knew. She'd have told Gisele she was a lucky damsel to have such a brave, steadfast lord.

Ah, Fleurette, I wish you could be here beside me now. Yet if the attack that killed the old nurse had not taken place, would Gisele even have met Brys de Balleroy?

Lady Cosette and Lady Aubine, who now stood just to the left of Gisele and Brys, had totally taken over preparing Gisele for the wedding. They'd pronounced the mulberry gown unsuitable for Gisele to be wed in, of course.

"'Tis a pity the green cloth my lord de Balleroy purchased for you has not been made up into a gown already," Cosette had remarked. "What a lovely bride you'd have been wearing that gown, to be sure! But we must make do with what we have, must we not? You and I are of a size, Gisele dear. I believe I have just the gown in my chamber—just wait—I shall be back in a trice!" she had said, dashing out the door in uncharacteristic haste.

"I don't know why this can't be delayed until the morrow," Aubine muttered while the other lady was gone. "Who ever heard of a bride going to her wedding without so much as a bridal bath? Still, I suppose you're clean enough," she said, squinting and sniffing at Gisele like an alewife checking her brew.

Cosette had been back in a few moments, as promised, bearing a gown of a green so light that it put Gisele in mind of willow leaves in spring. It had silver embroidery at the neck and just above the elbows and a matching silver girdle. She brought with it a veil of gauzy white with a stiffened, silver headband.

"Ah, it suits you better than it ever did me, my dear!" Cosette sighed, clasping her hands together as she gazed at Gisele in misty-eyed admiration. "Let us hurry and arrange your hair. Your bridegroom is doubtless already in the chapel, impatient to make you his wife!"

"From what the empress told me, it seems my lord de Balleroy has already made her his wife in fact, if not in the eyes of God," Aubine commented in her tart fashion.

"Hush, Aubine, none of that." Cosette reproved the other woman. "Whether or not my lord de Balleroy and Gisele anticipated the ceremony, they will still be united and blessed by God in holy matrimony! I'd guess their love was so strong they could not wait!"

Gisele had blushed, thinking miserably how untrue it all was, at least from Brys's standpoint. Brys did not love her—if he'd truly "cared" about her as he'd told the empress, she'd doomed his affection for her by her impulsive act.

The priest's voice crashed into her thoughts. "Lady Gisele, you must make a response here, yea or nay. *Will* you have Brys de Balleroy to be your wedded lord, to love, honor, and obey him, as long as you both shall live?"

"I…I will," she said, feeling the heat rise up her neck as she stammered the words, wondering how many other times he had asked her the question before she had finally heard him. She dared a glance at Brys, and found him staring down at her, his lip curved slightly in amusement. She could see no disdain in his eyes, but he had to think her a witless simpleton for allowing her mind to wander now! She had not even heard Brys say his vows. But he must have done so, for now he was slipping a heavy ring of gold upon her finger, a ring whose emblem she could not even discern through the tears that stung her eyes.

Just as dawn was piercing the eastern sky, the impromptu wedding breakfast ended in the empress's apartments and Brys was brought back to his chamber by Matilda and her chamberlain. Gisele had already been taken there by Cosette and Aubine.

Normally, a drunken, bawdy throng of male wedding guests accompanied the groom going to bed his bride, but Gisele was grateful for the lack of such an escort. Exhausted by the night's events, her nerves were strung thin and taut as lute strings, and she did not feel she could have borne the lewd jests and leering eyes.

"My naughty Brys, this time you'll not be interrupted, that I promise!" she heard Matilda proclaim at the door. "Naturally, we shall not expect to see you until much later, if at all, today!" she added gaily, pushing Brys inside. "Now go in and bed your *wife*, my lord!"

Aubine and Cosette had drawn themselves up in front of his bed, as if shielding Gisele from him.

"Gisele?"

Instantly the older ladies sprang apart, almost guiltily, revealing Gisele sitting up against the pillow-strewn headboard. With the morning sunlight beginning to stream through the narrow window slit, she felt horribly exposed in the night rail of sheer, gauzy linen that had been loaned to her by Cosette. The ladies had insisted she leave her hair loose over her shoulders.

He was staring at her and swallowing as if he had an apple stuck in his throat. She followed his gaze and saw that one of her nipples showed quite plainly through the thin fabric.

Blushing, she hastily pulled her hair forward, covering her breast, knowing that it was ridiculous to do so. He had already seen—and touched—much more than just one nipple. And as her husband, he now had the right to see every inch of her. He owned her, just as he owned his horse.

A few hours ago, you did not mind his seeing, and his touching, her traitorous heart reminded her. *You reveled in it, just as you did in the garden just yesterday afternoon.*

"'Tis time we were going, Cosette," Lady Aubine whispered, pulling at the other lady's skirts. Lady Cosette had been smiling raptly, first at Brys, then at Gisele—almost as if she were the proud mother of the bride.

"Yes, I'm sure we should leave the bridal couple alone together," Cosette trilled, still beaming. "Much love and happiness, dear Gisele," she said, kissing her on the forehead and giving her a swift hug that touched Gisele's heart.

And then they were gone, and Gisele was left alone with Brys.

For a moment, they just stared at one another.

"My lord..." Gisele began, hesitating as he crossed the room in a few swift strides. But he did not stop at the bed; instead, he drew the shutters against the burgeoning sunlight and turned to face her in the sudden gloom.

"My lady wife, I believe you have some explaining to do."

She took a deep breath. "I…I'm so sorry about what happened, my lord." It sounded so pitifully inadequate. "I never meant to embroil you in my troubles."

"Is that what you call it, 'embroiling' me, *wife?* Fool that I am, when I awoke to find you standing there, I thought you *wanted* me—wanted me to make love to you. Instead, I find that you sought my bed only to give yourself a defense against an accusation of murder!" Anger blazed in his eyes.

"I—I didn't kill the burgher—the man in the abbey—"

"I rejoice to hear it," he retorted, his voice an icy lash.

She flinched at the naked fury in his tone, and dropped her eyes, not wanting him to see the tears that stung them.

"I deserve your ire, I know, my lord. I accept it. But I want you to know why I did what—why I took refuge in your bed." She took a deep breath, and raised her eyes to him again. "I didn't kill the man, but I saw him killed. Geoffrey de Mandeville killed him, my lord."

He closed his eyes for a moment, as if she but confirmed his suspicion. "But why?"

Gisele could only shrug. "I can only guess, from the words I overheard. I had gone into the abbey to fetch the empress's prayer book—we had been in there earlier—and saw the earl and the other man coming out of a side chapel. They did not see me. They were quarreling—the burgher threatened to expose him. 'If you think you can sell London to the highest bidder,' he said. And then the earl stabbed him."

Gisele saw Brys stiffen as she repeated the burgher's

words. "'If you think you can sell London to the highest bidder?'" he echoed. "That is what he said to de Mandeville, right before the earl killed him?" There was an edge to his voice, a dangerous gleam in his eye.

She nodded, feeling some of his anger slip away from her.

"Then what happened?"

"I...I was behind a pillar—'tis why he didn't see me—and I was just going to remain there until the earl left the abbey. But I dropped the prayer book, my lord, and de Mandeville heard the sound, and knew that someone had seen the horrible thing he did. I...I ran, Brys," she said, unable to hold back her tears now as she relived that terrifying pursuit through the darkness, into the hall, and up the stairs, remembering how she had expected every breath to be her last. Her ankle still throbbed from the punishment she had given the tender joint.

"He didn't want to leave any witnesses to what he had done. I knew he would kill me...if...if he could catch me." She buried her tear-drenched face in her hands.

The rushes beneath his feet rustled as Brys walked over them. Gisele felt the rope mattress sag as he sat down on it. Then she felt the miracle of him putting his strong arms around her, and it made her weep that much harder.

"You must have been terrified, my poor Gisele...."

She nodded against his chest, unable to say more for a moment. Then she raised her head. "I...I thought if I went to my chamber, he would either break down the door and slay me there, or have me taken by the guard and accuse me of the murder. Either way, I was certain I wouldn't live to clear my name. I couldn't be sure if he had seen my face clearly, or just knew what color gown I was wearing. And so I—''

''Came to me and shed your clothing,'' he finished for her, nodding, a light of bitter understanding in his eyes, ''Making sure that it appeared you could not possibly have been the one in the abbey, for you lay naked in Brys de Balleroy's arms.'' He cleared his throat. ''I applaud your quick cleverness, my lady. Not many women would have had your...presence of mind.''

It did not feel like a compliment. Stung in spite of her sense of guilt, she retorted, ''I wish now I had let him cut my throat along with the burgher's. You would not now be saddled with a wife you did not want.''

She saw him flinch.

He stood up, raking a hand through his hair and pacing back and forth in front of her. He seemed to be struggling for words. Then all at once he was back, kneeling in front of her, taking her hands in his to force her to look into his eyes. ''Gisele, don't you know I would have defended you to the death? Fought as your champion against any charge of murder?''

She saw anguish there, and regret, but there was something else there, something she hoped was at least a faint trace of love for her. The realization made her want to weep anew.

''I didn't know for sure that you were there,'' she told him. ''For all I knew, you had gone back into London after we parted this afternoon, going about your...business about which I know so little. If you had not been there he would have found me there, eventually.''

Understanding lit his deep-brown eyes, and he nodded. ''I'm glad I was there, then. I just wish you had told me....''

His voice trailed off, but she knew he meant *why you were really there.*

"I should have, my lord." Then, as he dropped her hands, and arose, she felt a flicker of unease. "Where are you going, Brys?"

"To inform the empress that de Mandeville is a murderer, and then to have him arrested. I'll be your champion, Gisele, if he demands trial by combat."

She was suddenly afraid for him, and leaped up to take hold of his wrist. "Oh, Brys—be careful..." She had no fear that the earl could not best Brys de Balleroy in a fair battle, but the earl was a treacherous man, not one governed by honor. She had a vision of Geoffrey de Mandeville fighting like a cornered boar when they tried to take him, caring nothing if he had to kill again to escape.

Gently but firmly, he disengaged her grasp. "I must hasten—it may already be too late. Now shoot the bolt behind me," he told her.

"You'll come back? You'll let me know...you're all right?"

He nodded, but it was clear he was impatient to go. She shot the bolt behind him as he had directed her, then unshuttered the window to banish the fearful shadows from the room. Finally, she lay down upon the bed, curled up like a terrified child, thinking she would pray until he returned.

The pounding roused her from a sleep so deep it took her several moments to remember where she was, and what had happened. The room was flooded with midday light.

"It's me, Gisele. Open the door," Brys's voice called.

She stumbled to the door and pulled back the bolt, letting him in.

"Is he—did you—" she began, her eyes scanning Brys for any hurt, and seeing none.

He shook his head, his face a study in frustration. "We've searched the palace and grounds, every nook and cranny. He's fled, the craven weasel. The hue and cry is out. Matilda has sent men-at-arms into the city and in all directions, seeking him."

The news both relieved her and frightened her all over again. Brys was safe; he had not been injured helping to arrest de Mandeville, and would not have to risk trial by combat if the earl had maintained his claim of innocence. But de Mandeville was out there somewhere, a vindictive, unprincipled man.

"I...I'll go now," he said, his hand already on the door, "and leave you to sleep. I just wanted you to know what had happened."

She saw the total exhaustion beneath his veneer of strength. "No. Stay with me, my lord," she said, going back to the bed and sinking down upon it.

He blinked. "Nay, Gisele, I... This is not the time—not after all—"

Would there ever be a time, she wondered? She shook her head. "No, I meant only that you need to rest, too. Lie down here, my lord."

Eyeing her warily, he came to the bed, and without taking off anything but his cuffed leather boots, he lay down next to her, on his back, but not touching her.

She willed him to open up his arms, to ask her to lay with her head upon his chest. It would have felt so good to have him holding her. But minutes later, when his regular breathing told her he slept, she was just glad he was there beside her.

Chapter Fourteen

When she awoke, he was gone, which didn't really surprise her. Once he had awakened, Brys would not play the adoring bridegroom, watching her while she slept.

Judging by the light she could see coming in the window, it was late afternoon. Soon it would be time for supper. Were they expected to appear in the hall, or would Brys arrange for supper to be brought to the room? Of the two choices, she definitely preferred the latter, for if they went to the hall, everyone would be staring. They would expect them to bill and coo like the lovers they were not. 'Twould be better if they dined in Brys's chamber, preserving the illusion that they could not bear to leave their private lovers' haven.

In any case, Brys would eventually return to his chamber, and Gisele did not want to greet him with bed-mussed hair and sleepy eyes. Rising, she went to the ewer and splashed water on a cloth and washed her face, then began to comb out the tangles in her hair.

Suddenly there was a knock at the door.

''Who is it?'' she said, trying not to sound as startled as she felt.

"De Balleroy."

Her heart pounding, she bid him come in, wondering what his mood would be.

"Ah, 'tis well you are up," he said, eyeing her as he strode into the room, looking as if he had not slept at all. He rubbed a beard-shadowed cheek. "There is just time for me to shave before the supper horn."

"But I thought…that is, the empress said she would not expect to see us today," Gisele faltered.

"There is a banquet for Saint John's Day this even, and I think we should attend," he said, his voice even. "There will be holes enough at the tables with the bishop and de Mandeville gone, and half a dozen other nobles as well. God knows where those others have gone, or why."

She nodded in acquiescence, her heart sinking, and began to rebraid her hair. She was his wife. His will must be hers.

The empress was in an expansive mood as she bid her court welcome to the banquet. "'Twill be a foretaste of our coronation banquet two days hence," she said with a grand gesture, her hand sweeping over the bounty on the groaning trestle tables. "Enjoy your food and the festivities that follow—and be sure to congratulate my lord de Balleroy and his lovely bride, the Lady Gisele, who are still enjoying their first full day of wedded bliss!"

Brys's smile was strained, but Gisele was warmed by the way he put his arm about her waist and waved to those applauding and cheering at them, for all the world the picture of the proud bridegroom. Thank God, he was not the sort to shame her in public, despite his resentment. Perhaps they would manage to maintain this facade of wedded bliss at court for a time, each of them serving the empress but sharing nothing but a cold bed, as they had this morning. Then, after some time had passed, perhaps he would beg leave to take her to one of his castles, either in England or in Normandy. There she would remain, alone except when he deemed it necessary to get an heir upon her. And once she had done her duty, he might never be with her again.

"Let us pray," intoned the chaplain, and proceeded to say the grace.

The diners had just sat down at the table when the open windows brought the sound of distantly chiming church bells to their ears. The tolling went on and on, until all realized they were not just calling the faithful to vespers.

"What can be happening?" Matilda asked, her eyes wide. "It must be an alarm of some sort! Has Stephen's wife and her accursed Flemings attacked from across the river again? Talford, send a messenger to find out, that we may come to their aid!"

But before the chamberlain could carry out her bidding, the steward ran into the hall.

"Domina! I've just had word from the soldiers you sent into the city to find the earl! All London is marching on the palace, armed with whatever they could find! They mean to tear apart the palace, Your Highness, and you with it! You must flee!"

As Gisele watched in horror, Matilda's face paled, but then she jumped to her feet. "Nay, we shall not run like rabbits! How dare they turn on me, their rightful queen, so soon before the coronation? Robert," she said, turning to her bastard half brother, the Earl of Gloucester, "organize the soldiers to march upon them, and turn them back! Talford, have all the entrances locked. De Balleroy—''

But Matilda's half brother put a restraining hand on her shoulder. ''Sister, we have not men enough to repulse a horde of commoners! The men-at-arms you sent beyond London in search of de Mandeville have not yet returned, and even if they were here, 'twould not be enough to resist such a determined force! Nay, we have time to get Your Highness safely away, and that we must do!''

Every nobleman in the room, including a grim-faced Brys, agreed with him.

Matilda argued, protesting that once she allowed the rabble to drive her out, she would have set a dangerous precedent and would never be able to return. She stamped her foot and refused to go, but when none would agree to stay and fight alongside her, she wept and fisted her hands.

''All right!'' she snapped. ''We shall make a run for it, then, to Oxford. *'Tis only temporary, do you all understand?* Talford, order the horses saddled! Those who are coming with me, you have but a few moments to go get what you must take with you—hurry!''

Brys had already yanked Gisele to her feet and was pulling her into a run. Pandemonium reigned as the hall emptied, the banquet forgotten.

Together, they dashed up the stairs. Gisele ran down to her old chamber to grab the things out of her chest there, then back to Brys's chamber, where he was throwing belongings onto his spread-out cloak on the bed.

She folded the mulberry gown and laid it in the pile, then asked, ''Is there room for this?'' Gisele showed him the folded bolt of silver-shot green cloth he had bought for her.

He nodded, his gaze softening. "We'll make room," he said. "Gisele, I'll keep you safe, I swear. I'll die before I'll let any harm come to you."

She felt tears sting her eyes as she gazed into his solemn face. He had been forced to marry her, but now he was pledging his life to protect her? Holy Virgin, what sort of a man had she wed?

"It's the devil's own luck my squire is on the road to Bristol now," Brys remarked. "I'd give much to be able to have him take you on to Tichenden."

"But how will your squire know where to find you?"

Brys smiled grimly. "It depends how close to London he is when he hears that the empress has retreated to Oxford. If he's closer to London, he'll check at my house in West Chepe first. Don't worry about Maislin—he can take care of himself."

She hadn't known he had a house in the city. What else didn't she know about her new husband? Nor had she been worrying about Maislin, but she just smiled and said, "Yes, one would have to be more than fool-hardy to quarrel with such a giant."

Within the hour, the empress's household was on horseback, heading northwest toward Matilda's head-quarters at Oxford. They'd regroup there, the empress promised, and plan how they would retake London.

But at the first crossroads, Matilda summoned Brys and Gisele forward and said, "My lord, do you think you would still be accepted in Stephen's wife's camp?"

Gisele blinked and patted her palfrey's sweaty neck to hide her confusion. Brys had been accepted among the enemy?

Brys glanced at her, then back at the empress. "Domina, it depends on whether Geoffrey de Mandeville ran straight to Matilda of Boulogne when he fled the palace. If so, he doubtless told her I had been at your court, and they'll have figured out where my allegiance truly lies," he said. "But he may not have joined her. He may have preferred to go his own way."

So Brys had been spying among Stephen's camp! It explained much of his secretiveness, Gisele thought. But she would not rest until she knew all.

Matilda considered what Brys had said, while her palfrey stamped restively. "De Mandeville is a lawless rebel. He won't likely want to trouble himself to help Stephen. I'll wager he's gone off to the fens, hoping to hide out until Stephen emerges the victor. He knows I won't take him back, now that he's been accused of murder," she said, with an acknowledging nod in Gisele's direction. "Brys, I want you to circle back into the city and see what's going on there. Infiltrate the Countess of Boulogne's party again. Learn their plans, then get word to me at Oxford. I need to have someone among them that they trust."

Gisele nearly dropped her reins in alarm. Matilda was willing to wager Brys's *life* on her guess that de Mandeville hadn't gone back to the other side?

"But Your Highness," she began, edging her palfrey forward, "surely you can't mean for my lord to take such a risk—"

Brys laid a restraining hand on her palfrey's reins and gave her a warning look. "I will do as you ask, Domina," he said. "If de Mandeville hasn't poisoned my name among Stephen's adherents—"

"But what if he *has?*" Gisele demanded.

"—I can remain among them and keep you informed,'' Brys continued, as if Gisele hadn't spoken. ''But I would ask that you keep my wife safe with you at Oxford.''

''Certainly, my lord,'' Matilda said. ''You know you may trust in us—''

''*No!*'' Gisele cried, surprising herself as much as anyone else. ''That is…Domina, you cannot mean to separate my lord and me so soon after we have wed? I—I want to stay with him! That is, with your permission, of course!'' she added hastily, seeing Matilda raising a brow at her temerity. '''Tis not that I do not wish to serve you any longer, but—''

''Nay, my lady, I absolutely forbid it—'' Brys began, his face darkening.

But the empress had held up a peremptory hand. ''Hush, Brys! Such devotion in a spouse—even if 'tis but the fervor of a wife still enjoying her honey moon,'' she added, with a chuckle, ''is all too rare! Far be it from me to part a devoted lady from her lord! You may remain with Lord de Balleroy, Lady Gisele, until such time as you are ready to resume serving me!''

She watched as the rest of the empress's ladies, including a sulky Manette de Mandeville, galloped off in the empress's wake, wondering if she would ever see them again. The way to Oxford might be fraught with peril, too, just as much as the path she had chosen to follow with Brys.

When she looked back at Brys, she found his eyes upon her. He waited until Matilda's party was out of sight around a bend in the road, then demanded between clenched teeth, ''What did you think you were doing, countermanding my wishes, wife?''

The sharp rancor in his voice sparked her own temper. ''I *won't* be shunted aside like an unneeded chest of clothing, my lord!'' she retorted. ''I'm your wife! And if you insist on putting your head in the lion's mouth out of some misguided sense of chivalry—''

''You're determined to put yours right along with it,'' he finished for her, his brown eyes taking fire from the setting sun. ''The more fool you, when you could be relatively safe with Matilda at Oxford.''

His scathing tone stung. ''My lord, you may hate me for what I caused to happen to you last night, but—''

He interrupted her, seeming genuinely surprised. ''I don't hate you, Gisele. But there *is* the possibility of real danger in this game of intrigue. I'm well able to take care of myself, but now, with you to look out for—''

''My lord, believe me, if I could transform myself into a man this instant, I would do so,'' she snapped. ''All my life I have been made to feel I had no value because I was a female, that I was nothing but an encumbrance. But worthless as I am, Brys, I care about you....'' Her voice trailed off as she closed her eyes tightly against the tears that threatened to spill.

Gisele almost jumped when she felt his hand touching her shoulder.

''And I, for you, though I know you will not believe it, Gisele,'' he said, his voice husky. ''I have been fighting my desire for you ever since I found you in the Weald, didn't you realize that? But you didn't want to become a wife, and I... Well, let us just say that even if you had changed your mind, I thought you deserved better than me.'' He lowered his voice and looked away, adding, ''Yet I could not resist buying you those presents in London, nor trying to seduce you in the garden. Damn me for a double-minded rogue.''

''Deserved better than you, my lord?'' she asked,

honestly puzzled. "Why on earth would you say that?" He was handsome, strong, a baron with lands in Normandy as well as England....

She could see by his suddenly shuttered face that Brys wasn't about to answer that question, and added, "Is it because you have been spying on the king's camp? Did you think I would see that as treacherous or dishonorable? Actually, I think it very brave and daring of you."

He shook his head and said, "I wish it were only that, my lady. But 'twill soon be dark. Let us go."

Chapter Fifteen

It was fully dark by the time they pulled up at the narrow-fronted house in West Chepe that stood between the goldsmiths' shops and the food shops.

"Go on inside, while I put your horse away in the stable around back," he told her as he helped her down from her palfrey. Weariness was writ all over her face, twisting his heart with a tenderness he could not afford to feel—not if he was going to keep his hands off her.

"Put *my* mare away? What of your mount, Brys? You are not staying?" she asked, a sudden flash of anxiety lighting her shadowed face.

My prideful little bride, he thought, gazing at her stiffly held features, lit only by a faint moonlight. I'd like nothing better than to stay and show you through my house—the bedchamber last, he thought. But if he remained, he would take her to bed, he knew—and this time they would not sleep so chastely together. And he did not want that to happen until it was what they both wanted more than their next breath.

"Nay—I need to go and discover what I may about the fate of the palace," he told her, "and why the Londoners turned on the empress when it was Stephen's queen who was burning Southwark, with the aid of her Flemish mercenaries. And whether de Mandeville has turned his coat yet again or not.''

Mention of the earl caused alarm to flash over Gisele's exhausted features, an alarm she didn't even try to conceal. ''Oh, Brys—''

''Do not fear on that score, Gisele,'' he reassured her. ''I'm sorry I even mentioned the possibility in front of you. He won't have gone to the enemy. As the empress said, he's a lawless rebel who won't commit himself again until there's a clear victor in this contest.'' In truth, he was far from convinced of that fact, but he didn't want Gisele to worry about something she could do nothing about.

''But—'' She eyed the dark, half-timbered dwelling, then looked back at him. ''Have you no servants? Is there no one within?''

''No, there's no one else who lives there. An old woman named Gytha comes in and cleans the worst of our excesses every fortnight or so. Her spouse mucks out the stables between visits, too.'' Suddenly he saw the place as a woman would see it—unfriendly and frightening in its strangeness. ''On second thought, come back with me while I stable your palfrey and tie up Jerusalem, then I'll come in at least long enough to light some candles for you and show you about before I go on.'' *And God help me, somehow I'll manage to keep my hands off you,* he vowed to himself.

Gisele awoke the next morning to the cries of ''fresh peaches from Normandy!'' and ''Spanish oranges and lemons!'' mingling with the rattle of iron-rimmed wheels over the cobbles. The light coming beneath the wooden shutters was muted; when she left the comfortable bed with its straw-stuffed mattress and threw them open, she saw that the sky threatened rain.

"Brys?" she called, wondering if he had returned while she was sleeping and had gone to bed in the adjoining chamber so as not to awaken her. No answer—and when she peeked inside the other room, she saw that its bed was untouched.

Wondering what she would break her fast with, she donned her chemise and found an old bed robe of Brys's in the chest at the foot of the bed to put over it. It would do until she had availed herself of the wash water Brys had left for her last night before riding off into the darkness.

She went down the steep steps and had just determined there was not a morsel of food in the house, only a jar of watered wine on the table in the main room, when a knock sounded at the back door.

Padding over the cool stone floor in her bare feet, Gisele peered through the narrow peephole and saw an elderly woman standing there clutching a cloth-wrapped bundle. Even through the narrow aperture, she could smell fresh-baked bread.

Gisele pulled back the bolt and opened the door. This must be Gytha, who took care of the house for Brys.

The old woman said something in English, which of course Gisele could not understand; then, at Gisele's blank look, unwrapped the bread and a wheel of fresh butter and made motions to indicate that they were for her breakfast.

"Thank you," Gisele said, hoping that the woman understood that much French, at least, or that her smile would convey her meaning.

"I bring soup...at noon," Gytha said then, in halting,

broken French. "Alf brings hot water, soon." She pantomimed bathing.

Gisele thanked the old woman again. So Brys had been thinking of her needs after all, Gisele thought, touched. *God keep him safe.*

Once the old woman had gone, Gisele munched on the still-warm bread, spread with the fresh butter Gytha had brought, and watched as Gytha's spouse, a taciturn, monkey-faced old man, brought in buckets of steaming water, two at a time, with the aid of a yoke across his back.

An hour later, Gisele had just finished her bath and was sitting in front of the fire, clad in her spare gown, drying her long chestnut hair, when she heard another knock at the back door.

It was still a long time until noon, Gisele thought, but probably Gytha had decided to go ahead and bring the soup now.

Remembering Brys's concern about the Londoners' tempers, Gisele cautiously peered out the peephole before drawing back the bolt. She could see no one standing there, even when she peered to each side.

Curious, she thought. Mayhap she was so eager for Brys's return she was hearing things. She went back to the hearth to finish drying her hair.

Five minutes later, the knock came again. Yet when she went back to the door and peered out through the peephole, once again, there was no one there. This time, however, she had been quick enough that she heard the sound of running feet and laughter. Pushing the bolt back, she went outside, but she could see no one.

Children of the streets, playing a jest. She remembered pulling just such a trick on her old nurse one time when Fleurette was napping.

Next time she would be ready for them, she thought, smiling wryly to herself as she shut the door, but did not slide the bolt home, so that she could open the door quickly and surprise them at their mischief. She waited by the door.

The next knock came some five minutes later, but she had a moment's forewarning, for the children were giggling as they crept up to the door.

Grinning at the innocent fun, she opened the door, and heard shrieks of alarm as a trio of imps, a girl and two boys, went streaking around the corner of the house toward the stable.

Roaring in mock rage even as she wished she had some sweets to give them, Gisele dashed out the front door in pursuit. Maybe she could make friends with them and amuse herself with them until Brys came back—though it wasn't likely they spoke even as much French as Gytha had.

Gisele rounded the corner in time to see them run past the stable, giggling. Then she saw a flash of movement to her left, between the house and herself. Before Gisele could dodge, she was grabbed by a strong hand that yanked her back against a man's hard chest even as his other hand was clapped over her mouth. She felt the cold, sharp edge of a dagger blade.

"Peasant whelps are ridiculously easy to bribe," Geoffrey de Mandeville hissed in her ear.

Her blood froze in her veins and she went still—all but her eyes, which darted from side to side as she prayed that someone—anyone—would wander into the stable yard and come to her aid. Even the children who had been paid to lure her outside might realize the richly dressed man was up to no good and summon help.

As if reading her mind, de Mandeville snarled into

her ear: "They won't be back. I told them once you came out, they were to run and keep running, or I'd take the farthing back. And now," he added, his breath hot on the back of her neck, "why don't we go inside and discuss the purpose of my visit?"

Gisele allowed him to push her back toward the door, horribly sure that she knew why de Mandeville had come.

"How...how did you find this place?" she asked, once de Mandeville shut the door behind him. As long as he was talking, he wasn't doing anything worse, and maybe she could find a way to save herself.

The earl sniggered. "Oh, it wasn't hard to find out that de Balleroy has this little hideaway where he can go to earth whenever need be. And when he disappeared from the palace along with the rest of the cowards, it wasn't difficult to guess that Matilda would send him back to keep an eye on things—or that you two would stay together."

Fear for Brys blossomed anew within her, like a deadly black flower. "But my lord is not coming back for me," she lied. "He didn't want to wed me, and he's left me here to fend for myself." She *had* to convince de Mandeville of Brys's disinterest in her, so he would leave whenever he was done destroying her, and Brys would be safe.

"So your little ruse to escape me cost de Balleroy his freedom, eh?" De Mandeville's chuckle had an ugly quality to it. "Well, well! But you're lying, *Lady de Balleroy.* The man is chivalrous to a fault, nor is he stupid enough to abandon such a toothsome wench as you," he added, running the flat of the dagger blade caressingly down her cheek while she struggled to suppress her shiver of disgust. She didn't want to give him the satisfaction of seeing her fear.

"Yes, he'll be back," the earl repeated. "But I could be persuaded to leave him safe—for a price."

Gisele blinked in confusion. "What...what do you mean?"

De Mandeville's lips curved upward in a smile that chilled her soul. "He's being rather duplicitous, isn't he? He *appears* to be the ally of Stephen and his queen while really being the loyal vassal of the empress—"

"*You* have no right to criticize anyone for duplicity," Gisele hissed at him. "Murderer!"

De Mandeville narrowed his eyes. "Now, now, little kitten, I'd sheathe your claws if I were you, since I'm about to offer you a compromise. A compromise that will give each of us something we want."

"What compromise?" she demanded, sickeningly aware of his greedy eyes roaming over her body with hot intent.

"Since I had to flee Westminster to avoid being charged with murder, I've been pondering whether to throw in my lot with Stephen's party again, or go off on my own. Naturally, if I offer my support again to the anointed and crowned king and his queen, I will have to reveal that de Balleroy is a traitor. If I don't..." His shrug was eloquent.

"Why wouldn't you reveal it, if you *believe* in Stephen's cause?" she asked, her tone scornful.

"Lady de Balleroy, the only cause I truly believe in is my own," he admitted with a cynical grin. "But if you'll go upstairs and give me what I've made it clear to you that I've wanted ever since we met, I will pledge you my silence, charming lady. I'll go off to the fens and never reveal your lord's true loyalty! What do you say, sweetheart?'' he asked, allowing the knife blade to drift as if by accident past her trembling breast.

Gisele could only stare at him in horror. *''You want me to lie with you to buy your silence?''*

''You have the power to save his life,'' de Mandeville purred. ''Without your…ah, cooperation, I will hie myself to Stephen's queen's camp, and tell her just what her 'friend' de Balleroy is up to. They'll execute him for his treachery. *With* your cooperation, I'll say nothing about him and disappear—knowing that *you* won't say anything more about the unfortunate necessity of my killing that greedy burgher in the abbey, either. I had to silence him, you know,'' he added conversationally, as if he was sure that Gisele would understand. ''He was going to expose me for the scoundrel I am!''

''You're a devil,'' Gisele breathed, as he slowly, steadily backed her toward the stairs with the dagger. ''And I'd rather die than allow you to touch me!'' Quickly, she spat in his face, and was pleased to see the spittle land directly in one of his eyes.

''Damn you, wench!'' He brought up his free hand to wipe his eye, and for that moment the hand holding the dagger against her wavered.

Gisele dashed to the side, running for the front door, praying she could slide back the bolt and wrench open the door before he could recover and catch her. Surely someone in the busy street would help her!

She had just succeeded in pushing back the bolt when he caught her in a flying tackle, sending her sprawling, screaming, amid the rushes. Geoffrey de Mandeville fell on her like a ravening beast, dropping the dagger amidst the rushes and clawing at her clothing with one hand while the other attempted to stifle her cries.

Gisele was determined not to tamely submit to rape,

however, and she bit the hand that was pressed into her mouth. De Mandeville recoiled with a shouted curse. She rolled away from him, desperately pawing through the rushes for the dagger he had dropped.

Her hand had just closed over its hilt when his clenched fist caught her under the chin, sending her reeling backward. Her head struck the edge of the wooden tub, stunning her as now-cold and soapy bathwater sloshed over the top.

Momentarily unable to struggle, she could only lie on damp rushes as flashing pinwheels of red and black capered across her vision, partially blotting out the wiry form of the man who crouched over her, about to destroy all that she had hoped to give to Brys.

Then the front door crashed open behind them, and she glimpsed only a blur as something—someone—launched himself at de Mandeville, wrenching the earl off of her and throwing him against the nearby wall.

"Whore's son! You'll die for this, and then I'll still have her!" de Mandeville screeched as he twisted around, making a grab for the dagger.

But Brys de Balleroy was quicker, and it was a fatal mistake for the earl to turn his back on him even for that second. Gisele heard a sibilant hiss as Brys pulled his sword from his scabbard. Just as de Mandeville faced him again, Brys ran him through.

Geoffrey de Mandeville went down with a groan, his eyes rolling back in his head. Then he was still.

Gisele watched her lord pull the blade out of the man's body and wipe the blood on her discarded towel.

"Is he—" She could not frame the word.

"Dead?" Brys nodded, still panting and flushed from the brief struggle. "Are you all right? Did he..." His eyes raced over her, searching for injury, and then probed her gaze.

Wordlessly, she shook her head, knowing what he was asking. Now the enormity of what had just taken place seized her. She stared at the unmoving body lying in the rushes, then back at Brys, her vision blurred with tears. "You killed him," she breathed. "You killed the Earl of Essex! Oh, Brys…" She choked on a sob while new fear for him clutched her with icy fingers.

"Hush," he said, pulling her close against his powerful chest and stroking her back while she sobbed. "I slew a vile knave, a murderer, who would have ravished you, then like as not slit your throat. Do not fear—all will be well…."

All the while he stroked her back and held her close, whispering soothing things to her, as one would to a child. She savored his heat as she shivered with shock.

"But I fought him, B-Brys…" It was vital that he know that, somehow. "And now, at least, he cannot…b-betray you to Stephen's camp…he said he would do that, if I did not l-lie with him…." She shuddered anew as fresh sobs threatened to shake her apart.

"Hush," he whispered into her hair. "It doesn't matter anymore what they believe."

"What?" she breathed, drawing back to stare at him. Didn't Brys understand? De Mandeville's death meant Brys would be safer now that the earl couldn't expose him as a spy!

He must have read the confusion in her eyes, for he held her gently by the shoulders and gazing into her eyes, said, "I don't care any longer who believes what about me—not after what nearly happened to you while I was gone! I'm not going to be the empress's informant anymore. I'm going to take you to safety, and then if

Matilda wants me to fight openly for her, she can count on my sword. If not…'' He shrugged, his eyes bitter.

"You're going to take me to Oxford—to the empress?'' she asked, wondering how she could dissuade him from going back to his original idea.

He shook his head. "Nay. 'Tis not sure enough. I won't have you starving through a siege if Stephen succeeds in surrounding the place. I'm taking you to my sister.''

Chapter Sixteen

"To your sister?" she echoed. Her hazel eyes were round and enormous in a face drained of all color.

"Yes, to Avelaine, at Tichenden on the North Downs," Brys told her, wondering if she would refuse to go. "You should be safe there, safer than you would be with Matilda, who will be playing the mouse to Stephen's cat."

He was surprised to see her close her eyes and sigh in obvious relief, and more surprised still to hear her say, "Thank the saints! I thought you planned to take me to my father in Normandy."

"Would that have been so terrible? To go home to your father and take refuge there, until England was safe?"

"I had rather you put me away permanently in a convent, my lord."

Her stark declaration, made without any touch of self-pity, made him wince inwardly and draw her close, while careful to shield her from the sight of the body lying a few feet away. He felt her resist for just a moment, and then she went to him like a bird seeking its nest.

"You and I shall not deal together that way, Gisele. I swear I will never make you go or stay anywhere you do not want to," he said against her hair.

"T-thank you, my l-lord," he heard her murmur, her voice still thick with tears.

"And now I think we must hasten to be gone," he told her. "I'd wager Gytha is planning to bring something for the midday meal, isn't she?" At her nod, he said, "We must be well away when she discovers the body."

He felt her start, and knew that she had succeeded, at least for a moment, of forgetting all about de Mandeville. She pulled away from him a little and stared up into his face.

"But...shouldn't you bury him?"

He shrugged. "We dare not stay here so long, and in any case I have nothing to dig it a grave with. Even if I did, what if Gytha—or someone else—comes into the yard out back while I am putting the body into the grave?"

She looked around him at the body lying amid the rushes, and shuddered. "I will go upstairs and get my belongings," she said tonelessly, and fled up the stairs. He watched her go, then covered as much of de Mandeville as he could with Gisele's discarded towel and carried him to the cellar. He hated to have the body inside his house, but he dared not go outside with it lest he be seen.

"'Twill take us two days to reach Tichenden, assuming we meet with no problems," he told her when they rode out of Southwark.

Gisele had been silent all the way through London, constantly casting furtive glances around her as if any second she expected to hear the hue and cry for them. When he had stopped to purchase food for the journey at a market stall, she had been anxious as a tabby cat hemmed about by big dogs. Now, however, she looked at him, saying, "What of tonight, my lord? Shall we pass the night at some monastery?"

He shook his head. "I'm hoping we can reach Hawkswell Castle before nightfall. That's where my friend Lord Alain, the Baron of Hawkswell, and his lady, Claire, live. They will welcome us—in fact, they may well press us to stay longer."

He had expected Gisele to bristle at the news, and she did. "So—I am to accept the hospitality of the lord who *rejected* me?" Then, her back rigid on her mount, she stared straight ahead.

He thought back to the day he had found her in the Weald, and he had realized she was the same Norman heiress whose hand Matilda had once offered to Alain. "Gisele, Lord Alain meant no offense to you," he said, turning her chin with a gentle finger so that she had to look at him. "Alain never met you. By the time Matilda offered you to him, he was in love with Lady Claire. When you meet them—when you see them together— you will understand that she was the only possible match for him."

She sighed again, and gave him a rueful smile. "'Twas just my injured pride speaking. No doubt you are right. They are better suited to one another than he and I should have been."

There was a wistful note in her voice that intrigued him. For all her proud sense of independence, a part of this woman he had married longed to belong, to be valued and treasured. Could he ever persuade her that *he* had begun to treasure and value her, even to *love* her, and that she could trust him? Would she ever be able to return his feeling, or would she be like a caged lark, content to eat from his hand, but always longing for the sky?

Dusk had cast deep shadows over the valley by the time Brys and Gisele reached the Hawkswell River. Just beyond it rose the gray curtain wall of Hawkswell Castle.

Gisele stared at the dark water, which stretched several yards across, in dismay. It had been bad enough to think of meeting the Baron of Hawkswell while she was travel-stained and weary, but now they would have to swim the river on horseback, and present themselves to Lord Alain and his lady dripping wet!

Brys must have read her face, for he said, "Don't worry, my lady, I know the best place to ford the river, and at this time of the year you won't even have to get your ankles wet."

He spoke truly. The water was several inches below her left foot at the deepest spot—also the point at which they heard a shout go up on the wall walk above.

"Alain's guard has spotted us," Brys explained, then cupped his hand and called, "Hello, the castle! I am Lord Brys de Balleroy! My lady and I seek shelter for the night!"

There was a pause, and then the figure peering over the wall called, "Aye, my lord de Balleroy, I remember ye well! We shall have the drawbridge down and the portcullis raised by the time ye and yer lady arrive at the gate, but where are yer men-at-arms? Can there be just the two of ye?"

"Yes, just the two of us!" Brys called back. "I will explain to Lord Alain—I trust he is in residence?"

"Aye, that he is, my lord, still enjoying his newborn son, born earlier this spring!"

"He and Lady Claire have a son? 'Tis joyous news!" Brys called back, and set his spur to his mount, gesturing for Gisele to follow him around the rectangular walls.

"I apologize for keeping you waiting, Brys!" said the Baron of Hawkswell, still clasping Brys by the shoulders after the two had exchanged a hearty embrace.

Gisele took this moment to study the man who had once been offered her hand in marriage. Almost as tall as Brys he was, and with that same warrior's physique. His hair was dark—in the torchlight she could not tell if it was brown or black. A well-favored man, though not as handsome as Brys de Balleroy. Then she became amused at her own line of thinking, so that when the two men turned to her, she was already smiling.

"And who is this lovely lady you have brought with you, Brys? Can it be that my old friend has been struck by Cupid's arrow at last?"

Brys looked briefly nonplussed at the last question, then recovered. "Alain, I would present you to my wife, Lady Sidonie Gisele de l'Aigle."

Alain was already coming forward, a ready smile curving his lips, when he evidently realized the significance of the name. He stopped stock-still, and his jaw dropped. Then he said, "Lady *Sidonie de l'Aigle?* But is she not—"

Gisele decided she had the right to enjoy this moment, and she did, watching the powerful lord embarrassed in his own castle hall.

"Yes, she is," Brys said with a mischievous grin, his

eyes meeting Gisele's in a moment of shared amusement. "The very same lady you refused, sight unseen. But do not trouble yourself, old friend. Your loss is my gain."

Lord Alain closed his eyes as if he were wishing the floor beneath the rushes would open up and allow him to drop out of sight.

"Lady Gisele," he said, coming forward and taking her hand. "How can I ever make a suitable apology for what must have seemed a churlish action? I can only plead for your understanding, for I had already been shot with Cupid's arrow myself, and was in love with the lady who later became my wife...I bid you welcome to Hawkswell Castle."

She smiled. She couldn't help herself, when he smiled so winningly at her.

"I thank you for the welcome, and no apology is necessary, my lord," she murmured. "As you said, your refusal had naught to do with me—"

"Alain!" called a woman's voice just then, and Gisele looked up to see a woman descending the stone steps that led to the upper chambers. She was carrying a small, blanket-wrapped bundle from which a tiny arm and downy head protruded. "I was putting the children to bed. Annis says we have visitors?"

Gisele studied the woman coming toward them, and knew that this must be Lady Claire, the woman who had stolen Lord Alain's heart. And no wonder—she was a golden-haired beauty, with startlingly blue eyes and a lissome figure.

"Why, 'tis Brys de Balleroy!" Lady Claire cried, rushing forward. "Brys, you are well come indeed! It has been too long since you have been within these walls, my lord!"

"Yes, it has, Lady Claire. I see you have presented my friend with a son," Brys said, gesturing toward the babe.

Lady Claire blushed with pleasure as she drew back the edge of the blanket so that the infant's face was more visible. "Isn't he the most beautiful child you've ever seen? His name is Verel—after my lord's young squire who died, you remember?" A flash of sadness crossed her face, to be instantly replaced by maternal pride as Brys beheld the baby.

"He is a beautiful child," Brys agreed. "And if he's fortunate, he will look more like you than his father...."

Lord Alain cleared his throat. "And my rude friend Brys has brought his bride with him, my love," Lord Alain said, gesturing to Gisele, who had hung shyly back. "Lady Sidonie Gisele de l'Aigle."

If Lord Alain had ever told his wife about her, it wasn't evident from the genuine, unwavering smile Lady Claire gave Gisele. "Oh! I beg your pardon, Lady Sidonie! You are well come, too, of course! I fear I was so eager to show off my babe to Brys that I didn't see you there!"

"'Tis no matter, Lady Claire. And I go by my middle name, Gisele, rather than Sidonie," Gisele said, liking her instantly. "My lord is right—a beautiful babe," she said, indicating the infant. A wave of longing seized her as she studied the sleeping infant held against the woman's breast. He looked to be perhaps three months old, with fat cheeks and a wealth of dark hair on his head, obviously a legacy of his sire.

"May I—?"

Lady Claire's smile rivaled the brilliance of the sun as she handed the babe to Gisele. "Of course! Is he not wonderful? And so is she, my lord!" she said, turning to Brys. "I'm so glad that you have found a lady to love! I wish you all the happiness my lord and I have known!" She crossed to Alain, and instantly his arm went about her, pulling her close to his side, and she looked up at him with naked adoration.

Alain's face was full of the same wholehearted love. "Sweetheart, our guests have been traveling since midday," Alain reminded her.

"Oh! Forgive me," Lady Claire cried. "You must be exhausted, and hungry, too! Annis," she said, speaking to the serving woman who had followed closely on her heels, "run to the kitchen and arouse Cook—"

"But it's late, and you were not expecting us," protested Gisele. "We must not keep you from your bed! If you will but show us to our chamber, we will not trouble you till the morning."

"And then we must be off," Brys added. "We journey on to Tichenden—"

"Nonsense! We do not have visitors to this castle often enough, and your visits, Brys, are rarer still!" Claire exclaimed. "I will not hear of your leaving for several days, unless you are able to persuade me you have a very good reason! And I would not sleep the night if I sent you to your beds hungry, like unwelcome mendicants! It will take no great time for Cook to fix something, and meanwhile we shall be treated to the story of how you met! And Annis, tell Frisa to ready the largest guest chamber, too!"

Her warmth enfolded them like a cloak. She did not seem to notice Brys and Gisele's stiffness with each other as she showed them to a place by the fire.

"Before my wife begins interrogating you," Lord Alain began, grinning at Lady Claire while she favored him with a mock glare, "I cannot help but wonder if all is well with you, my old friend? You travel with no escort, not even your young giant of a squire?''

''I sent Maislin on to Bristol, to deliver a letter to Stephen,'' Brys said. ''I'm hoping he will catch up with me at Tichenden.''

''So, you're still playing that dangerous double game?''

''I had been, but no longer,'' Brys told him, then launched into a description of the growing unrest in London, exacerbated by the raiding Flemings, and culminating in the court's flight from Westminster.

''So, Matilda has been repudiated again,'' Lord Alain said, his face troubled. ''This time by the common folk. The poor, would-be queen—her life has not been an easy one. But I am glad you are taking your lady wife out of harm's way.'' He turned to Gisele. ''And now perhaps you had better tell my wife the story of your meeting, Lady Gisele, for she will give me no peace until she hears it!''

Feeling very self-conscious, Gisele told of returning to consciousness in the forest after the massacre to find Brys standing over her.

Lady Claire was aghast. ''The saints bless us, but you are lucky to be alive! God be thanked that Brys came along before those brigands found you!'' she exclaimed.

Her beautiful face relaxed somewhat as Gisele went on, telling how they had gone on to London and about her first days at court. Gisele admitted she and Brys had been married only two days, but she did not mention how their marriage had come about.

''Ah, isn't it romantic, Alain! Clearly, their love was fated since that first day they met!'' Lady Claire bubbled, her face shining.

''Wife, you think all the world should be made up of

pairs of lovers—and their children, of course,'' Alain said fondly, caressing Lady Claire's cheek.

''Of course! What could be better?'' she responded. ''And now your best friend and his lady can enjoy their honey moon right here at Hawkswell!''

'''Honey moon?''' Gisele repeated. She had heard the empress use the phrase, too, but didn't know what it meant.

Lady Claire beamed. '''Tis a term I learned from our Saxon-speaking servants, who believe the first month of marriage is the sweetest! But I have found, after being wed to my lord long enough to bear his son, that the sweetness need not end with the first month, and so I would wish you two to discover!''

Gisele looked down at her lap, hoping she looked like the shy, blushing bride, but in reality she was trying to hide her dismay. She had been able to bear the thought of staying here with Brys's friends when it seemed they would only be here overnight, but Brys had not resisted Lady Claire's request that they stay longer.

How could she bear to be around two such genuine lovebirds as the Lord and Lady of Hawkswell, when she knew Brys had only wed her at the empress's insistence? She would be humiliated if Lady Claire guessed her secret—that Gisele and Brys were more like strangers than man and wife! Once again the longing swept over her to experience the sort of love the Lord and Lady of Hawkswell had so clearly found in their married life. Would she ever enjoy such warmth and easy understanding with Brys?

Just then the servant Annis returned to the hall, accompanied by another woman who must be Cook. Both bore platters of food. In the ensuing bustle of arranging chairs at the table and setting out the food, Gisele was able to regain her composure.

The supper of cold ham, accompanied by tarts and manchet bread and butter, was simple but nourishing. They spoke no more of events in London; instead, Lord Alain and Lady Claire chattered about their children. In the course of the conversation, Gisele learned that Lord Alain had been a widower, and Lady Claire had become a mother to his young son and daughter when they had wed. And now, of course, she had given Lord Alain another son this spring.

As soon as they were finished eating, Lady Claire ushered Gisele up the winding stone stairs, calling over her shoulder, "It's your usual chamber, Brys—you remember? Come along when you're done talking with Alain."

Brys felt his friend's eyes upon him while Gisele followed Lady Claire from the hall.

"I sense there is more to this story?"

Brys allowed himself a rueful grin. "You could always smell a secret, couldn't you, old friend? Yes, there is more." *More than I can even tell you,* he thought, but he would tell him what he could.

"You may have heard that Geoffrey de Mandeville, the Earl of Essex and Constable of the Tower, had recently cast his lot with the empress?" When Alain nodded, he went on. "What Gisele did not say is that he conceived an unholy passion for her as soon as he saw her at court. I suppose he thought she would be an easy conquest, but she wanted nothing to do with him. I warned him away from her, but just before we fled London I was forced to kill him."

Alain was clearly startled, but he said, "I'm sure that for you to do such a thing, you felt you had no choice.

I've met the man, and he was always a schemer. May he find no peace in the halls of hell.''

Brys nodded grimly, and explained further how Gisele had witnessed de Mandeville murdering a burgher—though he left out the part about Gisele coming to his bed to seek refuge. He completed his tale with the account of finding de Mandeville in his London house, trying to rape Gisele.

Alain shook his head in wonder. "And that was but hours ago? Do not fault yourself, Brys—you did what you had to. And do not worry, you will have sanctuary here at Hawkswell for as long as you care to stay."

"Thank you," Brys replied, grateful for his friend's understanding. "I don't think anyone among the queen's camp knows of our friendship, so it's not likely they'd come here looking for me."

Back in London, in the house in West Chepe which Brys and Gisele had left so hurriedly, Gytha was sponging dried blood from the earl's chest.

Geoffrey de Mandeville groaned, and tried to backhand the old woman, but missed, and groaned again the louder. *"Gently, you old crone, or I'll strangle you! When is that poppy juice going to ease this pain? Are you sure you gave me enough, you stingy hag? Give me some more!"*

Gytha could barely understand the nobleman's French, but she could tell he was in pain, and cursing her for it. More of the drug might well stop his breathing, and that was not altogether a bad thing!

When she'd come to the house to bring the promised soup to Lord de Balleroy's wife, and instead found the Norman nobleman's crumpled, bloody form lying amid the rushes, she had screamed—and had nearly died of fright when the "corpse" had moaned in response to her noise.

That had been hours ago, but she'd been busy ever since, nursing him and fending off his pain-crazed blows. She'd enlisted her man Alf's aid to move him upstairs. Gytha could only guess what had passed between de Balleroy, a man she knew to be good and kind, and the man who now lay in de Balleroy's own bed.

Whatever reason you had for spitting him with a sword, my lord Brys, she thought, I'm sure this scathy niding deserved it! It was just a pity the blade didn't go a little more to the center, and pierce his heart! She wondered where de Balleroy and the beautiful lady with him had gone. *God keep you, wherever you are.*

"Send your man to the Flemish camp in Southwark!" de Mandeville bellowed just then. "They must be warned—de Balleroy is a traitor! Do it now, or you'll be sorry!"

Gytha wanted to ignore the Norman's ravings, for they meant naught to her. What did she care who sat the throne? She just wanted to live in peace. On the other hand, though, perhaps the man lying on the bed was as powerful as he claimed. He might hang her Alf if they did not do as he ordered. And if he died, the Normans might take it out on her, her man, and all the common folk in the West Chepe. She would have to do as he said, and take care to ensure he lived.

Chapter Seventeen

Gisele was not surprised to find herself alone when she awoke, but when she descended the stairs into the hall, Brys was not there, either—nor was Lord Alain. Lady Claire, however, was at the table, flanked by two standing children, a girl and a boy. They were attractive children; the girl's hair was as dark as her sire's, while the boy's hair had lighter glints in it. They presented an interesting contrast to their fair stepmother.

"Ah, good morn to you," Gisele said, rising. "Peronelle and Guerin, make your greeting to Lady Gisele, Lord Brys's wife."

The little girl, who looked to be about four, made a charming if clumsy curtsy, while the boy, who was perhaps six, bowed more smoothly, murmuring, "Lady Gisele, I give you good morrow," in a voice that sounded like a childish imitation of Lord Alain's. There was something about him, though—perhaps it was the determined set of the mouth—that reminded Gisele not only of Brys, but also, curiously, of the Empress Matilda. I must surely still be fatigued from the journey, Gisele mused as she returned their greetings, to be thinking such a thing!

Lady Claire excused them, then watched fondly as they scampered out of the hall.

"They're beautiful children," Gisele said, wondering how difficult it had been for Claire to assume her position as their new mother when she had married their father.

"Thank you. And they're such *good* children, too, for which I can only thank their late nurse. *I* knew naught about mothering when I came here! I can hardly bear to think of sending Guerin off to be fostered when he is seven next year… Of course, if we are still in the midst of civil war by then, though, my lord says we shall keep him right here at Hawkswell."

A man who put the safety of his son above the conventions of raising a son to manhood? Gisele felt her liking for Lord Alain growing.

"You must be wondering where Brys is," Claire said. "He and my lord went out hunting at dawn. Oh, they said we needed fresh meat, but the truth, naturally, is that Alain has a brace of hounds whose prowess he wanted to show off, and all men love to go a-hunting, do they not?"

Gisele murmured something noncommittal; she hadn't known her mysterious husband long enough to know his preferred pastimes.

It didn't seem that Claire was waiting for her answer, however. "But never mind, we shall not miss them. I have been so long without news of the world outside these walls, I shall keep you busy talking! And Brys tells me you have a beautiful length of green fabric just waiting to be cut and sewn into a *bliaut* for you. I count myself a competent needlewoman, so if you would like, I can help you make it."

"I would appreciate that," Gisele said, pleased at the

thought that she would have something to wear besides her dark brown traveling *bliaut* and the mulberry one she had been wearing that fatal evening... Had it only been three nights ago?

"Well then, as soon as you have broken your fast we should get to work. Verel is taking his morning nap, but after he wakes I cannot promise we won't be interrupted." She looked more closely at Gisele's face. "Ah, but you have lovely eyes, Gisele—a green gown will really bring out their hue."

They soon adjourned to Claire's solar above the hall. By the time the babe awoke and was brought to Claire, wailing with his demand to be fed, Gisele had been measured, the fabric cut, and the decoration at the neck, hem and sleeves planned.

"Here, let me sew while you nurse him," Gisele offered. "I am not such a good seamstress as you, but it won't matter on a seam."

Gisele took the cloth from Claire while the other woman settled the baby in her lap and opened the front of her gown to allow him access to her breast. Gisele was intrigued to see that Claire's talent with a needle had made it possible for her to conceal openable flaps in the bodice of her gown with inset bands of embroidery. She tried not to stare at the unusual sight of a noblewoman breast-feeding her own child, but she felt tears sting her eyes at the poignant picture they made.

Once the child had begun suckling steadily, Claire went back to querying Gisele all about court life and the famous personages that surrounded the empress. Gisele did her best to describe life at Westminster in a colorful but accurate way, even though she had been there so briefly.

At the same time, she tried to ignore the envy she

felt toward the kind woman sitting in front of her. Lady Claire had so much—children, a comfortable castle with competent servants, and most of all, a husband who clearly adored her enough to have risked the loss of Matilda's favor by marrying a daughter of the enemy....

"I imagine the ladies at court would think it hopelessly lowborn of me to suckle Verel myself," Claire said, a trifle self-deprecatingly, apparently noting the way Gisele tried to look at everything but the babe at her breast. "I could say none of the women of Hawkswell had given birth recently, but that's not true," she admitted with a shrug, meeting Gisele's eyes almost with defiance. "The truth is I just *wanted* to. Children grow up and are gone so fast, especially boy children who must be fostered elsewhere, and—"

"Oh, don't apologize!" Gisele protested, blinking back her tears, aghast that Claire would think she disapproved of her. "I think 'tis wonderful! I..." Her voice trailed off as, in spite of all her efforts, a tear escaped down her cheek, a tear that Claire looked up just in time to see.

She felt Claire's free hand reach out and touch her cheek. "Ah, you'd like to have your own wee babe, would you not? Be of good cheer, my new friend—I'll vow you'll have one...oh, by May next, if not April, unless I miss my guess about Brys..." she added in a teasing, between-us-women tone.

Gisele bit her lip and looked away, pretending great interest in a tapestry on the wall, but she had not fooled Claire.

"Oh, blessed saints, now I've shocked you with my careless tongue. Please forgive me, Gisele! I meant no offense. Alain is always saying I say exactly what comes into my head. I feel I have known you for years, but we *did* meet just last even."

"Nay, there's naught to apologize for, Claire. 'Tis merely that..." She did not know how to finish her sentence. Surely the golden Claire had never known a moment's doubt that Lord Alain wanted to be her husband!

"Gisele...if you will not mind my plain speaking...'tis not uncommon for a newly wed man and woman to have certain...ah, *awkwardnesses* as they learn to...*give* themselves to one another...in the marriage bed, I mean." Now Claire was blushing as furiously as Gisele felt herself to be, but she pressed on nonetheless. "But fortunately having a babe growing in one's belly need not wait upon being entirely comfortable with one another, my dear...."

Gisele felt Claire's eyes on her, gauging the effect of her words. Oh, dear Lord, what was she to say? Could she continue to pretend to be just a shy new bride?

"What's wrong, Gisele? Aren't you happy with Brys? Did you not wed him willingly? Dear God, are you...unable to bear children for some reason?"

For some reason the last question, uttered in a voice full of sympathy, made Gisele want to laugh hysterically. She managed to stifle all but an ironic chuckle as she tried to find the right words. She suddenly wanted to confide in this gentle, kind woman. She *needed* to trust someone as she had trusted no one since Fleurette had died.

"I suppose 'tis safe to say I cannot have children, and for the simplest of reasons—we have not...that is, my lord has not...I am not yet his wife in the fullest sense of the word."

Her bald statement hung in the air like a visible thing.

She watched Claire struggle for the right, tactful thing to say.

"But...you have only been wed for three nights, have you not? Brys is the kindest, most considerate of men, next to my lord. I cannot imagine him forcing himself upon his bride, just for the sake of his masculine pride at showing virgin's blood on the sheets the next morn! But I am still being much too blunt. If you had not known each other long, I can guess that he planned to woo you and seduce you slowly and carefully...but last night...heavens, you must have been too exhausted after such a journey to even *think of*..."

The last was true enough; Gisele had been asleep when Brys finally came to their chamber, and had been only dimly aware of him lying down next to her. He had made no attempt to rouse her. But she could not let Claire continue to misunderstand—she needed her advice too much.

"Nay, 'tis not what you think," she admitted, forcing herself to look Claire in the eye. "Brys *is* a considerate man, yes, but he...he did not wish to marry me. The empress forced him to."

Claire was silent for such a long time that Gisele went on, wanting to get it all out in the open, the whole unfortunate tangle. "Oh, he was willing enough to make love to me, before...before we were caught in bed together. But he had no intention of more than a quick tumble. And now, if he was not· the considerate man you say he is—and the loyal vassal of the empress—I do not doubt he would have our marriage annulled." She gazed into her lap, only to feel Claire's hand upon her shoulder.

"I'm sure you are telling me the truth—as you see

it, anyway,'' Claire said. "But I doubt it's as hopeless as you seem to feel it is, Gisele.''

"No?'' Gisele did not bother to hide her skepticism.

"No, of course not!'' Claire said. "Oh, men might start out just attempting seduction—my own Alain was certainly guilty of that,'' she added, much to Gisele's surprise. "But you are very comely, and as noble as he, and you are married.'' She smiled suddenly. "I'm very sure that time and propinquity will take care of...your initial difficulties, my dear.''

She hesitated, studying Gisele. "But a woman wants to feel a man make love to her for more reasons than that she is there and she is his wife, doesn't she?''

Gisele nodded slowly.

"Then I will tell you that I saw the way Brys looked at you last night when I first came down to the hall to meet you. There was something in his eyes, Gisele, when you were not looking back at him. He watched your every move—not like a man who is suspicious or resentful of the one he is watching, but like one who hungers for something...something he thinks he may not have....''

Gisele could only stare at her, afraid to hope. But... "Something he may not have?'' Surely Brys knew he had the right to take her, gently or forcefully, any time he wished?

"But in any case,'' Claire continued in a lighter tone, "once he sees how mysterious this green gown makes your eyes, he will not be able to resist you!''

It was midafternoon by the time Brys and Alain rode back over the drawbridge into Hawkswell keep, Alain holding the rope of a packhorse which bore the stag they had tracked and slain together.

"Come, let us go to our wives and boast of our prowess," suggested his host, gesturing for Brys to follow him around the outer ward rather than beneath the gatehouse into the bailey. "If I know my Claire, at this time of day she will be sitting in the orchard. She spends so many afternoons there I finally had a bench made for her to sit on there."

Sure enough, when they had passed the gardens, circled the stock pond, and come at last to the rows of fruit trees, there were Claire and Gisele, sitting under an apple tree that had boughs full of still-green fruit.

"I see the hunt was successful," Claire called, pointing to the packhorse's burden as they rode up.

Brys had a vague impression of his hostess Claire, her needle poised above a length of cloth he vaguely recognized as the same he had bought for Gisele in London. He heard Alain telling how they had pursued the wily stag over hill and dale until his arrow had finally brought the stag down and Brys had given him the coup de grâce.

But Brys's eyes only really saw Gisele. Alain's infant son was sleeping in her arms, his dark head against her breast. She looked so natural, so maternal, so happy as she gazed down at the babe after one quick, shy look from under her lashes at him.

Brys's mouth went dry. She would look just this way holding *our* babe, he thought. If only he knew how to bridge the gap between them and make their marriage a true one. If only he really deserved to be the Baron of Balleroy…Lady Sidonie Gisele de l'Aigle, heiress of her father's lands, would surely not want to bear the sons of a bastard, even a bastard whose father had been the king.

The babe reached out in his sleep and laid a chubby

hand against her breast, and Brys felt his pulse quicken, imagining how that would feel if it was *his* hand resting there.

"I trust you have passed a pleasant day, my lady?" he managed to say at last.

She nodded. A faint color crept into her cheeks. "Lady Claire has been kindly helping me sew a new gown with the cloth you bought for me. 'Twill be very beautiful, I think."

Ordinary enough words—but why could he not look away from her? He managed to mumble his agreement.

"I'm sure Annis will have some water heated in anticipation of your return," Claire was saying to the men as she rose, gathering up the unfinished gown. "There is just time for both of you to bathe before supper. Gisele, I'll need to go and make certain the meal preparation is well under way—men get so hungry when they have been out on the chase! Why don't you go with Brys? I'm sure he'd rather have you...ah, *assist* him than Annis."

Chapter Eighteen

Gisele could not believe her own ears. She had not expected the noblewoman to place her in such a position after the trusting way she had confided in Claire!

"Oh, but surely I had better go and help *you?*" she protested to Claire, aware of Brys's eyes on her and knowing he saw the heat racing up her neck.

An imp of mischief rode on Lady Claire's smile. "Oh, no, I don't think so. Cook doesn't usually need much direction, and she has plenty of help in the kitchen. She just sometimes needs to consult with me as to how soon we want the meal to be served. Here," she added, holding out the green cloth. "Give me Verel, and would you mind taking your gown-in-progress inside?"

There was nothing more Gisele could do to avoid going upstairs with Brys, not without being obvious, and Gisele knew Claire knew it. She only hoped her hands did not visibly tremble as she handed Claire the sleeping baby and took the silk cloth from her.

A pair of grooms had appeared to take Alain's and Brys's lathered mounts and the packhorse. And so the two men dismounted, each falling in step with his wife as they walked back through the outer ward, underneath the gatehouse and into the inner bailey. Lord Alain and Lady Claire seemed to have much to say to one another, as if they had been apart days instead of hours. In contrast, Gisele was miserably aware of the uneasy silence that stretched between Brys and herself.

"Thank you, Annis, I will assist my lord," Gisele informed the serving woman minutes later as she and Brys entered their chamber and found her waiting beside a tub of steaming water.

The serving woman smiled. "Very well, Lady Gisele. I have left my lord a change of clothing," she said, pointing toward a folded *sherte* and longer tunic that must have come from Lord Alain's wardrobe. Then she bowed her head and left.

They were alone.

What do I do now? Gisele wondered. She knew what was normal for the lady of the castle to do for an honored guest, but she was Brys's wife—should she help him undress, or merely wash his back?

"I—" Brys and Gisele said in unison, then each broke off, darted a glance at the other, then looked down at their hands.

"My lady, you need not assist me," Brys said at last. "I can do this myself." As if to underline the fact, he stepped over to the backless chair by the tub and began pulling the tunic over his head.

Had he taken her embarrassment out in the orchard for reluctance, or distaste at the thought of touching him? She had not meant to convey that!

"Nay, my lord, please allow me...." she said, going to him and taking the tunic from his hands, then folding it neatly before turning back to Brys as he began pulling the *sherte* he wore beneath it over his head.

He sat on the chair, bare-chested and wearing only his *braies* and short boots—such a splendidly masculine sight that Gisele barely managed to suppress a gasp.

He seemed to be waiting for something, but when Gisele just stood there, looking for a cue as to what he expected, he bent his knee and placed the ankle of his other foot over it and began tugging off his soft leather boot.

"Oh!" she said, dashing forward, realizing this was something she should have done. "I'm sorry…please allow *me*." Smiling slightly, he extended his other foot to her and watched as she pulled off his remaining boot.

He stood again, and untied the hose that were fastened at the top of his *braies,* then loosed the drawstring at his waist.

Gisele swallowed, knowing what she would see next should be a familiar sight to her by now, three days after their wedding. However, Brys surprised her by turning around before letting the *braies* slide down to the rushes at his feet. She had a glimpse of tight white buttocks before he walked away from her and climbed into the tub.

He leaned back against the wooden side, closing his eyes and sighing as the water sloshed around him. "Ahhh, that feels *so* good.…"

'Tis time to go and kneel behind him to wash his back and help him wash his hair. It's only a bath, she told herself, but her feet felt rooted to the spot. She stared at the back of his head and water-beaded shoulders, willing herself forward, but unable to move.

"Gisele," he called over his shoulder, his voice soothing. "Truly, 'tis all right, sweetheart. You need do nothing, if you would but hand me the soap.…"

She did so, and watched numbly as he soaped his

chest and arms, then leaned over, splashing water on himself with great gusto. Following that, he dunked his head, and soaped his hair, and reached out for the pitcher of water set nearby to rinse it.

Spineless fool, she called herself. Would Lady Claire behave this way?

"Nonsense, my lord. I was but woolgathering," she said briskly, taking the cake of soap from his hand. She knelt at his side and submerged the soap, working up a lather, but careful not to glance at that part of him that gleamed beneath the surface of the water. Then she moved more directly behind him.

"Lean forward, my lord, and I will wash your back."

Brys complied, and she began to spread the lather over his powerfully built warrior's shoulders.

The first surprise was the way he seemed to revel in her touch, slackening the muscles of his shoulders and neck still further and groaning in his pleasure.

The second surprise was how much Gisele found *she* liked the feel of his skin beneath her hands. Intending to stroke just hard enough to spread the soapy lather, she found her fingers automatically deepening their pressure in response to his reaction. She kneaded his back and shoulders with hands suddenly sensitive to the merest quiver in each inch of muscle.

"Ah, sweetheart, if only you had all night to do that, this chamber would be paradise indeed...." he murmured, as his head lolled back, so close to her face that his dripping, smelling-of-soap hair tickled her nose.

His ear was a bare inch from her mouth, and suddenly the bronzed-pink curve of it was irresistible to her. Hardly aware that she did so, Gisele closed the distance between her lips and his ear and kissed it.

He stilled for a moment, and then murmured in a

teasing voice, "Was that a mouse that just nibbled upon my ear?"

"No, my lord, 'twas a butterfly," she replied sweetly. "*This* is the mouse." And she closed her teeth around the lobe of his ear and bit down, lightly but sharply.

"'Tis no mouse but a vixen," he growled, just before turning and capturing her face between wet hands. A second later, while the water sloshed around his waist, Brys's lips took hers.

Again, a surprise, that his lips could be so sweet and hard at the same time. Her amazement had her lips parting and her body arching toward him, just as his hands left her face and slid down her shoulders to her arms, pulling her to him.

Dimly, she was aware of the warm wetness of the water soaking through the bodice of her gown and the undergown beneath, dampening her chemise, but she didn't care. All that was important in her world was the way his tongue was caressing hers, and the way his thumbs, extended from where his hands gripped her arms, stroked the sides of her breasts.

"Ah, sweetheart, I tried..." he muttered, as if to himself, as if giving up a battle.

How well she knew that feeling! She had attempted to resist him, to fiercely hold to her ideas of independence.... She rejoiced that each of them had given up a fight that no longer made any sense.

"I have no right..."

No right? But who had more of a right than he? "You are my lord husband, you have every right," she told him, between breathless kisses. "Pay no heed to the foolish words I uttered when I first came to England."

He closed his eyes, still holding her by her arms. "Very well..." Then, with a mighty splash, he was heaving himself from the tub, heedless of the water cascading down his sinewy thighs, and bearing her down against the rushes between the tub and the bed.

"Is...is there time?" she asked, suddenly not wanting to be interrupted by the distant but raucous blast of the supper horn when he was making her his at last. Not that food had any meaning for her at the moment, but it would be rude to fail to appear—especially since Lady Claire would know *exactly* what was keeping their guests abovestairs. Or was Lady Claire hoping this very thing would happen?

Brys shook his head gravely, his eyes holding hers. "Nay, there isn't—not to do all I intend to do before the night is over, my lady," he said, perhaps guessing her thoughts. "I can but give you a taste of what will be...."

Then he was pulling up her dampened gown, and gently pushing her knees apart, all the while holding her gaze with his. His hand was cupping her, *touching her,* parting the folds of flesh, one finger stealing inside her like a thief, robbing her of what little calm was left to her.

She rolled her head restlessly against the rushes, wanting the torment to end, yet paradoxically wanting him closer. The torment became a delicious torture that built upon itself until she was mindless, conscious only of the crescendo rising within her. He had had one arm around her, holding her while he stroked her, but now he knelt over her. Then his mouth replaced his hand and his tongue touched what his fingers had been stroking only heartbeats before.

Gisele went rigid with shock, but could not find her voice to object. Then she felt something shatter within her as her whole body became a molten fire. She opened her mouth to scream as the spasms took her, but she had breath only enough to moan. At last, her body went limp, and she was powerless to keep her eyelids from falling closed.

He was holding her close a minute—an hour?—later, when she finally regained strength enough to open her eyes again.

"My lord…it seems *you* did the tasting.…"

He laughed against her neck. "*This* time, anyway…"

Below them, the supper horn blew.

"We'll find an excuse to retire early," Brys promised her, his arm about her, as they descended a few minutes later to the great hall.

Gisele smiled, trying not to think how she must look in her water-splotched *bliaut,* with her lips swollen from his kisses. Her flesh still tingled as she walked. She hoped she had managed to put her hair sufficiently to rights beneath her veil, so she would not look like a dairymaid fresh from a romp in the hay!

Thankfully, the lord and lady of Hawkswell, seated with the two older children to one side of them, seemed not to notice anything amiss.

Gisele found herself charmed by Lord Alain's children, so grave and courteous, but so obviously fascinated by their visitors.

"I wish I was as beautiful as Lady Dizele, Mother," announced little Peronelle, gazing worshipfully down the table at Gisele. "I want my hair to be the same as hers, not this color," she added, pulling a lock of black hair loose from her braid and holding it up, self-disgust writ plain on her face.

"That's Lady *G*isele, darling," corrected Lady Claire. "And your hair is very pretty, too, a gift from your father. Black as a raven's wing, as he often says.'' A fond look passed between husband and wife.

Gisele felt a warm glow within, wondering if she and Brys would have a daughter like this one day...perhaps they would begin her this very night? Or a son as well-made as young Guerin? She did not care if she gave Brys a son or daughter first—she just could not wait to be carrying his child under her heart....

''Black as a magpie's wing, more like,'' Guerin chortled beside her. ''And she's just as noisy!''

Peronelle aimed a childish swat at her brother, which Claire intercepted with a mild frown of reproof at both of them.

But Guerin was not crestfallen for long. ''Lord de Balleroy, your Jerusalem is the most handsome warhorse I have ever seen—and Father says he will come to your whistle!''

Brys smiled, and thanked the boy without a trace of adult-to-child condescension, which warmed Gisele's heart. '''Tis true,'' he said. ''An old Crusader taught me that trick. One never knows when 'twill come in handy.''

The boy blew out a breath, admiration lighting his face. ''I wish I might have a colt of his when I am made a knight, my lord.''

Brys grinned. ''If God preserves my destrier and me a few more years, I do not see why that wouldn't be possible, Guerin. Assuming your father has no objection, of course.''

Lord Alain was not loath to permit it. ''I wouldn't mind one of Jerusalem's get myself, for that matter,'' he mused. ''I have a mare coming in season...''

But Guerin did not want to lose Brys's attention to a discussion of horsebreeding between adults. His face rapt with wistful hero worship, he announced, "My lord, I am almost old enough to be a page soon. 'Tis your household I would join."

"Guerin!" Lord Alain's voice was stern. "Of all the audacity! You will apologize to Lord Brys for your effrontery. Where you are fostered is a matter to be discussed between your father and the lord involved, not for a mere pup such as yourself to decide!"

Guerin made his apology, but his young mouth was set in stubborn lines and his eyes were stony.

Suddenly Gisele knew just who his expression reminded her of. The realization chilled her and extinguished the desire-filled joy that had cloaked her since leaving their chamber.

"You may be excused from the table, son," Lord Alain announced. "Peronelle, I see you are finished, too. Go with your brother. I will come up presently." He sighed, his face as troubled as Claire's, as he watched his son, accompanied by Peronelle, stalk from the hall.

Gisele saw Brys glance at her before saying, "Alain, I know you do not intend to foster him until the situation in the realm is more settled, but unless you would rather place Guerin higher than with a mere baron, I would be honored if you considered me worthy to foster him."

His words were but confirmation of Gisele's suspicions. Of course he wanted Guerin to come into his household!

Alain's pleased response in the affirmative was but a buzz in the background as Gisele replayed the scene in her mind, seeing the boy's face over and over again in her mind. That stubborn set to his mouth, that defiant stoniness in the eyes, that willfulness... She had seen them all before—in Brys's face.

She remembered her impression from this morning, that there was something familiar about this boy she had only just met, something that reminded her of Brys—and of Matilda, too, she admitted, but willfulness was a common royal trait.

She stared at Lady Claire, wondering if she had ever noticed the resemblance between Brys and the boy. Did Alain know who had fathered his first wife's love child? He must not. If he even suspected, how could he welcome Brys with such open arms?

"I...I fear I am coming down with a headache," she said, rising to her feet. "I pray you will excuse me. No, 'tis not necessary to go with me, my lord," she said, fending off Brys's proffered hand with a wave of her own. "I shall be all right on my own. Stay and talk with our hosts, won't you?" She prayed she would not lose her supper, or weep, before she escaped the hall.

Chapter Nineteen

Brys stared at Gisele's retreating figure. What the devil had ruined her joyous, excited mood? For he was fairly sure she didn't have a headache. The change had come about too swiftly, and she had appeared upset, not in pain. Could it be she objected to the idea of Guerin coming to their household to be fostered? He would have to make sure she understood that the boy's coming was many months away, if ever, because Alain and Claire would never let the boy come until peace had been achieved in the realm, one way or the other.

He stood, intending to follow her to their chamber, but hesitated, indecisive. She had told him to stay with Alain and Claire. Did she merely need some time alone, for whatever reason, so that his following her might make things worse?

But what if he was wrong, and she really was ill? What if she had swooned from the pain, right at the top of the stairs?

Claire, apparently sensing his dilemma, rose to her feet. "Let *me* go to her, Brys."

Alain reached out a hand to his friend. "Yes, let

Claire see what may be amiss. She has possets for headaches that work wonders, I vow."

But nearly an hour later, when Claire returned and found them sitting in front of the fire, she still appeared concerned.

"I gave her a tisane, my lord. She's sleeping now." Someting about Claire's face, however, made Brys think *she* hadn't thought Gisele's complaint genuine, either.

An hour later, he found Gisele lying on her side in their bed, her face to the wall. Her breathing was slow and regular, and yet...

Brys would have wagered his right arm she wasn't truly asleep.

"What have you been doing today, my lady?" Brys asked her the next afternoon, when he and Alain returned to the hall after a morning spent hawking in the wood beyond Hawkswell's walls.

Gisele, who was rebraiding little Peronelle's hair, looked up from the dark plait she held in her hands, her face carefully expressionless. "Lady Claire and I finished making a *bliaut* out of the green cloth you bought me."

"Yes, just in time," added Claire, sitting just beyond her, embroidering the neckline of a new tunic for her lord. "And 'tis beautiful, if I do praise our needlework myself—*and* the quality of the cloth you chose, too, of course. Just wait till you see your lady in it, Brys! Gisele dear, you must wear it on the morrow for the lord's feast!"

At Gisele's blank look, Claire said, "To celebrate the completion of the hay mowing. All of Hawkswell's folk will be supping in the bailey tomorrow evening. 'Twill be very merry, with minstrels singing while we sup and jugglers performing afterward, and there will be games...."

"Yes..." Gisele darted a glance at Brys, then her eyes went back to her braiding.

"Lady Gisele, would you please come to my chamber?" Peronelle said, as Gisele finished her task. "I want to show you what *I* will wear tomorrow! My mother made it, and said I should save it for the feast." She prattled on, pulling Gisele with her toward the stairs.

"Child, cease plaguing Lady Gisele!" chided Claire in mild tones. "You have attached yourself to her like a burr to a lurcher hound this day! I'm sorry, Gisele. She sees so few other women besides me and the castle folk...."

"Nay, I don't mind," Gisele murmured. "Until later, then, Claire...my lord..."

Brys could swear she had been relieved to escape his presence. He stared after her in frustration, wondering how he could break the ice that seemed to have formed around Gisele's heart. *Tonight,* he thought. *Tonight in our chamber I will find out what is tormenting her.*

He turned back to find Claire's eyes upon him. "Peronelle seems as taken with your lady as Guerin does with you," she said. "She's scarce let her out of her sight, and Gisele is so good to indulge her. I think she would love to have a child of her own, Brys."

"Claire..." He did not know how to begin.

But Claire seemed to know. "If you're about to ask if I know what's troubling her, Brys, I must save you the trouble and confess I do not. She's said not a word to me since last night, though she answers my questions. Yet she insists there's naught amiss. But be of good cheer, my lord. I truly believe there is love in her heart for you."

There *had* been, he'd dare swear. There had been more than mutual lust between them that time in the garden at Westminster, and yesterday in their chamber, when she had been as eager for him as he for her… But something had chilled that love last night at supper like an early frost blights the last rose of summer.

Even if he could succeed in bringing that love back to life, though, would it die again when he told her his shameful secret?

"We shall have to leave for Tichenden the morning after the feast, my lady," Brys said, changing the subject. "As much as I would like to linger, I cannot put off our departure any longer. I must see Gisele safe with my sister, then get back to help the empress." Would there still be this icy distance between his wife and himself when he left Gisele behind at Tichenden?

The candle still burned on the nightstand after Gisele lay down on the bed and pulled the bed linen up.

Brys reached across the bed, caressing Gisele's shoulder. "Gisele, I—"

She went rigid. "I am weary, my lord."

"I only want to talk to you, to discover—"

She sat bolt upright, shrinking away from his touch. "I…I am ill, my lord—I must go to the garderobe!" she said, hurrying from the chamber.

He waited, leaving the candle burning, while night settled around the castle. Through the narrow arrow loop window he could hear a nightingale calling its mate. Minutes crawled by while he waited for Gisele to return.

His day had begun at dawn, and he was weary, too. He wanted to wait for Gisele to come back to bed, to find out once and for all what was bothering her. But the minutes crept by, and the wine he had drunk at supper, the comfort of the bed, and the soft night wind wafting through the window, all conspired to make his eyelids heavy. He'd just rest his eyes for a moment. He'd hear her when the door creaked as it opened, or feel her additional weight as the rope mattress sagged to accept her body.

He slept.

Gisele knew she had made a big mistake the moment she came down the stairs into the great hall, dressed in the silver-shot green *bliaut* with the Irish silver necklace nestling amidst the vertical bands of darker green embroidery at the neckline. Brys's eyes told her he found her beautiful, and how much he hungered for her.

She had not wanted to disappoint Claire, who had unselfishly done the lion's share of work on the garment, by not wearing it. Claire had been unfailing in her kindness to her—even though Gisele knew her demeanor must have seemed strained to her hostess after that supper two nights ago.

Had it been wrong of her to wear the green *bliaut,* knowing how well it became her, since she did not want to spark her husband's desire? She wanted to flee back to their chamber and don her dull-brown traveling dress, but of course she could not very well do that. And so she had taken the arm he proffered and let him lead her outside, feeling his eyes on her.

The sky had been red at dawn, warning of rain, but thus far it had not made good on its threat to put a premature end to the lord's feast. A gentle, sultry breeze fluttered the edges of the table linens, weighed down by hams, roast ox and capon, breads, puddings and fruits. The bailey was thronged with the folk of Hawkswell Castle, great and small, finding their places at the rows of trestle tables.

Lord Alain and Lady Claire's son and daughter sat laughing and talking with the village children, and almost indistinguishable from them. But how different their destinies would be from that of the children of the hayward and the brew mistress, Gisele thought. All too soon each of them would leave Hawkswell—Guerin temporarily, as he trained for knighthood, Peronelle more permanently, once she was married to some nobleman with castles and lands of his own.

A pair of traveling minstrels, having hastened to the castle after hearing of the upcoming feast, entertained the crowd with mellow tenor voices. During the meal, they sang lays praising God and the Virgin Mary, and the castle's priest beamed approvingly, but once he dozed over the remains of his meal and his empty wine cup, they began concentrating on songs of love.

Since, love, our minds are one,
What of our doing?
Set now your arms on mine,
Joyous our wooing.
O flower of all the world,
Love we in earnest!

Imagining Brys's arms clasping hers, Gisele felt herself blushing furiously. Hoping he hadn't noticed, she darted a glance at Brys.

He was staring straight ahead, but as the minstrels began the next verse, she was startled to feel Brys touch her on the shoulder, then lean over to whisper in her ear, "Our minds are not one, my lady, but I would they were."

She stared at him, not knowing what to say. How could she describe the journey her heart had gone on since meeting him, a journey whose final step she had just completed when she had taken his arm to come into the bailey? She had struggled against loving him when it would mean the loss of her freedom, yet begun to love him all the same. When they had been forced to wed, she had been willing to accept the inevitability of giving in to that love, even knowing marriage to her would not have been his choice.

Two nights ago, when she had reached her dismaying realization about what Brys had done in the past, she had waited for her love to wither within her breast. But it had not. Stubbornly, it refused to die, even knowing what she knew. She loved him anyway.

Perhaps it was a woman's lot in life to be captured by a certain smile, by the heat deep within a pair of brown eyes, by the remembrance of the power of a kiss, or the touch of one man's hands. Even the greatest villains of history—Herod, Nero, the infidel sultans who persecuted Christians in the Holy Land—had presumably known women who could not resist their charms. And Brys was no villain, just a man who had committed a grave sin. But no one was sinless, were they?

She would give in to her love and desire for him, even knowing what she knew. She couldn't, and did not want to, put him off any longer with such silly maidenly ploys as pretending to be asleep.

Tonight she would surrender, would lay her pride at his feet and her body beneath his, and he would do as he would to her. Brys would satisfy her desire, she was certain. Her love would grow all the more once she had truly become his wife.

Gisele thought her sweet submission would at least engender in Brys a certain tolerant affection for her. She wanted more, so much more—but she would be content with that. And perhaps it would be enough that she could accept with grace having young Guerin in their household. The sin of his father was not Guerin's fault, after all.

She was about to reply, to give him some hint of her yielding, but Lord Alain had risen from his high-backed chair and was holding his hands out for attention.

"And now, while our musicians pause and refresh themselves with some wine and sweet cakes, perhaps we should play some games? What of Hoodsman's Bluff, my lady?" he inquired, looking down at Claire.

Cries of agreement punctuated the suggestion.

"Perhaps next, if the weather permits," Lady Claire agreed, after a wary look at the darkening sky. The wind had picked up slightly, ruffling her sleeve as she held up a bowl from which ribbons, attached to rolled-up strips of parchment, dangled. "But first, I have prepared a game of Ragman's Roll. Everyone must come up and pick up a piece of parchment, on which is written your fortune. Those who can will read theirs aloud, or Father Paul will read it for you."

There were chuckles as Lord Alain gently woke the slumbering cleric.

"One lucky person, man or woman," Lady Claire continued, "shall win freedom from all work for three days, with any necessary tasks to be taken up—cheerfully, mind you—" she added with a smile, "by your fellows! The winner shall be indicated by having a star inscribed on their parchment, rather than a written fortune!"

A cheer went up, and all the common folk rushed to form a line in front of the lord's table. Everyone, from the swineherd to the reeve, wanted to be the lucky one who drew the parchment strip with the star.

"You are diligent in your duties, and shall be rewarded," the priest read out loud to the potboy, earning him a skeptical sniff from the cook.

"Rewarded with the back o' my hand if he comes in with his nose in the air, more like," she said with a snort, but beamed when her own fortune was read from the unrolled paper: "You are queen of your own kingdom."

"Aye, and rules with a rod o' iron!" was the potboy's gleeful retort.

The reeve's fortune promised him marriage with a comely maiden, causing his brow to furrow, for he was a confirmed bachelor of forty winters. The sergeant of the garrison was praised as a kindly saint, resulting in howls of derision from his men-at-arms.

At last, just as a rumble of thunder sounded overhead, the goose girl picked the paper roll inscribed with a star, and ran around the bailey, whooping joyfully. Then the castle priest drew his, and announcing that the paper indicated he was destined to go to bed early tonight, ambled off to his quarters amidst more laughter.

Now only the lords and ladies had not received their paper fortunes.

"How did you manage to ensure each one received such a fitting fortune?" Brys inquired of Lady Claire when he and Gisele went up to dip their hands into the near-empty bowl.

Lady Claire shrugged. "'Tis pure luck this time. At Christmas when we played, Father Paul drew a roll inscribed 'You are Argus-eyed and ever vigilant,' and the castle folk couldn't help themselves—they laughed till they cried. His dignity was much injured, I can tell you. Come, 'tis time to learn your destiny, Lady Gisele."

Gisele reached out and picked a purple ribbon attached to one of the few remaining rolls. Her hand shook slightly as she smoothed it out, then she read: "Love never fails."

Oh God, please make it be so, she thought.

Then it was Brys's turn. "Be yourself, and those who love you will love you still."

He looked thoughtful, but said only, "And now the lord and lady of Hawkswell must choose their fortunes."

Lady Claire had just reached for a dangling ribbon when a crack of thunder erupted directly overhead. In the next moment, the heavens opened.

Amidst shrieks of confusion and dismay, the village folk ran for the drawbridge, all but the dairymaid's aged parents, who could not move so fast. The lord and lady of Hawkswell hastened to their sides, helping them to the gatehouse where they might wait out the downpour in relative comfort.

Brys and Gisele started to run toward the hall, but a sudden, shrill shrieking stopped them. Unseen by his parents, Guerin had apparently slipped on the suddenly wet cobbles and gone down, bloodying his knee and frightening his sister.

By unspoken agreement, Gisele and Brys dashed to the children. As nearby lightning illuminated the scene with a brief, phosphorescent flash, Brys scooped up the boy, while Gisele took hold of Peronelle's hand, and they ran for the shelter of the hall.

Half an hour later, after Guerin's knee had been washed and bandaged and both children had been comforted and turned over to their mother, Gisele stood in their candlelit chamber and watched Brys kindle a fire in the brazier.

Her heart ached as the same scene played itself over and over again in her mind: Brys swooping down to rescue the boy, then running with him, the boy's face so near his, so like his.

"Come over and get warm, Gisele," Brys said, holding his hands to the heat. "We're both drenched. 'Twould be wiser still if we both got out of these wet clothes." His eyes, questioning, sought hers over the flickering flames.

Gisele found she could not look away.

"You…you were very kind with Guerin, Brys," she said into the sudden silence. "You like him very much, do you not, my lord?"

He nodded, obviously puzzled. "Of course…he's a wonderful lad," he said carefully, studying her. "I like little Peronelle, too—she'll break hearts one day." Then he bent over in front of her and reached for the hem of her *bliaut,* "Gisele, let me help you out of that wet gown—"

Gisele put out a hand to halt him. She had to get this

out into the open, or they could go no further. "That is to say, my lord, 'tis all right, I understand. That you like him—*love* him," Gisele amended. "'Tis natural, I suppose."

Brys straightened. His eyes, in the flickering light, were almost black. "Gisele—*what* are you saying?"

She looked up at him as tears stung her eyes. "I mean, my lord, that I know Guerin is *your* son, not Lord Alain's! 'Tis only natural that you should love him and want him to be fostered in your household!"

Chapter Twenty

Brys stared at his wife, certain he could not have heard her aright. *"What did you say?"*

Her chin levered up a notch or so, and she looked straight into his eyes. Tears stood in hers, making them look like rain-drenched brown stones.

"Come, my lord," she said. "You can hardly deny the resemblance. He has your chin, your mouth, your stubborness, your mannerisms. As I've said, I know why you love him and would want him with you. I just do not understand how you can come here, all smiles and friendship with her Lord Alain! Is Alain so blind he does not see who sired the boy, or has he merely come to terms with you about it?"

Now Brys knew why Gisele had started acting so strangely two nights ago at supper. It hurt that Gisele would have thought such a thing without giving him the chance to correct her misunderstanding, but how much more pain Gisele must have felt!

He wanted to take her into his arms and kiss her pain away—but he knew he must not. Not yet. If only he didn't have to tell her why she actually should *despise* him!

Staying where he was, he chose his words carefully. "Guerin and I are related, yes." Before the flash of bitter triumph in her eyes could flare higher, he added, "But he is not my son."

While Gisele was still blinking in confusion, he continued, "Before I say anything more, I must have your oath that no matter what happens between the two of us, you will never reveal to anyone else what I am about to tell you. Guerin could be in grave danger if you do. And the empress and her cause would suffer."

She stared at him for a long moment, then went and picked up his sword, which stood point-downward in the corner of the room. "Draw out your sword and hold it with the hilt upright," she told him.

He did so, and for a moment the sibilant hiss as the sword left its scabbard drowned out the thudding his heart made in his ears. He held it before her as she had instructed.

Gisele kissed the intersection of the blade, hilt and guard, and said in a solemn voice, "By the Cross formed by this sword, I swear to keep secret whatever you are about to tell me, my lord."

Satisfied, he began, "Guerin is Alain's son, right enough, conceived when Alain was newly knighted— and dazzled by a lonely older woman, the wife of Geoffrey, Count of Anjou."

He saw revelation dawn in her eyes as her jaw fell open. *"Guerin's mother was Matilda?"* Gisele breathed.

Brys nodded. "Born after Henry, the heir, at a time when the count and Matilda were separated geographically, as well as emotionally—though admittedly, the count and countess have never gotten along very well for very long. Matilda bore Guerin in secrecy, and gave him into Alain's keeping, knowing that if anyone else found out about his birth, it could destroy her.''

Now Gisele nodded. ''Her husband might well have divorced her. And Stephen—''

''Would have gained added weight to his cause, to be able to call the empress an adulteress.''

''How sad for the boy, never to be with his mother....'' she mused. ''Does he know?''

Brys shook his head. ''Not yet. Perhaps one day 'twill be safe to tell him.''

Gisele still looked perplexed. ''You said you and the boy were related, but you are not his father—''

''Can't you guess?'' He bit out the words as the old pain threatened to strangle him. ''I am yet another of the late king's many bastards. Which makes me Guerin's half uncle.''

She was thunderstruck. *''Your father was King Henry?''*

He could not hold back the bitterness welling up inside him, bitterness that had been bottled up within him all his life. ''Yes, damn his lecherous royal heart! But that hardly makes me unique, does it? My mother, however, unlike his other paramours, did not want it known that she had been a king's mistress. She persuaded Henry to marry her off to my father, the Baron de Balleroy, and I was born on the 'right' side of the blanket after all—at least in the eyes of the world. But the baron knew what he was getting into, and he hated me for what I symbolized to him. *I* was the reason he had been forced to marry another man's cast-off woman.''

He saw pity and compassion mingled in her eyes before she said, in a careful, even voice, ''Yet he kept you his heir.''

''He felt he had no choice. After me, he fathered

three daughters on my mother, and he did not want Balleroy's future weal to depend upon whatever lord my eldest sister wedded. He made me swear I would never reveal the secret of my birth.''

"He sounds much like my father," Gisele commented. ''But…did you not tell me you had a younger brother? Your father did not disinherit you when he was born.''

A bitter laugh escaped Brys. ''He could not. Ogier was born six months after my father's death. Oh, he knew my mother was with child, right enough.'' He allowed himself a bitter smile. ''But on his deathbed, he said that my mother had only given him 'puling girls' and that this one would be yet another. He would not agree to release me from my vow, even if the babe turned out to be a male—''

"Couldn't your mother have told the truth? She wasn't bound by your vow.''

Pain needled through his heart. ''That wasn't possible. She died giving birth to him.''

"I see.''

"Do you?'' he said, suddenly weary. He turned from her and went to the window, leaning his forehead against the cool stone while he stared out into the night. ''Do you see now why I never wed? I never felt *worthy* to marry, to give some lady my name, knowing I was not really entitled to it. I loved you from the moment I met you, beautiful Gisele, but I did not feel I had the right to take you to wife. For who was I but an imposter? A bastard not even entitled to my supposed father's legacy!''

"Yet you would have seduced me, in the empress's garden that day,'' she retorted with brutal honesty.

"Yes," he admitted. "I am but human, Gisele, and I wanted you."

"You would have made love to me—"

"Then left you free to wed some nobleman who was no bastard, who had a right to his lands and his title."

"What do you think I'd care about that, after I had been *yours?*" she cried. *"Do you think I could wed some other man after I had lain in your arms? Once I had loved you? My lord, I am not made so!"*

"No more am I, but I would have given you up for your good, sweet lady."

"Good? You think my good consists merely of marriage to some great noble? You would have given me up to despair!"

He saw the truth of it in her eyes. "*Do* you love me, Gisele de l'Aigle?" he asked her, a rueful half smile on his lips. "Can you still, after what I have told you?"

She looked him straight in the eye, and he felt her soul reach out to his. She shivered suddenly, and he did not know if it was her damp garments or fear that caused the involuntary movement.

"Yes, I do, and I can," she said.

"You could have the marriage annulled, you know. I married you under false pretences."

"I suppose I could, but—"

He interrupted her. "Before you say anything more, Gisele, I would have you know that I am going to have to tell Ogier the truth—that he is the rightful lord of Balleroy. I cannot live with this secret any longer, knowing I am defrauding Ogier of his birthright."

He held his breath. Once the words had left his lips, he knew that Gisele could turn from him in scorn. She might not wish to be merely a landless knight's wife.

But even if that happened, he already felt freer, as if a great weight had dropped from his shoulders.

"I did not love you because you were the Baron of Balleroy, Brys. I love you whether you are 'Sir Brys' or the Lord of Balleroy—or Brys the peasant, God help me! And in any case, you will be the lord of l'Aigle one day, since I am my father's heiress. Will that be sufficient for you?"

He stared at her, hardly daring to believe he had heard her aright.

"*You* are sufficient for me," he said, really allowing himself to smile at last. "Let me show you how true that is."

He held out his arms, hardly daring to breathe, but Gisele didn't hesitate. She moved into him as surely as waves must come to shore.

"My Gisele, I love you...." he breathed, gazing down at her, his lips scant inches from hers.

"Then make love to me, my lord, my Brys...*make me your wife,* fully and completely."

His mouth searched for hers, and found it waiting for him. Their lips and bodies met fiercely, with all the elemental force of a wave breaking upon a rocky beach. After all the hours and days and nights of wanting, all at once they could not get close enough, fast enough. They were drowning in the sensations caused by their questing lips and hands. But they soon made a mutual discovery—their still-sodden garments clung to their skin and could not be easily pushed aside to allow the touching and stroking both craved.

"As I suggested earlier," Brys murmured against her neck, while he cupped her breast, feeling its heavy warmth even through the wet green silk of her gown and the undergown beneath it, "'twould be wiser if we removed these soggy clothes...."

She gave a little laugh, then moaned as his thumb circled the sensitive areola. "Yes...but 'tis the most curious thing, my lord...I am no longer cold, but hot, as if I have a raging fever...."

He chuckled, while reaching for the laces up her back that hugged the silk close to her upper torso. "I've contracted the same fever, sweetheart—'tis love fever, I'm sure of it."

"And the cure—?" she asked, as he pulled the laces free and pushed the gown off her shoulders. It probably would have slid over her slender hips to the rushes at her feet, but for its clammy dampness, which caused it to pool at her waist.

"I'll show you, my sweet lady," Brys growled. Rock-hard, he pushed the gown the rest of the way down, then reached for the hem of her undergown, pulling it over her head with barely restrained impatience.

Gisele gasped as the air struck her damp skin, making gooseflesh and causing her nipples to tighten even more than they already had, but Brys did not let her suffer the chill longer than it took him to pick her up and carry her to the waiting bed. There he laid her carefully down, then stripped off his own sodden tunic and yanked his chausses loose from their tie-points while she admired the powerful, flexing muscles of his warrior's body. Finally, his eyes never leaving hers, he pushed the *braies* down over his lean hips and onto the rushes.

He was fully erect, his manhood standing out from his body. Gisele could not help but feel a tremor of fear, wondering how much it would hurt to take his full length inside her.

Brys lay down on his side and reached for her, pulling her close to him—but gently, even reverently. Her body, which had tensed in anticipation of roughness, relaxed a little while it grew used to the heavy thud of his heart against hers, his warmth infusing her with added heat.

And then Gisele grew aware of the tingling sensation of her nipples where they brushed against the hair on his chest, and the heated throbbing of his shaft against her belly. She did not dare to look down at it; she kept her eyes locked with his. He was still, waiting for her, obviously wanting her to indicate when she was ready for more.

Emboldened by his patience, Gisele moved against him, ever so slightly, and was rewarded with a groan of pleasure as he closed his eyes and reciprocated, rubbing against her, his shaft like a smouldering brand. Then he was kissing her, and reaching between her legs, still ever so gently, his fingers tangling with the curls there, then parting her and stroking her.

The sensation made her arch against him. Her limbs felt heavy, but she wanted to be closer, *had* to be closer. She raised her upper body, so that her breasts pushed against him. Distracted from her lips, his mouth strayed down to fasten around her nipple, suckling until she wanted to scream from the sheer joy of it. She stroked his damp hair as her upper leg stole over his, allowing him fuller access.

''Brys!'' she gasped as his finger stroked her, and she could feel the wetness he was eliciting from her. She strained toward him, clutching at him as his clever hand made her wetter, hotter. She was dying...she would die if he did not quench the fire that was building within her. Suddenly she knew that his manhood, which she had feared would pierce and hurt her, was the only thing that could bring her ease. She wanted all of him. He must fill her now, or she would burn to ashes.

"Please…" Gisele moaned, shifting, hoping he would understand what she wanted, understand what she barely understood herself.

"What is it you desire, *wife?*" he said, his voice caressing the word, infusing it with an infinite cherishing.

"You…" was all she could bring herself to say. She could not imagine herself putting it into words.

"But I am right here, love," he said, smiling at her, thrusting against her, so that he stroked the entrance to her womanliness, but did not go inside.

"Closer…more…" She couldn't breathe, couldn't feel anything else but what he did to her there, not the smoothness of the bed linens, not the slickness of their passion-dampened chests.

"Like this?" He thrust again, tantalizingly closer to crossing the threshhold.

"No…yes…" Gisele clutched his back, his buttocks, urging him nearer.

"But which is it, love?" His own breath came with more difficulty now. "Mayhap, if you cannot tell me, you should show me?"

Could she be so bold? But she must, or she would never know an end to this torment! Quaking within, she moved her hand from his lower back and placed it between them, her fingers fastening around his shaft.

He groaned aloud. "Yes, Gisele, sweetheart, that's the way…. Be bold, love—*show* me what you want me to do—"

Taking in a huge gulp of air, she moved the tip of him against her, at the same time thrusting against him.

"Ahhh…I see…I know what you need, now," he

said, his voice thickened and husky, his breathing ragged as her own. Clasping her tightly, he rolled above her, still keeping himself between her legs. "Hold on to me, sweet love...."

And then came the piercing she had so feared, and it hurt terribly for an instant, but in a heartbeat, he was kissing her and soothing her with his lips, his voice, telling her how wonderful she was, and how wonderful she would soon feel.

Gisele wanted to tell him *No, you don't understand, the pleasure came first, and now it is gone, the pain vanquished it.* She could feel him lodged within her, thick and hot, as the sudden pain ebbed.

He began to move, and she pushed at him in protest, fearing the pain would escalate again, but suddenly she realized it didn't hurt. Pleasure stole over her, small waves at first, like the furthest reach of a rush of water upon the shore, then receded as he withdrew, only to recur more compellingly as he came into her again, building and building while, unaware of her own panting cries, she thrust back. The wave was burning her and drowning her all at once, submerging her in fiery pleasure until she wanted only to die of it.

His breathing came hard now, as hard as he was within her, as if he were running a race with her, against her, in her.

"Brys—" she cried against him, as she felt the huge wave approaching her, breaking over and taking her under until she shattered in his arms, feeling him flooding her with his own pleasure.

Chapter Twenty-One

A surprise awaited Gisele and Brys when they descended the steps to the hall the next morning.

"*Maislin!*" Brys exclaimed, spotting his young giant of a squire arising from one of the trestle tables, having apparently just broken his fast.

"My lord!"

Gisele watched the two men embracing.

"He came in late last night, after you two had retired," Claire announced, then added with a smile, "but he didn't want us to disturb you at your rest."

Gisele felt herself blushing as she thought how little *real* rest they had gotten last night. After she and Brys had made love, they dozed in sated exhaustion, only to wake later and find themselves unable to keep their hands from one another. Compared with their first feverish coupling, this lovemaking had been slower and gentler, but infinitely sweeter.

They arose at dawn, intending to get an early start on their journey to Tichenden. But as Gisele stood up, Brys had caught sight of the dried blood—her virgin's blood—streaked on the inside of her thighs. He had insisted on helping her sponge away the stains. Gisele

had been so touched by his tender care that she kissed
him, which led to a renewal of passion....

"Aye, my lord, I would have reached Hawkswell
sooner, had I not had to take shelter from the storm,"
Maislin was saying. Then he looked at Gisele.

"Good morrow, my lady. You...you fled London
with my lord?" His curiosity was obvious, and Gisele
did not wait for Brys to enlighten his squire.

"We were married at Westminster the night before
the Londoners marched on the palace."

Maislin's jaw dropped, then he beamed at both Gisele
and Brys. "Congratulations, my lord!" he exclaimed.
"You could not have taken a finer lady to wife! Countess de Balleroy, I am your faithful servant," he said,
going down on one knee before Gisele.

She could not help but laugh. "Thank you, Maislin."

"Well, you're just in time to go on to Tichenden with
us, Maislin," Brys told him, "where I will leave my
lady wife with my sister."

Maislin's face looked uneasy. "My lord—"

Brys cut him off, demanding briskly, "You had no
trouble reaching Stephen at Bristol?"

"Nay, I delivered the letter and found him well."

Meanwhile, Gisele was still reeling inwardly from
hearing that the events of the past night had done nothing to change Brys's mind. How could he leave her for
some unknown length of time, now that they had at last
found one another? She *must* find a way to dissuade
him from his plan, she must!

"But I'll say this, my lord," Maislin added, "it was
chancey enough getting out o' London, let alone dis-
covering where you'd gone on to, what with the folk in
Chepeside chatterin' about how de Mandeville had been

found wounded in your cellar, and settin' up the hue and cry for you—''

"*Geoffrey de Mandeville lives?*" Brys cried. "I thought I'd killed him, the whore's son!''

The squire shook his head, his face grave. "Nay, the tale being told is that his wounds brought him close enough to hell to be singed by the flames, but he's recovering. What happened, Lord Brys?''

Chilled at the news that her attacker still drew breath, Gisele nevertheless saw the quick, concerned glance Brys darted at her. "I'll tell you later. But for now, my lady and I had best break our fast, so we can all depart. Your news makes me that much more eager to see my wife safely disposed with Lady Avelaine.''

"Um…my lord…" Maislin appeared more than a little uncomfortable, "Lady Gisele is a sweet and kind female—gently raised. Are you sure you want to…that is, Lady Avelaine isn't…''

Brys's face darkened. "My lady will be fine in my sister's care, Maislin," he said in a tone that brooked no further discussion.

His abruptness left Gisele to wonder just what sort of woman Brys's sister Lady Avelaine was, to make the giant squire so obviously reluctant to take Gisele to her!

It was hard to leave Hawkswell and its lord and lady, and their family—particularly for Gisele, who had learned so much about love through Alain and Claire's example. Hugs and fervent promises to visit had been exchanged by all until at last Lord Alain realized his friend was eager to be off.

They reached Tichenden without difficulty, but after nightfall, owing to the late start they had gotten. Though a smaller keep than Hawkswell, Tichenden's walls appeared just as sturdy. And when the sergeant-at-arms who lowered the drawbridge to let them in called, "This is a wondrous surprise, my lord de Balleroy! Lady Avelaine will rejoice to see ye," Gisele was encouraged to think that Maislin had been worried for naught.

However, the woman who ran into the bailey to meet them, her hair all askew beneath her veil, looked anything but glad to see them.

"You might have let me know you were coming, my lord brother," she announced, hands on bony hips, her chin thrust pugnaciously forward.

"I would have, if there had been time to send Maislin on ahead, Avelaine," Brys began in an even voice, "but there wasn't. Times are somewhat unsettled, you know. Please make your greeting to the Lady Gisele, my bride."

Avelaine seemed to see Gisele for the first time, and give a smothered squawk. "You're *married?* This is your *wife?* I thought she was but a—" She put her hand over her mouth, then muttered in a grudging voice, "I bid you welcome to Tichenden, Lady Gisele. I am Lady Avelaine, the eldest of Brys's sisters."

As Gisele returned the woman's greeting, she studied Brys's sister. She would not have guessed this woman was related to Brys. The reddish hair was the only similar element in their coloring, but Avelaine's hair was of that much lighter, nearly blond shade often called ginger, where Brys's was auburn. Her features were much sharper than his, her eye color a pale blue in contrast to his brown eyes, her manner brisk.

"Won't you invite us into the hall, sister?" Brys prompted. "We've been on the road from Hawkswell since morning, and I'm sure my lady is weary. I know I am."

"Oh!" Ruddy color invaded Avelaine's pale face as she was brought to remember her duty. "But of course—it is *your* hall, after all, my lord brother," she said, gesturing them toward the stairway that led to the door. Taking Gisele's hand in on his arm, Brys led her past his sister.

"But as for you, you hulking lout," they heard her say to Maislin, "I haven't forgot how you tracked the mire onto my fresh rushes the last time you were here."

Gisele glanced over her shoulder to see Avelaine advancing on the squire, who had been about to lead their horses to the stable.

Gisele paused, but Brys urged her forward. "Those two have always gotten along like cats and dogs. Never fear, Maislin can take care of himself."

Sure enough, Gisele heard the squire say, "My boots are as clean as traveling on my lord's business these past few days can make them, lady. By the arm of Saint James, I see you haven't grown one whit kinder. Still unmarried, I'd warrant? 'Tis no wonder, and 'tis like to continue, with that harpy's tongue!"

"*Oh?* And *you* have the kindness of an angel, I suppose?" came her tart retort.

Gisele saw Brys watching her with amusement after she glanced back at the wrangling pair yet again. "My lord, should he—?"

"Oh, I gave Maislin free rein ages ago, to speak to her as he was spoken to," Brys said. "After all, as the son of a baron, his birth is as good as hers. Don't worry, she'd be sorely disappointed if he meekly bowed to her temper," Brys assured her.

However touchy Avelaine's temper, she was efficient. Within half an hour, she had them sitting down in the hall and being served heated venison stew, accompanied by a fresh loaf of crusty bread, cold, sweet butter and currant tarts.

"This is delicious, and quite restoring," Gisele complimented Avelaine, gesturing toward her nearly empty bowl of stew. "You obviously have your kitchen servants well in hand." Gisele guessed Avelaine was a woman who cherished the feeling of control, and if she wanted to get on a good footing with her husband's sister, perhaps she could do so by praising her on how well she ran Tichenden.

Avelaine's mouth tightened into a thin line for a long moment before she said, "They are *your* servants now, my sister-by-marriage. On the morrow I shall surrender the keys to you," she added, gesturing at the bunch of keys that rode from a ring on her worn leather girdle. "Unless, of course, you would prefer them tonight?" she added quickly, starting to remove the ring.

"Avelaine, 'tis not necessary to be so ab—" Brys began.

But Gisele interrupted him, fearing a reproof from Brys might make a shaky beginning worse. "Oh, no, of course not! I wouldn't dream of assuming I should control this keep, where my lord assures me you have ably served as chatelaine for so long—"

Avelaine cut in stiffly, "As my brother's wife, *you* are the lady of Tichenden now. It would not be proper for me to continue to be in authority. And mayhap I would like to rest from my duties, after all." But her face said otherwise.

"The morrow will be soon enough, Avelaine," Brys said. "I won't be leaving to rejoin the empress for a couple of days, at least, and you can take your time acquainting my bride with her new responsibilities. Now, if I may change the subject, where is Ogier?"

Gisele was startled to realize she had quite forgot Brys's younger half brother, the one whom he had confessed to her was the true heir to Balleroy and Tichenden, too.

"In bed, of course, where any normal boy ought to be," Avelaine retorted. "That is, if he has not left it after I bid him good night. I will check before I seek my own bed."

Gisele saw a look pass between brother and sister, and wondered what it meant.

"I'm sure that's not necessary, Avelaine," Brys replied. "At fourteen, Ogier is too old to be shooed back to bed like a toddling weanling."

Startled, Gisele looked down at her half-finished tart. She hadn't realized Brys's brother was as old as that. Had he perhaps stolen out of bed to go lie with one of the serving wenches? He might well be old enough to be up to such tricks, particularly if one of the castle's women had seduced the youth.

But why wasn't he being fostered in some other castle? Some boys his age had even progressed from page to squires, if they were strong and clever. Jésu forfend, but was he simple of mind? If so, no wonder Brys was conflicted about turning the barony over to him!

"I'll see him in the morning, then," Brys said, concluding the discussion about his younger half sibling. "And now, have you had word of our sisters at Fontrevrault?"

"I have letters waiting from both of them, asking when we will be coming to Normandy to visit, and the abbess writes that they make satisfactory progress in their studies. Neither one seems to have a vocation for the religious life."

She seemed disappointed by that, but Brys was not.

"Then I shall find them good husbands one day, if God so wills it."

Later that night, when Gisele was still soaking in a tub of hot water the efficient Avelaine had arranged to have waiting in their bedchamber, she broached the subject gingerly.

"What do you mean, is Ogier different in some way?" Brys responded, quirking a brow.

"I mean, is he...well, is he...I mean, most boys that age, of noble birth, do not live at home...." she said, hoping she would not offend Brys. "Is he not in good health, or somehow not of...sound mind...as he might be?"

To her surprise, Brys, who had bathed also and was drying himself, laid back his head and laughed. "Not of sound mind? Ah, that's rich, sweetheart! Nay, Ogier's mayhap a sight too sound of mind, if anything! He can speak four languages, including Latin, fluently, and can quote long passages of Homer—in the original Greek, of course. No, there's naught wrong with Ogier's mind! But your first guess was nearer right, he wasn't in good health at the time when he should have been sent out to be fostered. He had some sort of lung disorder in which he had wheezing attacks. But that seems to be getting better as he gets older, and so we have hopes of beginning his training when peace comes again to the realm, as long as..." His voice trailed off, and he looked troubled.

She wondered what he had been about to say, but had not. "Perhaps you can send him to Lord Alain and Lady Claire?" Gisele suggested, relieved that Ogier was not, after all, simpleminded.

"Yes, perhaps. We could trade boys, Guerin for

Ogier,'' Brys mused. "At least at Hawkswell, I know Alain would not allow other boys to torment Ogier for being older than they, yet behind them in their training. If only…''

"If only what?'' Gisele prompted, puzzled that he kept leaving his sentences incomplete.

"Oh, nothing. And don't worry about Avelaine,'' Brys told her. "She can be sharp and prickly, but 'tis just her way of testing you. She's too used to ruling the roost in my frequent absences. As my countess, you *are* the lady of Tichenden now, so bark back at her if she tries to snap and snarl.''

The thought of having to have a contentious relationship with Brys's sister filled her with dismay, especially if Brys was going to be gone.

"But Brys, she hates me! And 'tis not fair that being so long in charge, she should be deposed just because you have married—''

"Don't worry about her, my sweet Gisele,'' Brys murmured, bending over the tub and kissing her damp cheek. "She'll get to know you, and she'll grow to love you just as I do. Well, not *precisely* as I do…'' he said, as he seemed to grow distracted by the path a bead of water was making down the slope of her breast. "Ahhh, sweetheart, come to bed,'' he said, pulling her out of the water and enfolding her in a length of thick toweling. "Now that we have washed the stains of travel from us, I have a mind to pleasure you…''

"As your wife, my lord, I must be of the same mind,'' Gisele agreed, giving him smile she hoped was as seductive as his.

Chapter Twenty-Two

Once again, Brys was gone when Gisele opened her eyes the next morning. It seemed she was destined never to wake and find her husband still in bed beside her.

But this morning, that was perhaps just as well. She was not sure she could have met Brys's eyes and make ordinary, everyday conversation with him, so soon after the intimate things he had done with her last night. She had never suspected a woman could lose consciousness, even briefly, from the sheer intensity of the pleasure!

The little death, he had called it when Gisele had come to her senses, cradled in his embrace. Gisele blushed anew.

After she dressed, she went down into the hall, only to find her sister-by-marriage already bustling about, chivying a pair of serving women gathering up the remains of breakfast.

"Good morrow, Lady Gisele," Avelaine sniffed. "I have saved you some bread and wine," she said, pointing to it on the table, "for, apparently, we arise much earlier here at Tichenden than you are used to."

"Thank you." Gisele seated herself and reached for

the bread, determined not to respond to the needling. The sun had just barely begun to show itself over the horizon when she had opened the shuttered window in their bedchamber a few minutes ago, so 'twas not as if she were a slugabed! She noticed, without appearing to do so, that the ring of keys which Avelaine had worn at her waist had been left lying at Gisele's place at the table, by the cup of wine.

"Brys—?"

"My brother is already about his business about the keep." *As you would be, if you were as diligent,* her manner said. "There is much for the lord of a castle to do, when he is not always here."

"I'm sure that is so."

Silence reigned.

"Come," Avelaine said, while Gisele was still chewing the last crust of bread. "I will show you around the castle, so that you may assume your duties." She glanced meaningfully at the ring of keys.

Three hours later, they were just reentering the bailey after visiting a sick old woman in the village that hugged Tichenden's walls.

"You should go and see if the laundress has completed her tasks," Avelaine said. "She's a lazy creature if one doesn't keep after her."

"Yes, I'll do that," murmured Gisele, a bit out of breath after the pace Avelaine had set. She had seen every nook and cranny in the keep, including the sally port, the secret, hidden-on-the-outside exit from the castle, made for emergency use in case the castle was besieged. She had met every soul that lived there, from the steward to the potboy. She was certain she would never be able to remember all the things Brys's sister had told her about the castle's management. And she was nearly certain she couldn't recall how to find the laundress's workroom, but she wouldn't admit that to the competent Avelaine. And it would be peaceful to be away from the woman for a while.

But just as Gisele started to walk away, she heard Avelaine call out, "You there, squire!"

From the sheepish look on Maislin's face, Gisele guessed the young giant had spotted Avelaine before she had seen him and had been trying to steal away without being seen.

"Yes, Lady Avelaine?"

"Go and inform your lord the midday meal will be served in one hour."

Maislin inclined his head to show he had understood, but said, "My lord is speaking with his brother in the chapel, lady, and I would not disturb him. Besides, he sent me to—"

"Nonsense. I am sure he would appreciate the reminder," Avelaine said, making a gesture to indicate that Maislin should do as she said.

"But—"

"I'll inform him, Squire Maislin," Gisele said. She had wanted to meet Brys's younger half brother, the one who was the true heir to Balleroy and Tichenden, and yet they had not encountered him on their tour.

"But the laundress—" Avelaine protested.

"I will go to the laundress when I have seen my lord," Gisele said, her manner mimicking Avelaine's briskness. "Sister, why not have Maislin bring up that heavy cask from the cellar Cook said she needed brought to the kitchen? I'm certain 'twould be child's play for him—but you had better show him which it is."

To her relief, Avelaine responded to Gisele's command. "Come, Squire, I will show you the one...."

Gisele smiled to herself. She would have to apologize later to Maislin for throwing him to the lions...or more correctly, the lioness.

Brys faced the youth in the dim, candlelit chapel.

Ogier had grown at least three inches taller since Brys had last seen him, and was now within an inch or two of Brys's own height. He seemed all leg and wrist—gangly, like a colt. And pale—too pale for a boy who would soon have to be out in all weather learning to swing a broadsword.

"I'm sorry to disturb your prayers, brother, but I thought we should talk, and that we could be private here."

"There's no need to apologize, my lord brother," Ogier said. "I was going to come find you soon, in any case. I wanted to congratulate you upon your marriage—and meet your lady wife. I wanted to talk to you, too—but first I thought I had better pr— Never mind," he amended hastily. "'Tis good to see you."

"And you," Brys said, studying the boy, seeing traces of a beard shadowing the youth's cheeks. "You have been well? No more wheezing?"

Ogier shook his head. "It's been a year since that last attack. Avelaine says she thinks I'm done with that."

Brys let his relief show in his voice. "'Tis well, for I would speak to you of your future, Ogier."

The boy brightened. "Ah, the very same topic I wished to speak to *you* about, brother! You see, I am old enough now to choose what I want to do with my life."

"You will not need to chose, for it is time for you

to know the truth,'' Brys said, ''about what is properly yours, and the responsibility that goes with it.'' He cleared his throat, and felt the pounding of his pulse in his temples. ''I have been waiting until you were old enough—and healthful enough—to know what you should have been told from the cradle.''

Ogier looked puzzled for a moment, then put out a long-fingered hand. ''Wait, Brys. I've already decided what it is I must do. I want to go back to Normandy and—'' he began, but Brys was determined.

''Certainly you shall go back to Balleroy.''

''No, not to Balleroy, but to—''

''Hear me out. Brother, I have lived a lie for too long, and it has weighed upon my soul. You of all people should understand why 'tis important that I unburden myself,'' Brys said, nodding towards the prie-dieu at which Ogier had just been kneeling. He had moved the cushion, Brys noticed, so that he had been kneeling against the bare, hard stone.

''Certainly I would not have you carry the burden alone,'' Ogier said. ''But should you not seek out the priest?''

''Nay. You must hear this first, for 'tis you I have wronged—regardless of the fact that I did it at…at our father's behest,'' he said, stumbling over calling the man ''our'' father. ''Later, perhaps, I will confess to the priest—though he may already have known,'' he added, almost to himself.

''I…I don't understand,'' Ogier murmured. ''You've been the best of older brothers, and a good lord to Balleroy and Tichenden, always fair…''

''Thank you,'' Brys said, knowing Ogier would not think he had been the ''best of older brothers'' when he was done. ''But I am not the rightful lord. You are.''

Taking a deep breath, he began to tell Ogier about the bargain the late king had made with their mother, and how a barony had been given to Brys that he was not entitled to.

Gisele, standing in the shadows at the entrance, ached for Brys. How hard it must have been to admit what he had to his young half brother, knowing the consequences! She knew she ought to leave before either man or boy noticed her, but her feet felt rooted to the spot. She wanted to be there to comfort Brys and assure him he had done the right thing, especially if the youth reacted with anger and scorn.

Ogier, white-faced, backed away from Brys. "*No!* It can't be! I cannot be the Lord of Balleroy!"

"But you *are,* Ogier, and with all my soul I regret being a party to the deception our fa—*your* father, imposed on me. I now humbly ask your forgiveness, and will accept it if you banish me from your demesne."

"But no! You don't understand!" the boy cried. "I have always been glad, and felt *blessed,* that I was not our—my— father's heir! For I could look forward to a time when I could serve an eternal King, rather than a temporal one! I was just waiting to see you, Brys, before entering the monastery at Fontrevrault!"

Now it was Brys's turn to look horrified. "You—a monk? When you could be Baron of Balleroy? Nay, 'tis just that you never thought you were the heir! Think of it, brother—as a nobleman you have lands, castles! You can marry, have children—"

"All those things are blessings, but I have chosen a higher blessedness, Brys," Ogier explained in a patient voice. "I would prefer a life of prayer and service even if you told me I was the true *king.*"

"But stop and reconsider what you propose to throw

away! You have a duty to Balleroy, and to Tichenden! To our sisters!''

''No. I'm sorry, but I cannot accept my inheritance.''

''Do you fear to make me a poor landless knight? I can earn my living with my sword, Ogier, but even if that were not true, my lady wife is heiress to l'Aigle,'' Brys argued. ''So rest easy about that.''

''Nay, 'tis not that. And you know, even if I *had* decided to accept the barony, you would always be welcome at my hearth. Don't you see? I must do what I am called to do.''

Gisele could see Ogier's comparative calmness was maddening and frustrating her husband.

''Even if the consequence of your...ah, vocation, is that your sisters are now landless and penniless?'' Brys demanded, his voice becoming harsh. ''The church would own the Balleroy inheritance, isn't that so? What if none of them wanted to become nuns? It doesn't sound as if either of our younger sisters have a religious vocation, and you *know* Avelaine would not willingly take the veil! Yet what else would be left to her?''

From his astonished expression, it was clear that Ogier had not thought of that. ''I think the church would not insist I bring my entire inheritance as dower. I might endow them with Tichenden, and deed Balleroy to Avelaine.''

''Leaving her prey to every land-hungry scoundrel in England *and* Normandy!'' Brys snapped. ''While you chant prayers in peace and quiet? No, brother, that is *not* the answer!''

Ogier was silent for a long moment, during which Gisele could almost see the struggle taking place within the young man's soul.

''There *is* another way, brother,'' he said, coming

closer and putting his hand on Brys's shoulder. "We could leave matters as they have always been, with you as the heir, with no one the wiser."

"Nay—'tis not right!" Brys protested, his face anguished. "All my life I have been looking forward to the day when I could do right by you, Ogier—not continue in duplicity!"

"But I know the truth now, and I have made my choice. I give you back the barony freely. Brother, do not give me a burden for which I am unfit. *You* are the warrior, not me." He gave a short laugh. "Look at us," he said, stepping back and making a sweeping gesture, first at himself, then at Brys. "Perhaps I was molded by my sickliness, but I found myself, and my calling, in the midst of it. *My* pleasure has been prayer and study, all my life. Yours has been weapons and horses and the outdoors, Brys. You are married. I—I love and respect women, but I cannot imagine being tied in holy wedlock to one. How well do you think our sisters would fare with me as lord? Is it right to marry some innocent lady, when I would rather be a monk than get an heir on her?"

"I think you have not considered it long enough," insisted Brys. "I must leave on the morrow, but perhaps if you thought about it all day, and give me your answer before you retire tonight, you will change—"

"I will not change my mind, brother—not if I think about it all my life."

"*Ogier—*"

Brys's voice was full of pain, and Gisele knew it was time to come forward.

"He is right, Brys. Now that he knows the truth and still chooses the monastery, you must keep the title and its responsibilities,'' she said, stepping from the shadows.

Both man and boy gaped at the sight of her. "I'm sorry to have eavesdropped, my lord,'' she said. "I only meant to come find you, and to meet my brother-by-marriage. Hello, Ogier. I am Lady Gisele.''

The youth rapidly regained his composure, and came forward with a smile. "Welcome, my sister-by-marriage.''

Brys, however, was not ready to concede. "But surely 'tis wrong to—''

"My lord, forgive me again, but don't you see, 'tis for the greater good? Balleroy and Tichenden will prosper under your care, and your sisters will be safe, and Ogier will be where he is happy, where he belongs. Isn't that right, Ogier?''

"I could not have expressed it better. Welcome to the family, Gisele.'' Placing both hands on her shoulders, Ogier kissed her on both cheeks.

Brys sighed heavily. "But what of our sisters? Do they not have the right to know? *You* may choose to give up your inheritance, but what of them? Do we have the right to deny them that right?''

Ogier rubbed his chin and looked thoughtful. "'Tis a good question, and I confess I do not know the answer. I would be willing to pray and consider about that, brother, as you should, too.''

"I will,'' Brys said, raking a hand through his hair. "Faith, there are no easy answers, are there?'' He let the sentence hang on the air.

"Avelaine bid me tell you, my lord, that the midday m—''

Just then they heard the sound of running footsteps reach them, and all three of them turned to see a red-faced, panting Avelaine skidding to a halt at the chapel door.

"Avelaine! Brys has agreed to let me enter the mona—" Ogier began excitedly, but stopped because of the distressed look on his sister's face.

"What's wrong?" Brys asked.

"What's wrong? Your big gawking lout of a squire fell while carrying a cask up from the cellar, not only splitting open the cask, but breaking his right arm as well!"

Brys groaned. "Where is he? Take me to him."

They found him sitting in the bailey, his back against the inner stone wall, his face sporting a decidedly green cast. Avelaine had already splinted the fracture with a piece of wood from the shattered cask and strips of rag.

"I have sent for the priest, who is skilled at setting bones," Avelaine announced, "but it seems like a clean break—there are no bones sticking through the skin to cause a fever. With luck, it should heal fairly quickly."

"I'm sorry, my lord...." Maislin said to Brys, looking miserable.

"'Twas not your fault, Maislin," Brys assured the squire, but Gisele could see Maislin's dismay echoed in Brys's face. With his squire out of commission for several weeks while the bones knit, Brys would be going back into battle without his trusted squire.

The rest of the day passed all too quickly for Gisele, who could not forget it was the last one she would spend with Brys before he left to rejoin the empress— unless she made him see that he must take her with him. And so she lured him upstairs to their chamber in an effort to plead her case while he was hot to make love to her.

But even when they were naked and she could see that he was *quite* ready to love her, he remained adamant. "Nay, sweet Gisele. As much as I would have you with me, a besieged castle in the winter is no place for you to be."

"Winter?" she said incredulously. "Why, 'tis barely July!"

"I have done some thinking since you chose not to go with the empress," he said. "If Matilda stays in Oxford, where she is now, 'tis certain it will be encircled by Stephen's forces. The siege will almost certainly drag on through winter, if nothing changes," he predicted, his face grim. "I do not want you there, once they have slaughtered all the livestock and start eating the horses, then the rats."

"I would not have *you* there, either!" she retorted, desperate to make him see reason. "I love you, Brys! Stay with me! To perdition with all this fighting for who owns the crown, and the death and destruction that go with it!" she cried, feeling the tears streak down her cheek.

"Don't weep," he begged her. "Not now. I cannot keep the barony if I hold my honor so cheaply. I have to go. You are better off here with Maislin and my sister, with the garrison to watch over you. And if worse comes to worst, and anything happens to me—"

"'Anything happens?'" she echoed.

He nodded, unsmiling. "It's extremely unlikely, sweetheart, but if I should fall, from here you and my sister can more easily make your way to the coast and take ship for Normandy if need be, than if you were up at Oxford."

"No! I want to be with you! I don't care if we are besieged—I do not want to be here, while you face danger at Matilda's side! Let me come with you. I can serve as one of her ladies again. She will need me, too!''

''No, my mind is made up, wife,'' Brys said, his mouth set, but his eyes pleading with her to understand. ''And now, let us not waste this time we have together,'' he coaxed, caressing her face and throat in that way he knew she could not resist. ''I would plant a babe in your belly ere I leave....''

Chapter Twenty-Three

❧

"**Y**ou're not happy to be left behind, either, are you, Maislin?" Gisele inquired of Brys's glum-faced squire. She was trying very hard not to give way to tears, and sought to distract herself by talking to the disconsolate young giant. They stood in the gatehouse tower, watching as the tiny dot that was Brys on his warhorse gradually disappeared over the rolling downs.

"Nay," he growled, sticking his left hand into the sling on his right arm to rub his aching wrist. "'Tis humiliating to be left behind to guard the women, when I should be going into battle with my lord! Uh, not that I wouldn't willingly die for *you*, my lady," he hastily added, "but that gorgon of a sister of his is another matter! And who will watch over Lord Brys, and make certain he eats his supper, and has a dry place to lay his head? Who will disarm him after a battle?"

Gisele winced inwardly, for the squire's words mirrored her own worries. "I pray it won't come to actual fighting," she said carefully, "but I'm sure my lord will find someone to assist him. Though no one else would do as well as *you*, Maislin," she assured him. "But how much help could you be to him with a broken arm? He promised to send for you, once the bone has knit, assuming all goes well here. Besides, I'm sure Lady Avelaine is no gorgon,'' she said, trying to hide her smile at the comparison. ''I thought she looked rather pretty this morning in that plum-colored *bliaut,* did not you?'' Gisele had a sudden inspiration, and went on before Maislin could declare he had not noticed what Lady Avelaine wore, ''Do you know, I think she's softening toward you? Why, this very morn she told me she thought you had beautiful blue eyes.''

Maislin's eyes left the empty stretch of downland he had been staring at. ''Beautiful eyes? Lady Avelaine said *that* about *me?*'' He looked dumbfounded.

''That she did,'' Gisele insisted, amused at the success of her little white lie. At the very least, she hoped to make it possible for Maislin and Avelaine to tolerate one another. She did not want to spend all her days settling squabbles between Maislin and Brys's strong-willed sister. At best—who knew? She just knew she had to find a way to distract herself from her aching grief at being separated from Brys.

''Avelaine, I have a compliment to pass along to you,'' she said later, when she and Brys's sister were in the stillroom, working on a brew Avelaine claimed made a bone knit faster.

Brys's sister looked suspicious. ''A compliment? Something my brother told you before he left?''

Brys's only mention of Avelaine as he held Gisele in bed that morning had been to beg her to be patient with his sister, but of course Gisele didn't say that.

''Nay, 'twas not Brys who said it, but his squire,'' Gisele said, stirring the concoction.

Avelaine frowned. ''What could that overgrown oaf

have to say that I would want to hear?'' she grumbled. But curiosity lit her pale eyes.

''Maislin told me he thought you looked particularly pretty in that plum color,'' Gisele said, nodding at the *bliaut*.

Avelaine looked every bit as amazed as Maislin had, and Gisele had to take a deep breath to keep from laughing.

''I'm surprised he noticed aught, he was so busy pouting that he couldn't go off to war with my brother,'' retorted Avelaine, but her tone was softer.

But Gisele didn't want to think about Brys, who was heading toward danger without even his trusty squire at his side. ''Tell me again how this decoction speeds the healing of a fracture?''

Brys reached Oxford without incident, only to find Matilda preparing to march on Winchester.

''Brys! Where have you been, you knavish rascal?'' she demanded. ''Where is Lady Gisele?''

Briefly, Brys explained about their near-disastrous encounter with Geoffrey de Mandeville in the house in London, and how he'd taken Gisele on to Tichenden via Hawkswell.

''So that's what de Mandeville did after he fled the palace,'' was Matilda's grim comment. ''Too bad you *didn't* actually kill him! And how is dear Alain? So you left your bride at your castle on the downs? I'll warrant she wasn't happy about that, eh?''

Patiently, Brys answered the volley of questions one by one, hoping the empress wouldn't notice he did not comment about Gisele's happiness. His heart ached too much, remembering how his bride had tried not to weep when they had made their farewells. Pale as a wraith,

Gisele had bit her lower lip and blinked back tears, but she had handed him the stirrup cup and thereby done her duty as his wife.

"Hmmmph," Matilda snorted. "I wish you had brought Gisele. I miss the girl. I had to send that little baggage, Manette de Mandeville, off to a convent. Two months gone with some knave's bastard, she was, and bold as brass when she refused to confirm whose it was!"

Brys couldn't help but grin at the thought of the wanton Manette, her belly swollen with a babe, immured among nuns.

"A pity," he murmured. "Now, what's this about a march on Winchester?"

"That's right—you're just in time to join us, for we leave on the morrow. I've given Henry of Winchester time to repent of deserting me in London, and even sent my brother Robert to invite him back to my side, but my patience has run out. He's holed up in his castle there and we are going to smoke him out!"

Chapter Twenty-Four

The nights were the hardest, Gisele decided as July turned into August and then into September. During the day, she could keep herself busy with the myriad duties of the chatelaine of Tichenden. There never seemed to be enough hours to plan the meals and oversee the cooking, the soap and candlemaking, and the regular changing of the rushes on the floors. Then there was the sewing and the tending of the sick and elderly in the village.

The reeve made regular reports of what went on in the fields. In July, the rye and wheat had been harvested, then the barley and oats. Threshing came next, then the grain was ground into flour by the miller, and baked into loaves for the feast of Lammas.

Avelaine helped, of course, and though she always deferred to Gisele as the lady of Tichenden, Gisele had the feeling she was slightly surprised at Gisele's fatigue at the end of the day. She knew Avelaine could have managed everything herself much more easily, and wished Brys's sister had not been so insistent about giving her the chatelaine's keys. Brys would take her on to Balleroy some day, and she would have been quite content to leave Avelaine mistress of Tichenden.

"You're not breeding, are you, dear Gisele?" Avelaine asked with a warm smile one September afternoon as Gisele put down the garment she had been stitching to smother a yawn. "Oh, I hope you are. Would that not be a delightful surprise for Brys, to come home to find you great with child?"

Gisele smothered the groan that threatened to pass her lips. She had had her fluxes twice since he had left, so she had reason to know that Brys had not left his seed growing in his belly as both of them had hoped.

"Nay, Avelaine, I'm not breeding. I...I didn't sleep very well last night, that's all."

Avelaine clucked sympathetically. "Ah, that's too bad. You're missing my brother, aren't you? I thought as much. There are violet shadows under your eyes."

Gisele nodded. "I thought it would get easier. But as time goes on, it just gets harder." She thought of the many times she had dreamed of him, when she could swear she actually felt his hands on her...and the ecstasy of him thrusting inside her.... She had woken up, reaching for him, only to find she was alone in the big bed. How Manette de Mandeville would have laughed at Gisele, to hear that Brys had taught her the pleasures of lovemaking so thoroughly that Gisele could not now do without him!

But those dreams of passion were preferable to the nightmares, when she had dreamed of him, wounded and calling out to her, and jerked awake in a cold sweat, her heart pounding.

"We hear so little about what is going on," Gisele said. "I don't even know for sure where he is."

"That peddler told us the empress has gone to besiege the bishop in Winchester,'' Avelaine reminded her. ''I would say he's likely with Matilda.''

''Probably,'' Gisele agreed. ''But I worry so much about him—about whether he is safe, whether he is getting enough to eat....''

''You love him very much, don't you?'' Avelaine said, reaching a sympathetic hand out to touch Gisele's wrist. ''Yes, I can see you do. I'm very glad my brother took you to wife, Gisele.''

Gisele smiled back at her, touched. She had grown genuinely close to Brys's half sister in the months since her arrival. Avelaine had gentled, become less prickly, and in the process, her sharp-featured face had relaxed and actually become more beautiful. Was she just relieved to have shifted the burden of running Tichenden to Gisele's shoulders? Gisele didn't think so. Avelaine had enjoyed being mistress of the keep. No, it had to be something more than that....

A soft knock at the door made both of them look up.

''Hello, Maislin,'' Gisele said. And then Gisele noticed, out of the corner of her eye, the transformation of Avelaine's face.

Avelaine's greeting had been matter-of-fact, but her eyes had lit up. Her lips, which she had once held in a perpetually tight, firm line, were curving upward. Her face had become suffused with color.

Why, she loves him!

''Ladies.'' The young squire bowed. In the last week or so he had cast off the splint and sling he had worn on his injured arm, and it was that arm he used now to extend a folded, red-wax-sealed piece of parchment to Avelaine. ''A pair of Benedictines just arrived, traveling from Chertsey to another house of their order, and they brought a letter from Ogier.''

Shortly after Brys's departure, Ogier had told Gisele and Avelaine that he had learned everything Tichenden's priest could teach him, and had asked if he might go to study with the brothers at Chertsey. Avelaine had been initially resistant to his going. However, when Gisele told her that Brys had just given Ogier permission to follow his vocation, that day before Avelaine had run up to the chapel to tell them about Maislin's broken arm, Avelaine had given her blessing, too. And so Ogier had gone off to nearby Chertsey Monastery.

Avelaine pounced on the missive. "Oh, let's see what he has to say! Did the brothers tell how my brother fares? Is he well? Still growing an inch a month?"

"That he is, my lady," Maislin said with a grin.

"Have you sent for refreshment for the monks? Bid them stay the night with us?" Gisele asked.

Maislin nodded. "They look forward to thanking you at supper, Lady Gisele."

"Then read the letter aloud, Avelaine. I'm eager to hear it, too."

Gisele tried to listen, but she could not help but be distracted by the expression on the giant's craggy countenance as he watched Avelaine read Ogier's affectionate epistle. He had once avoided Brys's sister like the pestilence, but now he gazed at her with absolute adoration. *He was in love with her, too!*

Well, well! When had this come about? Had she been so busy with her duties as chatelaine—and so filled with longing for Brys—that she had missed the signs that her earlier attempts to achieve peace between Avelaine and the squire had blossomed into love?

She wondered how far their mutual fondness had progressed. Maislin was only a squire, and a year or two younger than Avelaine. Though he could rightfully expect to achieve knighthood some day—and a keep of his own when his father, the Baron of Andover passed on—he could not yet even call himself "Sir Maislin," let alone "Lord." And Avelaine was a baron's sister. Despite her obvious love for Maislin, would she consider being bound in wedlock with her brother's yet-unknighted squire a mésalliance? What would Brys think?

Hearing Avelaine reading the closing of the letter, Gisele decided to try a little experiment.

"We have some time before supper. Let us answer the letter, so the good brothers may take it back to Ogier," Gisele suggested.

"Oh, yes, let's do," Avelaine agreed enthusiastically, but neither she nor Maislin offered to fetch pen and parchment, though it would have been chivalrous of Maislin to offer.

"I'll go and get writing materials," Gisele said, rising, inwardly amused. Maislin did not mean to be discourteous—he was just blind to anything but the opportunity to be alone with the object of his adoration.

"Thank you, sister," Avelaine murmured, but her tone was distracted.

Gisele was careful, as she left, to leave the door of the sewing chamber slightly ajar.

She made sure she was gone much longer than it would have ordinarily taken her to go up the stairs to her room, locate quill, parchment, sealing wax, ink, and sand to dry the ink, then return. When she approached the sewing room again, she did so quietly, peering into the room without knocking to alert them of her presence.

What she saw was more than she could possibly have hoped for. In her absence, they had rearranged them-

selves so that now Maislin was seated with Avelaine in
his lap. Locked in an embrace, they were kissing with
passionate abandon. Avelaine's arms were around Maislin's neck, while his big hand cupped her breast, knead-
ing it to the music of her soft moans.

With infinite care, Gisele crept away from the door,
until she had returned to the stairway several yards
away. Then she made as much noise as she could, even
calling down the stairway to a nonexistent servant so
that even in the midst of their passionate frenzy, Avelaine and Maislin would hear her coming.

She could hardly smother her smile when she reen-
tered the room to find Avelaine with her stitching once
more in her lap, remote as a plaster madonna, while
Maislin stoked the coals in the brazier. Only the high
color in both their faces, and the tendrils that had escaped from Avelaine's always perfect plait, gave them
away.

Maislin soon excused himself to attend to other duties, and Avelaine did not even appear to notice his
going.

She and Avelaine had been sewing new *shertes* for
the men of Tichenden, who were given new garments
by the lord and lady of the castle every Christmas. Since
Gisele had been just one seam away from completing
the garment she had been working on when the letter
had arrived, she sat down and finished it, folding the
russet garment and taking it over to the oaken chest
where such things were kept.

When she lifted the lid, she caught sight of an edge
of heavy black cloth which showed beneath the folded
shertes Avelaine had already made.

Curious, Gisele pulled it out, and was startled when

a white wimple and scapular fell out of the folds of the black woolen gown. It was a nun's habit.

"How did this come to be here, Avelaine?" she asked, holding out the garments. She wondered briefly if the woman had once taken the veil, and then run away, but Avelaine's words soon dispelled that wild thought.

"Tichenden has always shown hospitality to travelers, as do most castles," Avelaine began. "Well, a few years ago, four nuns stopped here because one of their number was desperately ill of a fever after falling into a stream. She died here. This was her habit."

"But...did they not bury her in it?"

Avelaine shook her head. "The other nuns thought it was accursed, and buried her in her shift. That seemed like nonsense to me. She caught a chill because of her drenching, that was all."

"And you kept it?"

Avelaine shrugged. "I thought at one time to take the veil. I was younger and idealistic. I used to try on the habit, and imagine what it would be like. But Father relied on me to be his chatelaine, and so I lost interest in being a religious. I thought someday to put it back in the hands of some nun, if not those of her own house. But since the strife in England has made traveling so dangerous, it seems religious women have not been straying far from their convents, so I have not had an opportunity."

"I see," Gisele said, refolding the garment and replacing it back into the chest, saying an inward prayer for the nun who had died so tragically.

"What news of the outside world do you bring us, brothers?" Gisele inquired that evening, once she had seen the Benedictines' trenchers heaped with ham and venison, and had heard all they could tell her about Ogier. "Particularly, what is happening in Winchester? The last we heard, the empress was preparing to march against Bishop Henry there."

"The word is she has done so," the older of the two, called Brother Ambrose, said. "She was received into the city without incident, but her efforts to speak to the bishop were met with defiance by His Grace. He holed himself up in his castle of Wolvesey there, and sent out messages to Stephen's queen begging help, all the while raining down firebrands upon his own city!" The monk's face reflected his shock.

"Dear God," murmured Avelaine, while Gisele fought to suppress the surge of fear she had for Brys, who was in the midst of all this peril.

The younger monk, Brother Timothy, took up the story. "An entire nunnery was destroyed by fire, and the homes of many others, as well. There are many dead, and famine threatens the city."

"And Matilda's army? What of it?" Gisele breathed, faint with alarm.

The monks shrugged. The fate of the army whose presence had led to such misery, even if they did not cause it themselves, was obviously of little concern.

"The last we heard," Brother Ambrose said, "the queen and her Flemings were preparing to march to rescue the bishop, and capture the empress and her army."

Hardly knowing what she did, Gisele arose, and the room tilted. "I have to go to him!" she cried. "He may be wounded!"

Avelaine, with Maislin at her side, pressed Gisele back down into her chair. "Don't be foolish, sister. Going toward that chaos should be the very last thing Brys would want you to do, even if he *was* wounded—which isn't probable. He is a powerful, skilled warrior, and he has always been able to take care of himself. I'll wager he is even now guarding the empress from the consequences of her own folly!''

"Nay, I must go!" Gisele tried to rise again, but her dizziness, as well as Maislin's firm hand, held her down.

"I swore to protect you *here,* Lady Gisele," Maislin said, bending over her, his genial face set in unaccustomedly stern lines. "And protect you I will, even if it means locking you in your chamber."

"You forget yourself, squire," Gisele began with icy fury, then her anger dissolved. Avelaine and Maislin were right. She must have been crazed to consider riding across war-torn southern England, when Brys was probably as hale as she was!

"I'm sorry," she said, aware that the two monks were staring at her, obviously aghast at her outburst. "You needn't worry—I'll stay here. I just wish I could know where my lord is, that's all."

"We'll hear from him soon, I just know we will, Gisele," Avelaine told her, obviously relieved that Gisele had decided to be reasonable. "I worry about him, too, but the knight hasn't been born who can best my brother in battle!"

Gisele smiled weakly back at her. "I'm sure you're right, sister."

Chapter Twenty-Five

Brys came toward her, his arms extended, a smile of welcome on his face. His mail reflected the brilliance of the sun. He must have found someone to keep the rust from it, despite his lack of a squire, she thought, as she began to move toward him, already anticipating the feel of his arms around her and his kiss on her lips. Then she froze, seeing the flaming firebrand flying over the castle walls in a red-gold arc, heading straight for him. She screamed a warning. He had plenty of time to dodge the death-dealing missile, but he seemed deaf to her cries and oblivious to her pointing. She ran to him, determined to try to knock him out of the path of the firebrand, but she was not quick enough. The ball of flame descended, and caught the edge of his linen tunic that extended below his mailshirt, turning him in an instant into a human torch. She screamed....

Gisele sat bolt upright in bed, drenched in sweat. She was not at all sure if she had screamed out loud, or only in her nightmare, but the sound of it was still reverberating in her head.

Thank God, it had only been a dream. Or had it? Despite allowing herself to be persuaded at supper that

Brys was all right, was some sixth sense trying to convince her otherwise? Was the dream a warning? If she did not go to him, would what she had visualized come true?

Still trembling from the horrible images of the nightmare, she slid down off the side of the bed and wrapped a blanket around her shoulders. The hour candle had burned down only a little. It was probably midnight. She would visit the garderobe, then try to calm herself enough to fall back asleep. If only she could avoid any further nightmares...

Carrying the hour-candle to illuminate her way, Gisele pushed her door open and stepped into the corridor. The garderobe was at the end of it, just past Avelaine's chamber.

The corridor was chilly, for evening had brought rain, so she hastened, eager to be back in her warm bed.

She was just entering the garderobe when a sudden draft blew out her candle.

Plague take it! Ah well, there was no reason to be afraid of the dark. She needn't fear her bare feet encountering a spider on the stone floor of the garderobe, now that autumn had come.

She was just reentering the corridor, and drawing near to Avelaine's chamber, however, when the other woman's door opened.

Perhaps her sister-by-marriage needed to answer nature's call, too? But no, 'twas *Maislin* who was leaving the room, carrying a candle, which revealed his blanket-clad form, and his bare, hairy legs beneath.

She was so surprised she could not smother her gasp.

Maislin whirled, holding up his candle. *"Who's there?"* he demanded.

"Good even, squire. What do you here, coming out

of Avelaine's room in the dead of night?'' she asked, determined to be mistress of the situation. She rather thought the answer was obvious, but she wanted to hear Maislin explain himself. After all, she was Brys's representative here, and he would not have been pleased to find Maislin sneaking out of his sister's bedchamber!

A squeak inside the chamber told her that Avelaine had heard the exchange, and the rustling of the rushes heralded Avelaine's rushing to the door.

Shamefaced, Maislin nevertheless straightened and faced her. ''My lady, I would not dishonor my lord's sister. I know my station is less than hers—at present— but we love each other, and intend to marry. If my lord will give his consent, of course.''

All traces of her old hauteur gone, Avelaine chimed in, ''It's true, Gisele, I love him, and would wed no other. Please say you will intercede for us with Brys.''

As lord, Brys was in charge of Avelaine's life. He could give her in marriage to anyone he chose, whether she willed it so or not.

''No part of the blame should attach to Maislin,'' the other woman added. ''He did not seduce me. *I* bid him come to my bed.'' There was a flicker of defiance in her eye, but Avelaine's blush was evident even in the flickering candlelight.

''I see.'' Gisele did not think Brys would refuse his consent, but she could not help but feel a trifle piqued that while she had been worrying about Brys, these two had been falling in love! And tonight, when she had been tortured by a nightmare of Brys burning to death, Maislin and Avelaine had very obviously been coupling!

''I...I was just about to return to my room, Lady

Gisele. This will not happen again,'' Maislin was saying, his eyes still downcast.

Gisele did not say anything, but when she turned to go to back to her chamber, Avelaine put a hand out to stop her.

"This seems to be a time for honesty, so there is more you should know," Avelaine said, gesturing for Gisele to come into her chamber.

When Gisele had done so, Avelaine said, "Ogier spoke to me privately before he left for Chertsey, sister. He gave me a letter from Brys. In it, he told me the truth about his parentage."

Gisele stared at her. "Then you knew…"

"That the late king sired Brys?" Avelaine shook her head. "No. But we knew our father didn't sire him. Gisele, we—by that I mean myself and Brys's younger sisters—we've always known."

"You *knew?* About Brys? But how—"

"We could tell he wasn't anything like our father, either physically, or more importantly, in the sort of man Brys is—honest, loving, trustworthy…." She smiled. "We used to make up stories, we girls, about how he was a lost prince of Avalon. How little we knew about how close we were to the truth!"

Gisele smiled, too, but for a different reason. Since meeting Matilda, she had no illusions about royalty. They were only human, with as many sins as virtues. Brys was a good man because he had decided to be, not because of his blood.

The question had to be asked. "But how do you— and your sisters—feel about Brys having the title, knowing what you do? Especially now that Ogier is entering the monastery?"

"I've known for a long time that Ogier wanted to be

a monk,'' Avelaine said. ''It doesn't change how I feel—how all of us feel—about our brother Brys.''

Gisele noticed Avelaine didn't call him ''our half brother,'' just ''our brother.''

''He is still, as far as we're concerned, the rightful lord of Balleroy and Tichenden.''

''Oh, Avelaine—'' Overcome with emotion, Gisele fell into the other woman's arms, and they embraced.

Gisele's mind was made up.

She waited perhaps an hour, until she figured everyone was once again asleep; then, shod in a pair of Brys's old boots, with clumps of rag stuffed in them at the toes to make them fit, and clad in her chemise with the blanket once more clasped about her, she tiptoed down the stairs to the sewing room. There she knelt at the oaken chest, and with the candle's light shining into the chest, pulled out the Benedictine nun's habit.

Closing the lid and setting the candle upon it, she pinned her braid in a coil at the back of her neck with pins of bone she'd brought tucked in one of the boots, then put on the unfamiliar garb: the white scapular and wimple, the scratchy wool habit, and finally the rope girdle with the crucifix at one end. She left the rope sandals in the chest, however, reasoning that her cross-country journey on horseback required Brys's sturdier footwear rather than the humble footwear the Benedictine Rule dictated.

The writing materials had been left on the table in the room, so next she sat down and wrote a note of leavetaking to the two lovers:

To Avelaine and Maislin, greetings:
   By the time you find this note I will, God will-

ing, be far away. Now that I know you will be
content with each other, I am going home to my
father's castle at l'Aigle, being unable to bear this
constant worry for Lord Brys's well-being. Tell my
lord he can claim me there, if he so desires, when
his duty to the empress has been satisfied. Please
know I am happy for you, now and always. Love
is a blessing to be cherished.

Gisele

She was not, of course, heading for the coast to take
ship for Normandy. She had no desire to see her father,
now or ever again, but she'd never spoken of her lack
of love for him to Avelaine or Maislin, and she hoped
they would believe what she had written. She knew that
Maislin would be honor-bound to come after her, and
she hoped to throw him off her trail long enough that
he would not be able to prevent her from going to Brys.

She hoped that by wearing the garb of a nun, she
would increase her odds of reaching Winchester safely.
England was full of lawless men these days, but surely
she would stand a better chance wearing a nun's habit!

Praying the hounds slumbering among the rushes
would not bark and rouse the sleeping servants, she descended into the hall. One or two dogs got up and
sniffed her curiously, but recognizing her scent, lay
down again. The servants, however, continued to snore
on their benches and pallets in the rushes. From the hall,
she crept out to the bailey and tiptoed into the stable,
where she saddled her sleepy palfrey, Lark, and led her
quietly down the aisle between the stalls.

But the old groom was a light sleeper, and he had
heard even the slight noise she had made. Now he came
rushing at Gisele and the horse from the back of the

stable, crying, "Hey, wench! Stop there! Who are ye, an' where do ye think ye're takin' the lady's beast?"

Gisele held the candle directly under her chin, praying the elderly man was the superstitious sort. She knew it would cast a ghastly, distorting light upon her face.

"Who are ye to stop a ghost?" she demanded in sepulchral tones. *"Hinder me not...."*

She must have made a convincing shade, for the old groom's eyes grew wide, then rolled back in his head, and he collapsed at her feet.

The palfrey snorted and shied, pulling on her reins, but Gisele held them firmly while she knelt down in the dirt and felt for the old man's pulse at the side of his neck.

It bounded firmly, if slowly, back beneath her fingers. Good! He had only fainted. It would give her a little time to escape before the old man came to his senses and told the sentries he'd seen the ghost of the dead nun.

Leading Lark, she headed for the sally port, thankful that Avelaine had shown her where it was and how to unlock it. Moments later, she was beyond the walls, still leading the mare. She would mount Lark once the horse's hoofbeats would be out of earshot of the sentry on the wall walk, for the clouds had lifted, leaving a bright full moon to light the rolling countryside.

"We have been here six weeks, Domina," Robert of Gloucester reminded the empress. "My attempt to make peace between you and the bishop was futile. The queen's forces may soon make an attack we are unable to repel."

Matilda's shoulders sagged, and she stared at

Gloucester, seemingly unable to muster the spirit to assert that Stephen's wife was *not* rightfully the queen.

"We need to retreat now, while we may do so in good order," Brys urged, coming to stand by Gloucester.

Matilda sighed. "You may be right, Brys. I've had word today that Geoffrey de Mandeville, that arch turncoat, is riding at the head of an army to augment Stephen's forces."

Brys stiffened. "So he has recovered well enough for that," he snarled. "Mayhap I will get a chance to make sure he's dead this time, when we leave Winchester."

"We haven't men enough to take on de Mandeville or anyone else," Gloucester reminded him. "Hold on to your grudge, my lord—you may yet get the chance to send him to Hell."

Brys nodded grimly. He knew the other man was right, but it galled him to know that the man who had almost raped Gisele still drew breath—for now.

Matilda straightened, and once again her bearing was regal. "We shall leave on the morrow."

Gisele had been careful to stay on the main road, where it was less likely she would encounter outlaws. She had no wish to repeat the experience she had had in the Weald.

Just let me reach Winchester, and Brys, Gisele prayed, *and I vow I will never disobey him again, Lord. Or tell a lie.* She had been riding for three days, and after getting lost a couple of times, she was now but two miles from Winchester. Her thighs and buttocks ached from the hours in the saddle. Her skin itched from the friction of the rough wool habit, giving her a new respect for those who chose the religious life and lived in such uncomfortable garments the rest of their lives.

Thus far, her disguise as a nun had stood her in good stead. Avoiding religious establishments, where her story might be scrutinized too thoroughly, Gisele sought refuge at night with poor folk, who took her story at face value.

But she had become weary of the lie. Last night, she had taken shelter with a charcoal burner and his wife, who shared their humble supper of raw onions and coarse bread with her. They had questioned why a Benedictine nun was traveling by herself, of course, and she had started to tell them the story she had prepared of how her small convent had been attacked by Flemish mercenaries, and she alone had escaped. Something about the honest concern in this couple's faces, however, made it impossible to repeat the lie.

"Dame Mary Agnes," the man said, using the name she had given him, "Ye left a keep where ye were safe, and rode all this way by yerself, simply because of a dream?" The peasant's face showed just what he thought of such foolishness.

"Aye, because she loves her man, Alf," his wife had countered, her worn face creased by a grin that revealed several missing teeth. "And you told me lords an' ladies never felt naught fer one another!"

The memory of the conversation made her smile now as she came to a bend in the road, and urged her palfrey into a trot.

She saw them too late—perhaps a score of men crouched behind a coppice of oak.

"*You there! Halt!*" cried a man in mail, running out to the road, accompanied by a man-at-arms.

She thought of ramming her heel into her mare's side

and trying to outrun them, but only for a moment. Something about the crossbow bolt that was aimed directly at her chest by the narrow-eyed man in a boiled-leather *byrnie,* standing behind the man addressing her, persuaded her that she would not get far.

"I am Lord de Warenne, sister. Where are you bound?"

De Warenne—a nobleman firmly on Stephen's side, she remembered.

"I am Dame Mary Agnes, infirmaress of the Wherwell Convent," she said, thinking fast. "I—I need to get to Winchester, to succor the sick and wounded there. Let me pass."

"No one wants to get *into* Winchester these days, sister. They're all trying to get out, even the nuns, after their convent burned," said the knight. "But as for you, I thought nuns never left their convents alone." He glanced downward, at her feet.

Too late, she realized her position in the sidesaddle revealed nearly the full length of her most un-nunlike footgear.

"I...we were set upon by brigands, who did not care about our habits," she lied. "My...sisters and the abbess were was killed. I lost my sandals, and these," she said, pointing at the boots, "were given to me by a charcoal burner, a good man and devout. I pray you, let me go and tend those who need my care."

"If you are skilled in nursing, sister, there will be wounded in plenty right here, and soon," the nobleman retorted. "My scouts inform me the empress's party has left Winchester and is heading this way. We intend to capture them, and no doubt they will attempt to resist. So I think you had better plan to stay here and do your nursing."

"Nay!" she cried. She *had* to get away, to ride and warn the empress and her escort they were riding into an ambush! Brys would be among them! "You must let me pass! I have not come this far to nurse soldiers, but the innocent, who never did anything to bring this miserable war about!"

"I'm afraid I cannot do that, sister," the man said regretfully, taking hold of her palfrey's reins. "I cannot take the chance that you will feel it necessary to warn the enemy!"

"I am a religious, and therefore neutral. I won't speak to anyone!" she protested. "Let go of my horse!"

De Warenne had apparently tired of arguing with her. "Get her off the road, and off her horse," he ordered the soldier. "Tie her up and gag her."

Gisele shrieked and drummed her heel into Lark's side, praying the palfrey would rear and make de Warenne lose his hold on her reins, but the nobleman had taken a firm hold of them near the bit and held on like a limpet. Out of the corner of her eyes, Gisele saw men running out to the road to help him, and knew she was not going to be able to get away.

The next thing she knew, she had been unceremoniously hauled off the palfrey, thrown over the soldier's back like a sack of meal, and carried off towards the trees. De Warenne handed the reins to another man-at-arms and was following the soldier carrying Gisele.

"Let go of me, you misbegotten knave, you beast!" she cried. "Or I'll—I'll *excommunicate* you!" Over her shoulder, she saw that Lark had managed to struggle loose and was now galloping willy-nilly down the road in the direction of Winchester. Why couldn't the palfrey have done that while she was still on her back?

"Tsk, tsk, sister. Such language!" de Warenne, who had followed along, admonished her. "I begin to doubt your devoutness—"

Another man, also mailed, laughed as he approached them. "You do well to doubt, de Warenne. I caught a glimpse of her face while you were talking, and I can tell you she is no nun. If you pull off her veil, I'll wager you'll see she is not shorn, as a proper nun would be."

Gisele froze at the familiar, hated voice—and looked up into the face of Geoffrey de Mandeville.

"Put her down," he ordered the soldier, who complied, dumping her on the ground as if she were indeed a sack of meal.

Slowly, almost as if he expected lightning to strike him because of his daring, de Warenne complied, leaning over to pull off the black veil, revealing her knot of chestnut hair behind the tight wimple.

"See? I told you she was no nun."

Desperately, clambering to her feet, Gisele cried. "I am *too* a nun! I just haven't taken vows yet!"

But a novice would not be wearing the same black veil as a professed Benedictine, and apparently de Warenne knew it, as well. He looked at her with eyes that were now full of doubt.

"You speak as if you know her, my lord," de Warenne said. "Who is she?"

Geoffrey de Mandeville smiled at her, an evil glint in his narrowed eyes.

"Lady Gisele de l'Aigle...my former mistress," he said in silken tones. "Did my rejection of you put you in such despair, my dear, that you went into the convent?"

"You know very well it did not," she snapped at him. "I was *never* his mistress," she said, addressing de Warenne. "Though he tried twice to force himself upon me. I am the wife of one of the empress's most loyal vassals."

"Ah, yes, Lord Brys de Balleroy, that traitor," de Mandeville purred. "You have heard of him, my lord? How the queen has put a price upon his head? The odds are good he will be with the empress when we capture her. Whoever takes him will be a rich man." The glitter in his eyes seemed to indicate he wanted to be that man.

His words sent a spear of ice into Gisele's heart. Had she come this far, only to see Brys taken and executed?

De Warenne's expression reflected distaste as he faced the Earl of Essex for a moment, then addressed the soldier, "Go tie her up, as I said. Place her in my tent. If we stand out here wrangling until the empress's party arrives, they'll get away."

Chapter Twenty-Six

As they rounded a curve in the road, Brys caught sight of the riderless horse coming at them at a gallop. "Where did that horse come from? Where's its rider? I don't like it—something's wrong, my lord," he muttered to Gloucester.

"Yes...possibly," Robert of Gloucester agreed, shading his eyes to watch the horse approach. "What do you suggest, Brys?"

"Get the empress out of sight, off the road. We'll keep going, and if there's nothing up ahead, we can come back for her."

Gloucester nodded, and turned to Matilda. "Domina, 'tis a good idea. They may be lying in wait for us up the road, and perhaps that horse bucked off its rider and got away from them."

"Nonsense, 'tis a lady's palfrey," Matilda said, also watching the horse. "We should press on."

Just as he was about to argue with her, the horse neared, and Brys felt a sickening jolt within as he identified the bay mare with the distinctive white star on her forehead.

"Wait—'tis my *wife's* palfrey!" he shouted, catching

Lark by her flapping rein as the mare skidded to a halt.
The mare had apparently recognized Brys's destrier Jerusalem, and was willing to be caught. "What can she
be doing he—"

But he never got to complete his sentence. Men-at-
arms erupted from behind the hedgerows on both sides
of the road, while mounted knights charged at them
from seemingly out of nowhere.

"Take the empress and run for it!" Brys shouted to
Brien fitzCount, who was riding closest to Matilda,
while he unsheathed his sword. "We'll stay to slow
them down!"

They could do no more than that, Brys had recognized at once. Even if all the empress's party stayed to
fight, they were vastly outnumbered, and many of the
knights and lords riding farther back were already
wheeling their horses to flee.

It was over in a few minutes. When Brys came back
to consciousness—he had never seen the blow that had
felled him from Jerusalem's back—the ground was lit-
tered with Gloucester's men, dead and dying, as well
as shields and weapons. He couldn't see Matilda or
fitzCount anywhere—pray God they had gotten safely
away. Flemish mercenaries were flinging jewel-studded
cups and priceless ornaments from the baggage wain.
At least, Brys thought, Matilda had had sense enough
not to cling to her valuables.

He recognized Robert of Gloucester being led off the
road in chains. So he had been taken alive. Thank God
for that, too.

Brys tried to bring his arms around to push himself
off the ground, and found that they were tied.

"So, you've come to your senses. Who are you?"

inquired a voice, and Brys looked up to see a man in mail standing over him.

"Who're you?" Brys countered in a voice that was little more than a croak.

"Lord William de Warenne."

"Brys de Balleroy," he responded. He'd never met the man before, but he seemed a straightforward sort. His head ached abominably, and a gash in his forehead stung as sweat dripped into it.

"I see. The Earl of Essex thought you might be among the empress's party," the other responded.

So, Geoffrey de Mandeville was here. De Warenne might not know Brys had been pretending to be on Stephen's side, but de Mandeville would make sure he did not remain in ignorance long. He felt the first flickering of despair. Gloucester might well be ransomed, but de Mandeville would see that Brys paid with his life.

Another man had approached, a figure Brys knew all too well.

"I have de Balleroy," de Warenne said shortly.

"Excellent!" de Mandeville crowed. "Her highness will be so pleased when I bring her his head!"

Brys shuddered. He only hoped he would die bravely, when the time came.

"Come with me," said the other, helping Brys to his feet while de Mandeville held his sword at the ready. "There is someone in my tent who will undoubtedly want to see you before you die."

Brys felt bile rising in his throat, knowing, even before de Warenne pulled back the tent flap and bid him enter, that it would be Gisele. He was going to die, and then Gisele would be helpless against Geoffrey de Mandeville.

At first, seeing the Benedictine-robed female figure,

he thought there must be some mistake, or the enemy's attempt at a jest. And then he saw that the face framed by the white wimple was indeed Gisele's.

Gisele's face went chalky when she looked up and saw Brys stumbling into the tent, followed by the two enemy noblemen. She jumped to her feet—awkwardly, because her arms were tied behind her back also.

She ran to him, gazing up into his face. "Brys! You're *wounded!*" she cried. "My husband is hurt, my lord! Bring me water, and bandages!"

"Don't bother, my fair one," de Mandeville said in his oily voice, coming forward from behind de Warenne. "He'll be dead soon enough, and it won't matter then if his face is clean or not."

"Did you hurt him, you misbegotten churl?" she said, and spat right into his face.

De Mandeville purpled, then lunged at her.

"My lord! We do not make war on women!" the other nobleman shouted, catching him by the hood of his mail shirt and yanking him backward.

De Mandeville shot a resentful look at de Warenne, then snarled at Gisele, "No, I'm not the one who marred his pretty face, for if *I* had been the one to un-horse him, I would have gutted him like a fish and left him to die. I may do that yet, but don't worry—I'll let you watch. And while he's dying, his last sight can be that of me violating you."

"There'll be time enough to plan how he's to die later," de Warenne snarled. "Come with me, de Mandeville. We have to decide what's to be done with Gloucester, until the empress agrees to exchange him for the king." He pushed de Mandeville out of the tent, then leaned back in and said to Gisele, "I'm afraid it will be necessary to bind his legs as well," he said apologetically, "but I'll send water and bandages, Lady de Balleroy."

"What...what about a priest?" Brys croaked. "I'm not to be put to death without being shriven, am I?" He didn't doubt de Mandeville would have denied him the opportunity to confess his sins, but de Warenne seemed like a fair man.

De Warenne's words dashed his hopes, however. "Sorry. We have no priest with us. I'm afraid the only consolation I can offer you is the company of your lady wife."

It would be enough, Brys thought, as a pair of men-at-arms came into the tent, and tied his legs together at the ankles. At least he could kiss her, even if he could not hold her.

Gisele's face, when they were alone again, was awash in tears. "They can't kill you, Brys! Not when I've come so far to find you!"

He shook his head sadly, wishing he could put his arms around her to comfort her, and be comforted by her. He'd gladly trade an extra hundred years in purgatory for the joy of embracing her once more.

"Yes, I'm afraid they can," he told her. "They don't ransom those they see as traitors."

"But you can't just tamely accept your fate!" she blazed at him. "One of us has to get loose, and free the other! Then we'll wait till they've gone to sleep..." She struggled against her bonds, but when it was clear she couldn't budge the knots, she turned panic-tinged eyes to him.

His heart sank. He could not do any better, for whoever had bound him while he lay unconscious had done his job well, even winding the rope around his hands so he could not work on the knots that bound Gisele.

"I'm sorry," he told her, turning so that she could see how he was bound.

Her shoulders sagged.

He had a sudden thought. "Where's Maislin?" Surely his squire was out there somewhere, and had somehow escaped capture. She could not have gotten this far without him, surely! Even now, he was probably trying to find a way into the camp to liberate them!

Or if not both of them, at least Gisele. If he knew she would be safe, Brys thought, he could die in peace.

She looked down at her black wool-swathed knees. "He's probably somewhere between Tichenden and the coast, trying to find me. I…I slipped out of Tichenden in the dead of night, leaving a message that I was going home to l'Aigle."

For a moment he could say nothing, so amazed was he at Gisele's temerity.

"I…I'm sorry, Brys," she said, "but I had to come to you. I'd had this dream, you see…I just could not wait tamely at Tichenden, thinking I could have saved you…. 'Twas foolishness—I see that now."

He could not be angry, not now, however much he wished she'd obeyed him. "No…you did it for love." He tried to lighten the atmosphere. "But did you have to take holy vows, just to get to me?" he asked, nodding at the black habit.

She gave him a wan smile, shaking her head. "You remember that nun who died at Tichenden? Avelaine told me about her when I found the habit in the sewing room chest. I dressed as a Benedictine so I could travel more safely."

He could almost weep at her naiveté. Luck—and a legion of angels—must have been with her, at least until she had gotten here.

Silence fell between them for a space, while beyond the tent, the sounds of revelry increased. Men were celebrating the victory by drinking deeply, as armies always had. He heard laughter—womens' as well as men's. It seemed a camp full of soldiers was never without its whores.

"I...I have news from Tichenden, Brys," she said. It was an obvious attempt to distract him, but he was willing to be distracted. "Happy news. At least, I hope you will approve." she said. "Your sister and Maislin...have fallen in love."

She had succeeded in distracting him, right enough!

"*Avelaine?*" he repeated incredulously. "My fire-breathing dragon of a sister has fallen in *love?* With *my squire?*"

She laughed in genuine amusement at his reaction. "I was surprised, too, my lord, but—"

Then he thought further. "*That young whelp didn't seduce her, did he?* By God, if he's dishonored her..." His voice trailed off as he realized he was not going to be in a position to enforce anything. "I'll haunt him," he concluded, and saw her blanch at the implication.

"No, my lord...'twas not like that...exactly," she said. "If anything, 'twas the other way around. But I believe his intentions are honorable. Please say you will approve of their marriage."

He sighed. "If that's whom she wants. God send he finds a new lord who can see him made a knight, then. Maislin and my sister—who would have thought it?"

"They seem genuinely happy, Brys. She's become softer, prettier, even... Oh, and she told me something, before I left that night—she knows about your father, Brys. Your *true* father. Your sisters all do. And none of them wants to change anything. They still want you to be the lord.''

He was still digesting that startling news when she added, ''Oh, and I allowed Ogier to go continue his studies at Chertsey. It seemed best—''

Just then Gisele was interrupted by a soldier entering the tent, carrying a bucket of water, a folded length of toweling and some rolled-up strips of linen.

''The water you requested, my lady,'' he said, bending over to lay them at her feet. Then he straightened, and seemed about to leave the tent.

''But...how can I use these things, if my hands are tied?'' Gisele asked the man. ''Surely you could untie me long enough to do that? I understand you must stand guard over me while I do it....'' she added, her eyes full of appeal.

The man's stolid face remained unmoved.

''My lord de Warenne said naught about untying you, my lady. But he bid me tell you—'' he turned to include Brys ''—that his sister was once despoiled by de Mandeville.''

''But what has that to do with anything?'' she cried. ''How can I cleanse my lord's wounds with my hands tied?''

''I don't know, my lady. I can only do as much as I am ordered, no more.'' Then he turned and left the tent.

Brys was as frustrated as Gisele, but mystified, too. Why had de Warenne said that about his sister? He was not surprised that the Earl of Essex had molested other women, but why had he felt it was important for them to know? Unless...

''Gisele,'' he said, hope blossoming in him like the frailest flower in a snowbank, ''can you somehow unfold the towel?''

"But why..." Something in his eyes, however, must have given her reason enough, for she bent over and bit into a fold with her teeth, unfolding the towel, *until a short, bone-handled dagger fell out.*

Chapter Twenty-Seven

"**W**hy?" was all Gisele could think to say. "Why would de Warenne give us this?"

Brys's voice was charged with hope. "Don't you see? He heard de Mandeville threatening you, and he told the soldier to say that *de Mandeville had despoiled his sister.* He's giving us a chance to escape, out of revenge!"

Gisele eyed the dagger dubiously. "But how..." She couldn't see how it was going to do them much good, if both of them were still tied up. And then she knew.

It would take some doing, and she prayed they'd have enough time. One of them would have to take the knife in his teeth—blade-outward, of course—and saw through the other's bonds.

Brys had obviously come to the same conclusion. "Turn around, sweetheart," he said, attempting to kneel, so he could pick up the dagger as he'd said.

But the rope around his ankles made it difficult to kneel and reach the dagger.

"Nay, 'tis better that I cut through *your* bonds first," Gisele told him. "That way, your hands will be free to fight if anyone comes through that flap." She didn't say what they were both thinking, that if Stephen's noble-men decided to interrupt their revelry long enough to execute Brys, it was unlikely they would send just one person to escort him to his death. "Besides, my legs aren't tied and I can at least run that way, if need be."

Kneeling, Gisele bared her teeth to pick up the knife. She had several false starts, and got more than a few particles of dirt in her mouth in her attempts to bite into the blade without it cutting her mouth, but at last she had it firmly grasped between her teeth with the blade out, and began sawing at Brys's ropes.

Outside the tent, the sounds of revelling grew louder.

The minutes ticked by and the sweat trickled down past the white bands of the wimple as she moved her head back and forth, sawing at the rope. Her jaws ached from clenching her teeth for so long. Once, she dropped the dagger and had to get it repositioned in her mouth again; another time, she slipped and accidentally nicked the tender skin of Brys's wrist.

He winced as the sudden pain surprised him.

"Sorry, love," she tried to say, but with the knife clasped between her jaws, it came out as gibberish.

He understood, though. "Don't worry about it, sweetheart. Just keep at it."

His encouragement wasn't necessary. She knew they could be interrupted at any moment. But finally, the thick rope was beginning to visibly fray beneath the blade, spurring her on.

It seemed like a year until the last strand of the thick knot finally gave way, and then Brys was able to shove off the coils of rope that had bound the fingers of his right hand, then the left.

Eagerly he took the knife from her, and sawed at the bonds at his ankles, making short work of it. "Now you,

Gisele,'' he said, and she turned so he could begin to free her, too.

Suddenly they heard the sound of footsteps outside the tent. Before they could hide the knife and put their arms behind them as if they were still tied, a man-at-arms came through the tent flap, carrying a covered bowl.

''My lord de Mandeville said I was to bring ye yer last meal, my lord, and feed ye too, since ye're tied. It's only pig swill, but—''

There was a blur of motion as Brys dropped the dagger and grabbed the bucket of water that had been left in the tent, flinging it with full force into the man's head. Icy water flew everywhere, splashing Gisele.

When her vision cleared, she could see the man sprawled at her feet, clearly unconscious.

''I don't know how long he'll be that way,'' Brys whispered. He went back to slicing through the ropes binding Gisele's hands, saying, ''Too bad it wasn't de Mandeville—I'd have gladly slit his throat. But that soldier doesn't deserve to die.''

She was touched by his basic decency. Most noblemen hardly saw a foot soldier as human, let alone a life worth saving—though she knew Brys would not have hesitated to kill the man if it had been necessary for their survival.

A minute later, her hands were free, and she was chafing her wrists, feeling them tingle and burn as the blood rushed back into her fingers.

Brys bent to peer under the edge of the tent. ''There seems to be no one nearby. Come—we'll run for the trees straight ahead, and then we'll see what to do from there.''

The night air was chilly as they crept through the

darkness, keeping low. A few yards away, a dozen or so men-at-arms sat around a blazing fire. Some of them had women, their bodices pulled open, lolling on their knees. A couple of the soldiers were roaring a drunken song while the others laughed at them.

Lights shone within tents beyond the fire. Doubtless Stephen's lords were in them, celebrating their victory, too.

When they reached the relative safety of the oak coppice at the edge of camp, Brys turned around and stared at the tents.

"If only I knew which one Robert of Gloucester was in," he muttered.

Gisele understood. He wanted to free the important nobleman, not only for his own sake, but so Stephen's lords would not be able to exchange him for their king. But heroic as the impulse was, trying to rescue Gloucester without having any idea where he was held would be suicidal for Brys. And his death would leave de Mandeville to do his worst to Gisele.

He sighed. "I won't take chances with your safety, Gisele. Perhaps there will be another time to free Robert, once we have rejoined the empress's forces...." He shrugged. "But if not, I'm fairly sure they won't harm him. He's worth too much alive."

She said nothing, wishing he didn't have to make such a choice, but relieved that he was not going to risk himself further. At this moment she did not give a fig for what Gloucester's capture would mean to Matilda's cause. She just wanted Brys to be safe.

Once the decision was made, however, Brys did not seem inclined to look back. "I wish we dared steal some horses," he said, staring now at the picket line to which all the horses had been tethered. "But there's too much chance they'd whinny and alert the soldiers."

"Lark isn't there," Gisele murmured. "I last saw her galloping down the road toward Winchester." She'd miss her. The mare had been foaled at l'Aigle and she'd been Gisele's ever since.

"I'll get you another palfrey, Gisele," Brys said, speaking against her hair as he held her close.

She leaned into him, glad of his warmth. "I...I don't see Jerusalem either, do you?"

"Nay. I don't remember anything after they knocked me off him—perhaps he's wandering around loose somewhere, too. But we'd better get going before they miss us."

After widely skirting the camp, they started walking up the road away from Winchester, alert for every sound that might indicate pursuit. But none came, at least in their direction.

Just as the sun rose, they came upon Jerusalem and Lark, grazing on the lush downland grass together, as contented as if they had been back at Tichenden.

At the end of October, Brys and Gisele finally found Matilda at Gloucester, where she'd eventually gone after fleeing Winchester.

"'Tis good to see you both safe—though I thought you had left your bride safe at Tichenden?" Matilda said, coming toward them in the great hall. "That *was* the plan, was it not, my lord?"

Brys smiled as he brought Gisele forward with him. "'Twas *my* plan," he said. "My lady had another."

Matilda chuckled. "And a better one, evidently," she said. "Just look at them, my lord," she said to Brien fitzCount, who stood by her. "I'm told they've been chasing all over western England after me, and neither has ever looked better. Particularly *you,* you knave,'' she said to Brys.

Brys grinned. "I would say 'tis my joy at rejoining you, Domina—and I *am* happy we find you safe as well—but truth be told, my lady just told me this morn that I'm to be a father," he said. "Such news does impart certain prideful glow, I imagine."

"Indeed," Matilda responded. "Congratulations, my lord, Lady Gisele. So you could not bear to be parted from your rascal husband, eh?"

Gisele blushed. "No, Domina," she admitted, then added, "I...I would wish to be one of your ladies once more, though, while my lord serves your cause."

Matilda's brow furrowed. "I would love to have you attend me, Lady Gisele, but as your lord cannot serve me in England at present, I don't think I can give you your wish, at least for a time."

"Domina, what are you saying?" Brys cut in. "I cannot serve you in England—why?"

Matilda turned to Brys. "You seem to be a marked man, my lord, now that the Countess of Boulogne and all of Stephen's men now know that you are no true adherent of Stephen's. The Earl of Essex, in particular, seems to want your head on a platter."

"No more than I want his," Brys growled. "Give me the chance to punish him for his treachery to you— as well as to my lady."

"He'll pay for his crimes, eventually, Brys. Such men always do. I've no doubt he will prove as untrustworthy to Stephen as he has been to me. But since you would be executed, not ransomed, if you were taken, Brys, I'm sending you to Normandy."

"But—"

Matilda raised a regal hand, halting Brys's objections. "You *and* your wife are going, and I'll hear no arguments," she said firmly. "You are dear to me, Brys, and I don't want anything to happen to you, especially not now that your lady is with child. But do not fear, I'm not merely exiling you to Balleroy. I have a job for you to do in Normandy—not unlike the role you played for me here in England."

Brys darted a look at Gisele, and she managed a surreptitious shrug. She had no more idea what the empress had in mind than he did.

"It can be no secret that Count Geoffrey of Anjou, my husband, and I do not...ahem!...get along very well," Matilda said, smiling ironically at the understatement. "Our mutual...ah, disinterest...often results in poor communication." She took a deep breath. "I have not seen my heir, Henry, or my other two sons, in some time. I wish to know how they fare—in much more detail than the dry letters Geoffrey sends infrequently. That will be *your* job, Lady Gisele."

"My job?" Gisele echoed, surprised. She thought the empress had been telling Brys what she wanted *him* to do.

"Yes, yours. I want to see my sons through your eyes—the eyes of another mother, my dear—while your wily husband keeps *his* eye on Geoffrey." She turned back to Brys. "Geoffrey does not always tell me about what he's doing in my duchy until long after the fact. I want you to go and serve as an official liaison between my husband and me, Brys. Fight alongside him if Stephen's allies in France threaten Normandy—but *keep me informed as to what's really happening,* not just what Geoffrey says is happening. And of course, let me

know when my godson—or goddaughter—is born,"
Matilda said, including Gisele in her last words.

"Of course, Domina. We are honored," she said.
Their child would have a royal godparent! And sending
them to Normandy on this dual mission was the perfect
solution, Gisele thought, as she bowed her head in obedience.

But would Brys think so? Would he resent being sent
away from the thick of the action?

She looked up, only to see him gazing at her, love
shining from his eyes before he turned back to the empress. "Your wish is my command, Domina. And since
my beloved will be with me, it will also be my very
deepest pleasure to obey."

Gisele sighed, knowing Heaven could not afford any
more joy than she felt at this moment.

"Oh, and rest easy about your keep at Tichenden,
Brys, while you are across the Channel," the empress
added. "I have agreed to exchange Stephen's freedom
for Robert's. I will make a condition of my agreement
that Stephen agrees to leave Tichenden unmolested."

Brys's smile broadened. "Thank you, Domina! My
cup runneth over, it seems! But if I might beg one further boon, since Tichenden will be safe, could you add
a letter of safe conduct for my squire and my sister to
join us in Normandy? It seems my squire has made my
sister fall in love with him, and I would see them wed,"
he said, with mock ferocity. "And if he's ever to be
more than my squire, I need him back at my side, in
any case."

Matilda raised her arms in surrender. "All right, all
right! I never thought I'd see the day when you settled
down in wedded bliss, my lord. And *you,* Gisele! I
know you were reluctant to marry Brys when I ordered

you to—and now look at both of you! Plotting to tie others up in the bonds of matrimony!''

Brys and Gisele exchanged a look of perfect understanding. "Indeed, Domina," she said. "We can think of nothing better to do."

Brys leaned over and whispered in Gisele's ear.

Blushing furiously, she turned back to the empress. "If Your Highness will excuse us?"

Matilda watched as they left the hall. "Brien," she said wistfully to her trusted lord and friend, "I think Brys just thought of something better for them to do."

Epilogue

Normandy, December, 1141

She didn't know why she had let Brys convince her to accept the old man's invitation, not when she would have so preferred to spend this, their first Christmas as man and wife, together at Balleroy.

"Welcome, and thank you for coming to keep Christmas with me," the old man said simply. "No doubt they celebrate more lavishly at court...."

Why, he's aged ten years in the few months I've been gone, Gisele thought, seeing her father clearly as he tottered toward them, leaning heavily on the arm of his seneschal. *And when did he shrink so?* She remembered him as taller than that, more formidable, a man who made his serfs—or his daughter—cringe when he raised his voice.

And what had happened to the gleam of disdain that had always been in his eyes when he looked at her? It was entirely gone now. Instead, there was an expression of simple interest on his face as he studied his daughter and the man at her side.

"So this is your husband, daughter?" he asked, while smiling approvingly at Brys.

He had never called her "daughter" before. There had been affection in the quavery voice, Gisele realized with a start of surprise, before her old wariness made her analyze his words again.

Ah, so that's it. I have a husband now, so I am finally worthy of his respect, she thought bitterly. Aloud she said, in cool, controlled tones, "My lord father, may I present Brys, Baron of Balleroy?"

"We are honored by your invitation, my lord," Brys said. The two men embraced, and Gisele was almost piqued to note that Brys was exhibiting none of the chilly reserve she had seen him show toward others who had earned his scorn.

"Come to the fire and sit down," the Count of l'Aigle invited them, gesturing at three high-backed chairs pulled up near the hearth. "It is a long way from Balleroy in this weather, and you must be chilled to the bone. Robert, bring wine and food," he said to his seneschal, as soon as the latter had assisted him into the middle chair, so that he was between Brys and her.

Gisele was more surprised to hear the kindly tone in her father's voice as he addressed his steward than if he had screamed at the man. What had changed him so?

But as soon as the seneschal had moved out of earshot, leaving the three of them alone in front of the flames licking at the logs in the hearth, the count interrupted her musing.

"Daughter, I received the empress's letter telling me of the attack upon you in the Weald, upon your arrival," he began.

Gisele waited. Now he would become the father she

had always known, who would find a way to blame *her* for the loss of his men.

"She told me how your old nurse was killed, along with the men, and how you might have suffered an even worse fate had it not been for the godsend of my lord de Balleroy's finding you." He turned to Brys, and seized one of his hands. "My lord, you have my undying gratitude," he said, kissing it.

"My lord, no thanks are necessary—" Brys began, but then the Count of l'Aigle began to weep.

Gisele stared. She had never ever seen this man shed a tear, not even when her mother had died.

The old man wept into his hands for a minute or two before turning red-rimmed eyes toward her. "You do not know what to make of your father, do you, girl? None of the fire and bluster you were expecting, eh?" He shook his head.

"I have done a great deal of thinking since receiving that news of your brush with death, Gisele," he continued. "As it happened, I had much time for consideration, because the day I received that letter, I had a heart seizure and lay near death myself for several days."

Gisele gasped. "But you never sent word—"

The count waved a hand. "For a while I was much too weak to do anything but lie there and pray. The priest had given me the Sacrament, and I expected he would have to send word of my death to you. And then, slowly, I got better...but in any case I have never been much for writing letters. Too much trouble, to try to say out loud what I wanted some priest to write down for me...

"Anyway, as I lay there, I began to realize what a fool I had been." He smiled at her, a smile full of gentle regret. "I had wasted so many years, not appreciating what I had. I know I made your mother's life hell—and I was never much of a father to you.''

Gisele felt her jaw drop.

Her father turned to Brys. "You see, I had never gotten the son I wanted. I failed to see what a rare gift I had been given, in Sidonie Gisele.''

Brys said, "She has been a rare gift to me, my lord.'' His eyes gave no hint that Gisele had ever told him any of her hurt at her father's dismissal of her value.

Her father sighed. "I know I can never get those years back. I can never apologize to the woman who gave her birth. But I could atone…'' He turned back to Gisele, and laid a gentle hand on her shoulder. "I wanted to see you, Gisele…to have one last Christmas here with you.''

Gisele felt tears sting her eyes. "But…but I hope you will have many more Christmases, my lord—Father,'' she corrected herself, and found that she meant it.

"Perhaps, if God is willing. But they will not take place here. In the New Year, I will enter the abbey at Bec, and if I am found worthy, I will spend the rest of my days as a monk. I am ceding l'Aigle to you, my dear Gisele. I know your dear husband will help you to care for it,'' he added, nodding toward Brys.

"But Father…'' she began, but found she could not go on. She was too choked with tears.

And then, suddenly, she was being embraced by the man who had never, in her memory, done so before.

"Do not weep, my dear Gisele. It is a decision that brings me much peace, not sadness. Besides, it is not good for the babe.''

She jumped, and pulled away to stare at him. "You know? But I had not told you,'' she said, her hand going involuntarily to her belly, which was still only gently rounded beneath the gown she wore.

Her father's austere features rearranged themselves into a grin. "There is a radiance about you, my dear. I noticed it immediately. It is more than just the glow of a woman in love with her husband—though I can see that you are that, too." He leaned over and kissed her cheek. "Come, no more tears. We will have a wonderful Christmas, here at L'Aigle before I go—and I'm sure the abbot will allow me visitors, so that I may get to know my new grandson—or granddaughter," he added quickly, with a smile to indicate either sex would bring him equal joy.

* * * * *

Historical Afterword

Unfortunately, the Empress Matilda (or Maud as she is known in some sources) never achieved her dream of being crowned. Once Robert of Glouchester, her bastard half brother, died, she realized the futility of her struggle and retreated to Normandy for the rest of her life. After her son Henry reached manhood, however, he carried on the struggle until he and Stephen reached a stalemate. At this point it was agreed that Stephen would be succeeded upon his death by Henry, and he was eventually crowned Henry II.

However much I wanted to kill Geoffrey de Mandeville off in the course of the story, he was an actual historical personage and did not die until later. He remained a treacherous schemer, and eventually revolted against King Stephen, too. He died of an infected arrow wound sustained while in rebellion against the king in 1144, three years after this story.

There is no proof that Mathilda and Brien fitzCount were ever lovers, though there are cryptic hints in historical texts that they might have been. It is certain, however, that fitzCount was very devoted to Mathilda, and consoled her after their disastrous flight from Winchester.

*Take a trip to Merry Old England
with four exciting stories from*

In January 2000, look for
THE GENTLEMAN THIEF
by **Deborah Simmons**
(England, 1818)
and
MY LADY RELUCTANT
by **Laurie Grant**
(England, 1141)

In February 2000, look for
THE ROGUE
The second book of
KNIGHTS OF THE BLACK ROSE
by **Ana Seymour**
(England, 1222)
and
ANGEL OF THE KNIGHT
by **Diana Hall**
(England, 1154)

Harlequin Historicals
The way the past *should* have been.

Available at your favorite retail outlet.

HARLEQUIN®
Makes any time special ™
Visit us at www.romance.net

HHEUR1

Looking For More Romance?

Visit Romance.net

Look us up on-line at: http://www.romance.net

Check in daily for these and other exciting features:

Hot off the press

View all current titles, and purchase them on-line.

What do the stars have in store for you?

Horoscope

Hot deals

Exclusive offers available only at Romance.net

Plus, don't miss our interactive quizzes, contests and bonus gifts.

PWEB

**3 Stories of Holiday Romance from three
bestselling Harlequin® authors**

Valentine Babies

by

ANNE STUART

TARA TAYLOR QUINN   JULE MCBRIDE

Goddess in Waiting by Anne Stuart
Edward walks into Marika's funky maternity shop to pick
up some things for his sister. He doesn't expect to assist
in the delivery of a baby and fall for outrageous Marika.

Gabe's Special Delivery by Tara Taylor Quinn
On February 14, Gabe Stone finds a living, breathing
valentine on his doorstep—his daughter. Her mother
has given Gabe four hours to adjust to fatherhood,
resolve custody and win back his ex-wife?

My Man Valentine by Jule McBride
Everyone knows Eloise Hunter and C. D. Valentine
are in love. Except Eloise and C. D. Then, one of
Eloise's baby-sitting clients leaves her with a baby to
mind, and C. D. swings into protector mode.

VALENTINE BABIES

On sale January 2000 at your favorite retail outlet.

HARLEQUIN®
Makes any time special ™

Visit us at www.romance.net

PHVALB

Return to romance, Texas-style, with

ANNETTE BROADRICK

DAUGHTERS OF TEXAS

When three beautiful sisters round up some of the
Lone Star State's sexiest men, they discover the
passion they've always dreamed of in these compelling
stories of love and matrimony.

One of Silhouette's most popular authors,
Annette Broadrick proves that no matter
the odds, true love prevails.

Look for *Daughters of Texas* on sale in January 2000.

Available at your favorite retail outlet.

Visit us at www.romance.net

PSBR3200

Harlequin® Historical

is proud to offer four very different
Western romances that will
warm your hearts....

In January 2000, look for
THE BACHELOR TAX
by **Carolyn Davidson**
and
THE OUTLAW'S BRIDE
by **Liz Ireland**

In February 2000, look for
WRITTEN IN THE HEART
by **Judith Stacy**
and
A BRIDE FOR McCAIN
by **Mary Burton**

**Harlequin Historicals
The way the past *should* have been.**

Available at your favorite retail outlet.

HARLEQUIN®
Makes any time special™

Visit us at www.romance.net

HHWEST6

Start the year right with
Harlequin Historicals' first
multi-author miniseries,

KNIGHTS OF THE BLACK ROSE

Three warriors bound by one event,
each destined to find true love....

THE CHAMPION, by Suzanne Barclay
On sale December 1999

THE ROGUE, by Ana Seymour
On sale February 2000

THE CONQUEROR, by Shari Anton
On sale April 2000

Available at your favorite retail outlet.

HARLEQUIN®
Makes any time special ™

Visit us at www.romance.net   HHKOTBR